Norah's Children

Norah's Children

a novel

Ann O'Farrell

iUniverse, Inc.
New York Lincoln Shanghai

Norah's Children

iUniverse books may be ordered through booksellers or by contacting:

iUniverse
2021 Pine Lake Road, Suite 100
Lincoln, NE 68512
www.iuniverse.com
1-800-Authors (1-800-288-4677)

This is a work of fiction. All of the characters, names, incidents, organizations, and dialogue in this novel are either the products of the author's imagination or are used fictitiously.

ISBN-13: 978-0-595-40654-8 (pbk)
ISBN-13: 978-0-595-85020-4 (ebk)
ISBN-10: 0-595-40654-8 (pbk)
ISBN-10: 0-595-85020-0 (ebk)

Printed in the United States of America

To John, the believer.

Acknowledgments

Every year, as the clock crept towards midnight, I wished the organizers of the Oscar Awards ceremony would fulfill their yearly promise to cut the speeches, limit all the gratitude and appreciation and let me get to bed before dawn.

Now that I have a better understanding of how many people it takes to get a simple book from a nagging idea to a published item, I wonder how the Oscar winners manage to include half the people who must have had a hand in their success. Here is my version of the neatly folded piece of paper that most of them seem to have tucked about their person, in case they are one of the 'chosen ones.'

My first thanks must go to my husband John, my first supporter, critic and editor. As the idea for Norah's Children grew, and I talked about it more and more, he was the one who gently pushed me towards the computer. When I stopped writing he read and re-read the subsequent sentences, paragraphs and chapters. His patience was unending and his grammatical skills indispensable.

Deanna Bennett introduced me to the Wordsmiths Writers Group in Tarpon Springs who simultaneously polished my ego and my syntax. Mike Savage was the first person 'in the business' who convinced me that the book might have a life outside of my dreams. And then came Jeanne Walsh, who led me to Dorothy Fenwick who led me to Tom Coyne, in whom I found my perfect line editor, a man with an amazing eye to detail and continuity, combined with a gift for insightful suggestions and unstinting encouragement. Howard Jones hounded me to pursue publication. Ted Radakovic was incredibly generous with his time, and expertise, to help create an image from my vague imaginings. To all of you, my very sincere thanks.

Any flaws or faults to be found in the text are a result of my incessant tinkering, even after it was edited. The faults are mine and mine alone.

Author's Note

This story has been waiting a long time to be told. **Norah's Children** is a novel which has, at its heart, a truth. There was a Norah, though I'm not sure that she even spelled her name that way. Norah did have five children, and five different families ultimately took in those children. What those families were like, or how those children were actually reared, I do not know. I heard whispers long ago and, like the fine silk of a spider's web, they clung to me. I finally gathered those fragile threads and wove them within a story of 'how it might have been.'

If there are villains and victims in the story, it is because every story must have its villains and its victims. If there is a hero or a heroine it is because every story should have at least one. The characters, as they are depicted in my story, are conjured from my imagination. No offence or hurt to the memory of any real person is intended.

The original children are all gone. I don't believe they spoke much about their separate lives. In writing this book I wanted to honor them, and the trauma and sadness they must have experienced. Children are our legacy, our joy, and our responsibility. They begin their lives totally trusting in, and dependant on, our integrity. Too often their trust is misplaced.

Ann O'Farrell. 2006

Glendarrig, Co. Galway,
Ireland.

May 1922.

Norah

"Dear God, let this be over soon. Dear Mother of God, be with me in my hour of need. Blessed Virgin, help me."

The pain faded.

"You're doing fine, alanna." Annie patted Norah's hand, "The babe will be well born before Brendan and the childer come home. Won't they be surprised?"

Pain gripped the exhausted young woman again, and she strained forward, teeth clenched, and muscles taut.

"Good girl, Norah, I have it. Hold still now, I have it."

The midwife quickly inspected the baby.

"It's a boy, a grand broth of a boy. Wait, you'll see now. There!"

She held up the dark, moist bundle for the mother to see; a tiny, perfect baby with a mop of dark hair. It was very still. Norah stared at the infant in horror. No! Not another stillborn! He'd moved so vigorously in her belly; he couldn't be dead. It couldn't happen again. She remembered the tiny, stillborn girl. She, too, had looked so perfect. She remembered wanting to bury the precious infant in her mother's grave, but the priest had said "no," said a dead infant couldn't be baptized. So it was barred from Christian burial, and from Heaven; condemned to spend eternity in Limbo. Norah's grief had been unreachable. Please God, don't let it happen again.

Annie Quinn laid the baby boy on the bed and rubbed him vigorously with a cloth. With a shocked intake of breath, the infant screwed up his old man's face and squalled his protest at the rough treatment. Norah cried in relief while the midwife busied herself tying and cutting the cord. She then put the baby to Norah's breast.

Annie washed both mother and child, replaced the tangled, sodden sheet and bedcover, and brushed and braided Norah's dark auburn hair.

When Brendan returned from the seashore with the children, the midwife was sitting by the fire.

"Well, Annie, is it done?"

She heard the tension in his voice and smiled.

"It is indeed, Brendan. Go and see for yourself. I'll be off now."

He ushered the four children ahead of him up the stairs to the loft bedroom. His wife lay resting against the sweat-stained pillow, the baby still nuzzled to her breast, discreetly covered by a fringed wool shawl. The small family stood at the entrance to the room. Norah smiled and beckoned them in. Sheelagh, the youngest, was first to greet her baby brother. Going slowly to her mother's side, she stretched an uncertain finger towards the miniature fist visible above the shawl. The baby clutched at the finger and Sheelagh smiled shyly up at her mother. The little girl held her extended arm very still. Mary came forward, smiled at her sister, and peeped under the shawl at the sleeping infant.

"What is it Mammy, a boy or a girl?"

"A boy," said her mother, glancing over the head of her eldest daughter towards her husband. He nodded his approval. A boy was good. Boys had strong backs. A boy would work with his father, alongside his brothers. It was good he had another son.

Pierce and Colm remained standing beside their father. They felt self-conscious standing at the entrance to the warm, sweat-scented bedroom. They were embarrassed too, to see their mother lying in the bed, with her hair loosely braided instead of in her usual neat bun. They were embarrassed to see her in the soft cambric nightgown with its ribbon fastenings open for the baby. Pierce looked up at his father.

"Will I go and settle the horse, Da?"

"Do son, and take Colm with you. Don't feed the animal too much, and be sure to water him well."

The boys left, their hob-nailed boots clattering on the wooden steps. Brendan spoke to his eldest daughter; "Mary, take your sister and get her ready for bed, then see what's in the pot for supper. There's a good girl."

Mary took the younger girl's hand and tugged her away from Norah's side. Glancing back for a last look at mother and baby, they left the room.

Brendan crossed to the bed and sat close to his wife. He gently pushed a strand of damp hair from her face.

"How is he, Norah love? Is he well?"

He, too, thought of the stillborn infant, and Norah's inconsolable grief. He knew children were a gift from God, but sometimes it seemed to Brendan that

God was too generous with his gifts. Though sorry that the girl-child had died, he also knew he needed no more mouths to feed. He'd not known how to deal with his wife's distress when it happened. He'd fervently prayed through this pregnancy that the child would live, at least until it was baptized. If it could ascend to Heaven and be one of God's holy angels, it wouldn't be so bad. It was Limbo that had grieved Norah so, *and* the burial in unconsecrated ground, like any murderer or savage heathen.

"He's well," she said. "But I want Father Mulcahy to baptize him in the morning, just in case."

He nodded. "And you, Norah, are you well?"

She squeezed his hand. "I'm grand."

He again brushed her hair with his hand. "You're the most important one to me. I'm fierce fond of you, you know. Always remember that."

Norah smiled, "love" was never mentioned, but she understood. She glanced down at the sleeping baby.

"If I weren't here, if something ever happened to me, you'd take care of them, Brendan, wouldn't you?"

"Why would you fret yourself about that, Norah love? Haven't you just told me you felt grand?"

"I know, but you would, wouldn't you?" she persisted, becoming agitated.

"Of course I would, my darling woman, of course. But nothing's going to happen to you."

Reassured, she smiled down at the baby, and touched his face with her finger.

"We have to pick a name for him."

Brendan looked at the child for the first time.

"Begod, would you look at the head of hair!"

"What'll we call him, Brendan?"

"Let's call him after my Da. He looks just like him," said Brendan.

And so, the last of Norah's children was born quietly into an uncaring world, and named Michael.

Mary

Mary stood Sheelagh in front of the hearth, removed her thin cotton dress, and dropped a worn shift over her head.

"You've half the strand in your hair, Sheelagh Kelly," she laughed, as a shower of sand fell from the child's tight curls. She brushed it from her sister's hair and shoulders and kissed her lightly on the forehead. "I'll get you some bread."

She lifted Sheelagh up onto the settle and went to prepare the child's supper. A table near the back half-door was as much of a kitchen as the home boasted, its worn oilcloth still faintly imprinted with a floral design. Mary took the pot of dripping from the overhead cupboard and unwrapped the bread from its cloth. She cut a thick slice and smeared a fine layer of the fat over it. She took it and a half-filled mug of milk back to her young sister who rested against the high back of the settle, almost asleep.

"Here Sheelagh, eat your supper, and I'll tuck you into bed."

The sleepy child gnawed slowly on the coarse bread, then put her hand out for the milk. Mary gave her the mug and watched as she drank. After a while Mary returned to the table, reached under it, and pulled out the ragged cloth that hung on the edge of the water bucket. Returning to her sister, she took the bread and milk, placed them on the settle, and wiped the little girl's hands with the damp cloth. Though the child was not yet two years old, her tiny hands were already ingrained with dirt, her fingernails black-rimed. Mary gently lifted Sheelagh's chin and cleaned the sleepy face, then handed back the bread and milk, and sat to watch her sister finish her meal.

"Hurry up Sheelagh, will ya? Da will be down for his supper in a minute and I want you in bed before he gets here."

A new baby meant more work for Mary who, at six years of age, already knew hard work. All the children had their chores, and one of Mary's was to care for her young sister. The two-year old still soiled herself, and Mary was tasked with keeping her sister clean. She tried to teach her to use the privy or the pot, but Sheelagh was slow to learn and often forgot, especially when she was tired as she was now.

"Hurry up Sheelagh, please," she pleaded. "You have to go to the privy before I take you up. I don't want you in there either when Da comes down."

Sheelagh continued to chew, ignoring her sister's anxiety. Mary waited a few more minutes.

"Right! Come on then, Shee."

The tired child still clutched a small piece of bread and the half-empty mug as Mary hoisted her down from the settle and ushered her through the half-door into the back yard. Entering the lean-to, she lifted her sister onto the privy seat.

"Stay there, and sit still. I'll be back in a minute when I've got the pig locked up."

Mary went to coax the animal across the small yard and into its sty. She hastily fastened the bar across the entrance and returned to her sister.

"All right, Shee?"

The child nodded.

"Good girl! You are the best little girl. Mammy will be proud of you."

She threw a handful of earth in the privy bucket and chivvied the small child back into the cottage. Leaving the remains of the supper on the table, she persuaded the youngster up the short flight of steps to the loft.

The children's windowless bedroom was tucked under the eaves of the thatch. It was almost filled by one, large bed where all the children slept together in a cozy tumble of coarse linen and wool coverlets. Each child had his or her own special place in the bed. Pierce, who was usually first up, slept nearest the door. Colm, who followed his adored older brother everywhere, lay beside him. Mary's place was at the far side of the bed with Sheelagh tucked securely in beside her. She wondered what it would be like when the newest child joined the crowded bedfellows who tossed, turned, kicked, and fought for their sleeping space each night.

She knelt beside the bed and tugged her sister down beside her. Making the Sign of the Cross, she watched to ensure Sheelagh copied her and then recited the night prayer.

> "Now, I lay me down to sleep;
> I pray to God my soul to keep.

> If I die before I wake,
> I pray to God my soul to take.
> God Bless...."

Here she waited for Sheelagh to contribute her part to the familiar litany.

"Daddy," said the small child carefully.

"God Bless ..."

"Mammy," said Sheelagh.

The two continued with the family names and those of deceased relatives until Mary closed the litany by blessing herself again, and her little sister clambered into the unmade bed. She was fast asleep in moments.

When Mary returned to the living room, Brendan was already seated in his large wooden chair beside the fire.

"Well, child, where's my supper?"

She crossed to the hearth and used the iron hook to swing the pot away from the hot embers of the fire. She fetched a ladle from the dresser drawer and a blue and white china dish from the dresser shelf.

"Will you have some bread, Daddy?" she asked, already at the table, unwrapping the cloth and lifting the knife.

"I will, Mary girl, but no dripping."

She cut the bread, put the thick chunk on the side of the blue dish, and returned to the pot. She carefully ladled a generous scoop of the gray, steaming, broth into the dish, ensuring none was spilled, and handed it to her father. He hastily blessed himself and began eating, using the bread to soak up the thin liquid.

"Well, don't stand watching me," he snapped. "Get me a jar, there's a good girl, before I die of a thirst."

Mary fetched a bottle of the dark porter from the wooden crate under the stairs. She also brought a chipped glass from the dresser and set them both on the floor beside her father.

"I'll take my supper to bed now, Daddy."

She was tired, and it was better to be up in the loft and away from him. Then she couldn't make him angry.

"Fine girl, but take the broom to this before you go." Brendan gestured at the small scattering of sand in front of the hearth, the sand Mary had brushed from Sheelagh's hair. "I don't want your mother to see a dirty hearth when she comes down in the morning."

She wearily fetched the broom of dried twigs, and swept the sand into the ashes of the fire. She returned the broom to its niche and prepared her own slab of bread and dripping.

"Goodnight Daddy; God Bless."

"Goodnight Mary; God Bless. Don't forget your prayers."

The solemn young girl retreated to the loft.

Having finished his meal, Brendan pulled a pouch of tobacco from his jacket pocket. He took down a small clay pipe from the mantle, and filled it with the coarse threads of the tobacco. Lighting a taper in the embers of the fire, he held it to the bowl, sucked vigorously, and created a dense cloud of blue smoke. He sat back and gazed leisurely around his small home.

The pig grunted, disturbing his thoughts.

"Dammit," he growled.

He pushed himself out of his chair and stepped to the half-door. The animal had escaped and was again rooting in the turf pile. Brendan opened the half-door, kneed the animal roughly away from the turf and into the sty. He fastened the entrance securely. The animal was fattening well. There would be plenty of meat in the Kelly house this winter.

Brendan returned to the cottage, closed the half-door, and took his seat again beside the fire. He remembered his sons. They were still not home. Where were they? He knew it didn't take that long to settle the horse. They only had to water him, walk him out along the road, and tether him in good grass. They'd better not be riding him again. He'd caught Pierce riding the horse once before, barebacked and clutching the nag's mane. He'd given his son a good hiding with the belt. He needed the boy to understand that the horse was a working animal, Brendan's livelihood. He and the horse worked long hours every day, hauling goods, and he didn't want the animal exhausted further by giving his eldest son bareback rides.

At that moment the latch rose on the front door, and Pierce and Colm stepped into the cottage.

"Where in the name of all that's holy have you two been?" he demanded.

The two boys stopped in the entrance staring at their father. He was a large man, well built, over six feet when he stood. Even sitting, he was an intimidating figure. Colm slowly tucked himself behind his big brother.

"Get in here the both of you, and close the door."

The boys shuffled forward.

"Sorry, Da," said Colm, as he gently pushed the door closed behind him.

Pierce stood stiff and tall and resolutely met his father's gaze. Under the myriad freckles his face was pale, but he was determined to show no fear. The nine-year-old waited for his father's interrogation. Though no stranger to the hidings Brendan doled out, he raised his chin in quiet defiance. He was determined not to cry.

Pierce

Earlier, Pierce had been glad to get out of the house. When they visited the new baby, he saw that his Mammy looked tired. That meant more work for him tomorrow, probably fetching water. When Mammy was tired, it meant he was the one who carried three or four buckets a day from the pump at the crossroads to the cottage. Four-year-old Colm often came with him and cranked the heavy iron handle, but he was too small to help carry the buckets, and Pierce strained under their weight. The cold water slopped into his boots as he walked. It soaked his wool socks and squelched between his toes, making his tight boots even more uncomfortable. He hated fetching water.

He cut chunks of bread for himself and Colm before he went to care for the horse. His younger brother trailed behind him as always. The cart stood on the muddy patch of land at the side of the cottage, its wooden shafts pointing skyward. The horse stood beside it loosely tethered. It ate from a nosebag half-filled with oats and eyed the boys distrustfully as they approached. The brothers clumsily removed the nosebag and set off to water the animal. When this was done, they walked out along the Ballyfin Road to find a suitable spot on the grass verge to tether it. Pierce had heard his Da call the verge "the long acre" that thin stretch of grass between road and hedge where any man's horse could be left to graze overnight without charge.

Pierce knew he must make certain of enough sweet grass at the chosen tethering spot with no yellow daisy weeds. The weed gave horses colic, and a horse with colic couldn't work. Pierce still remembered the hiding he received from his father the morning they found the animal lying at the side of the road, its stomach distended, eyes rolling, and bubbles of foam flecking its mouth. The boys were always watchful for the deadly weeds now and kicked and trammeled underfoot any that they found.

"Can we have a ride, Pierce?"

"No, Colm, haven't we been at the beach all day? Isn't that enough for you?"

"Ah, *please*, Pierce, just a small one. Da won't know. I won't tell, swear to God."

"I'm the one that'll catch it, not you," said Pierce, but he was already hoisting Colm onto the animal's lean back. "Budge up," he said, and Colm edged forward until he was almost sitting on the horse's neck.

Pierce clutched a large handful of the animal's mane and swung himself up behind his younger brother. Putting both arms around Colm, he groped for the reins, gave the horse's rump a whack, and they set off at a slow trot.

"Make him gallop," laughed Colm, gripping fistfuls of the mane, and squeezing his scrawny knees into the animal's neck. Pierce kicked the horse again, and it moved a little faster, bouncing the two boys hard against its bony back.

The exhilaration of the ride and the feeling of freedom had both boys grinning broadly as the horse trotted along the country road.

Now he stood in front of his father.

"Where were ye?" said Brendan, his voice quiet. Norah was sleeping, and there was no point in waking her. She needed to rest.

Pierce raised his chin and stared at his father, unblinking. Brendan noticed again how the boy had his mother's sea-green eyes and red hair, though the boy's was a tangle of tight curls like his baby sister's.

"Sure we were finding a spot for the horse, Da. There are yellow flowers all out along the road. We went for miles."

"So, the horse is miles out the road?"

Pierce reconsidered. "Well, no, Da. We looked and looked, but then we came back and just picked a spot and flattened the weeds. Colm kicked them into the hedge so the horse wouldn't get at them. Didn't ye, Colm?"

Colm looked up at his brother, then at his father, his eyes wide with fright. He nodded.

"Come here to me, Colm boy," said Brendan, beckoning his younger son with the stem of his pipe. The boy took a hesitant step forward. "Were you on the horse, Colm boy? Did you ride the horse this evening?"

Colm's head was bowed. He shook it vigorously.

"Look at me, son, when I'm talking to you."

Colm lifted his head slightly, glanced up at his father, and started to cry.

"Don't lie to your Daddy, Colm. God hates liars, so does Father Mulcahy, and so do I. Liars don't go to Heaven, Colm. I'm sure Father Mulcahy told you that?"

The boy nodded and glanced sideways at Pierce.

"Don't be looking at your brother," Brendan snapped, then spoke more softly. "Were you riding the horse, son?"

Colm slowly nodded his head again, sobbing.

"Get up those stairs, lad. There'll be no supper for you tonight, and don't wake your mother with your bawling, or it's the sorry boy you'll be."

Colm stumbled up the stairs wiping his snot and tear-stained face on the sleeve of his shirt, trying hard to stifle his sobs. Brendan turned to Pierce who still stood firm staring at his father.

"He couldn't even get on the back of that horse on his own, let alone ride it," he said, unbuckling his leather belt.

Norah

The next morning Norah rose early, as usual. She filled the blackened kettle with the last of the water from the bucket, raked the ash from the fire, and placed clods of dry turf on the embers. She set the kettle onto the fire to boil, and all the while she cradled the new infant in her shawl. When these first tasks of the day were done, she sat into her chair facing the fire. Its woven rush seat was in sorry need of repair, holed in several places, but it was comfortable for nursing. She loosened her shawl and fed the baby.

Brendan came down the stairs buttoning his shirt.

"Is the tea made?"

"The water will be boiled soon," she replied.

"I suppose I have to wear this?" he questioned, indicating the starched collar that hung loosely around his neck.

She smiled and nodded. "Aren't you going to have your son christened, Brendan Kelly? Would you do it looking like a tinker? Your studs are in the dresser drawer. Your tie is in your jacket pocket."

Brendan rifled through the drawer. "I don't know if it will still fit. I haven't worn it since Sheelagh's christening."

Norah smiled again. "That's only two years. Sure you haven't changed a whit since the day we wed. Of course it will fit."

Brendan glanced at the photograph on the dresser, a sepia-toned picture of Norah and himself on their wedding day. We looked well, he thought, but he remembered his starched collar being too tight even then. Brendan squinted as he studied the photograph more closely. His curly hair had been center-parted and slicked to immobility, and his walrus moustache was so full it covered his mouth. He fingered the luxuriant growth that still covered his top lip and smiled to himself, a grand moustache. His hand went to the stubble on his chin, no longer clean-shaven like the picture. He sighed and returned to fumbling in the cluttered drawer for the studs. "I have them."

His glance went back to the picture. He was still wearing the same brown trousers as in the photograph and his wedding day boots. The pants were the worse for wear now, shiny with age, grease, and dirt. The boots were unpolished, well-patched, and butter-soft, but good for a few years yet, he hoped.

"You'll have to put them in, Norah. I'm all fingers and thumbs with these cursed things."

"I'll be done feeding the baby in a minute. I'll do it then. Did Eileen say Father Mulcahy would be there this morning?"

Eileen Flynn, the priest's housekeeper, guarded the priest and his privacy with the ferocity of a mastiff. None got to see "Father" without first being cross-examined by Eileen. Very little was said or done in the parish without her knowledge either. She and Norah were good friends.

"He will."

"Did you tell Eileen it was a boy?"

"How could I, woman? Sure, didn't I call into the priest's house on the way back from the strand? I didn't know myself. I just told her the baby was on the way and, God willing, we would need it baptizing this morning."

"Right!" She said, as she fastened her blouse. "The baby's fed. If you hold him a minute, I'll make the tea, then I'll fix your collar."

"Don't disturb yourself," he said, reluctant to take the small infant until he had to. "I'll make the tea. You keep ahold of the child."

When the tea was drunk, Norah attached Brendan's collar to the shirt with the studs. He retrieved the tie from the jacket pocket and eased it carefully over his head, making sure the knot stayed intact.

"So, Michael is his name then, is it?" he asked, tightening the knot.

"It is."

He struggled into the jacket. "Is he ready?"

"He is. Will you ask Father Mulcahy to Church me on Tuesday?"

"I'll not get into that with him, Norah, that's women's business. You can say it to Eileen, and she can arrange it with himself."

Norah was barred from entering the church, even for her own child's christening, until she was "Churched," cleansing her of her sins and atoning for the sins of Eve. The ceremony could not take place until a week after the birth.

"And, Norah love, get Pierce to fetch water before he goes to school. I don't want to have you carrying heavy water buckets today." Brendan took the infant gingerly from his wife. "I'll be back soon. Have the lad fetch the horse too. I'll hitch it up myself when I get back. Right then," he said, squaring his shoulders and clutching his infant son to his chest as if fearful he would drop him, "Michael it is."

Brendan dipped his finger in the holy water font by the front door, blessed himself, and surreptitiously splashed a little over the baby.

Once he was gone, Norah prepared breakfast for the children, boiling a large handful of coarse-ground oats in a pot of water to make their porridge. As the children came sleepily down the stairs, she ladled a scoop of the thin gruel into their bowls, sprinkled it with salt, cooled it with milk, and handed it to them. The three youngest took their places on the wooden settle beside the fire. Pierce, still smarting from his father's beating, chose to stand.

When their porridge was finished, Norah poured the last of the milk into four cups and distributed them. She sank into her chair and watched the children drink. She was tired.

"Will you fetch water before you go to school, Pierce-lad?"

"I will, Ma. Am I to fetch the horse too?"

She nodded. "Mary-love, will you pack a bite for yourself and Pierce to take to school?"

"I will, Mammy. Will I look after Sheelagh first?"

"Yes, please, child."

Colm clambered down from the settle and hurried to his mother. "Can I fetch the water with Pierce, Mammy, please, Mammy?" he asked.

Norah took the cup from the small boy's hand. "You can son, but don't get under his feet."

"Come on, Sheelagh, let's get you dressed," said Mary taking the child's cup and lifting her down from the seat.

Whilst the children went about their chores, Norah prepared Brendan's lunch and set about making fresh soda bread. The dough was sitting on the griddle over the fire, cooking, before Mary and Pierce were ready for school.

When they picked up their lunches from the small table that was their kitchen, Norah gave them a sod of turf. It was each family's daily contribution to the fire which kept the school warm on icy, winter days. She tugged Mary's shawl tighter around her shoulders and hugged both children close.

"Be good. Learn your lessons. Mind yourselves," she said as she did every day when they left for school. She kissed them and watched as they blessed themselves at the small font, opened the latch on the front door, and left.

Brendan returned soon afterwards. Barely in the door, he handed the baby to Norah and freed himself from his collar and tie.

"Begod, that's better. I thought I was going to choke on the blasted things. Is there any tea left in the pot, Norah?"

"Was Father Mulcahy there?"

"He was. It's all done. Michael Kelly he is."

"And did Eileen stand for him?"

"Eileen is his godmother and my brother Pat is the godfather, though there wasn't enough time to ask him to be there."

Pat was Brendan's only brother who still lived in the village, the other five brothers having long since gone their own ways: two to America, two to England, and one, Eamonn, had died at the Somme.

She poured his tea. "There's no milk left. I'll get some from Aunty Bridgie when I go there this morning.

"Are ye able for that, Norah?"

"I am, of course. Sure, amin't I well used to childbirth now? I can't be molly-coddling myself."

"Well, I can take you part of the way on the cart. I've to collect manure from Haggarty's farm." He turned to the two youngest children who sat on the bottom step watching, "And don't you two be annoying your Mammy today. Be good; do you hear me?"

They both nodded.

"Right then! I'll let the pig out, and we'll be off."

"Wait, Brendan, finish your tea. I'll do the bucket."

Norah tucked the baby firmly into her shawl then tipped the breakfast remains into the slop bucket. She quickly cleaned and prepared vegetables from the basket under the table and tossed them into the black kettle over the fire. She added the scrapings to the slop. Brendan took the bucket from her and turned the contents into the pig trough in the back yard.

Once ready, they set off for Doonbeg sitting on the bench seat of the cart. Norah cradled the baby in her shawl, and Colm and Sheelagh sat, tucked securely, between their parents. At the crossroads, when Brendan helped them down from the cart, he gave Norah a hasty kiss.

"Always remember," he said. She smiled and nodded. He tapped the horse's rump with his stick and headed off towards Haggarty's. Norah took Sheelagh's hand, and they set off to walk the last mile to Aunty Bridgie's.

Aunty Bridgie

Bridget Clancy stood at the door of her shop watching people come and go along the busy main street of Doonbeg. She was a small, round, woman dressed from head to foot in black. When her mother died, many years before, she had donned the traditional full black of mourning and continued to wear it from that day on. A thick, black, wool shawl for winter was merely exchanged for the slightly thinner one she wore in summer. The rest of her attire was the same year round, an ample black blouse fastened to the neck and a long, shapeless black skirt. She wore black wool stockings and sturdy, black, laced-up shoes that were just visible beneath the hem of her skirt.

She watched Norah come towards her along the street and waved.

"You've had the child, alanna?" She asked in surprise as soon as her niece was close.

Norah nodded and tugged back the edge of the shawl to show her Aunt.

"What is it, Norah, a boy or a girl?" the old woman said as she beamed down at the small puckered face.

"A boy, Michael."

"God Bless him." she said, blessing herself. "He's the image of my father; God rest his soul."

"Brendan says he's like *his* father," smiled Norah.

Bridget's eyes went from the baby to the mother. "And how are you, Norah child? Should you be here at all today?"

"I'm fine, Aunty Bridgie. Don't I always help you in the mornings?"

The small shop was in what had once been the old lady's front parlor. For years now she had sold an assortment of small goods from salt to soap and buttons to biscuits. A section of the room was even partitioned to create a tiny dairy with whitewashed walls and several flypapers hanging from the ceiling. Here, on a cool, marble-slabbed countertop, she kept her eggs, cheese, and butter. On the floor under the countertop stood two milk churns, and a half pint and pint ladle hung on the side of the churns ready to scoop measured quantities of the fresh milk into customer's jugs.

"Come in; come in." Bridgie pushed the door open and stood to one side. "Come on, children; step inside."

Norah and Bridget followed the two youngsters.

"Go through to the back room;" Bridget closed the shop door, "and I'll make us a cup of tea."

Norah stopped short and gripped at the counter. She winced and bent forward. Bridget put her hands out to steady the young mother, "What's wrong child?"

Norah straightened. "Just a little cramp. I'm grand."

The children had stopped and turned. Bridget chivvied them on, "Go on in. You know the way, Colm."

Colm opened the door and led the way into the small, cozy back parlor.

"Sit down there beside the fire, Norah, and rest yourself."

"I'm fine, really I am, Aunty Bridgie. Stop fussing."

"Fussing? Fussing, am I? Your poor sainted mother, God rest her, would never forgive me if I didn't take care of you, Norah Kelly. Fussing indeed!"

Norah surrendered and sat into the red, plush-velvet armchair tucked close to the range. It was Aunty Bridgie's chair.

Bridgie turned her attention to the children. "Why don't you childer go and play in the back yard." She opened the half door; "But don't chase the chickens. You know it stops them laying. Then your old Aunty Bridgie gets all cross." She smiled, fished in her voluminous apron pocket, and brought out two sticks of barley sugar. "There, will that keep you occupied for a while?" She handed one to Colm and unwrapped Sheelagh's before giving it to her. The two wandered out to the long back yard sucking on the sweet treats.

Bridgie returned to the range and lifted the black kettle. "I'll have the tea brewed in a minute, child. You rest there for a while."

The old brass clock on the mantle chimed the hour. Norah glanced up and saw an envelope tucked behind the clock.

"Did you get a letter, Aunty Bridgie?"

"From my brother, your Uncle Liam, his once-a-year letter. Not a lot of news, but it's always nice to hear from him. London seems a terrible long way away." She took the lid from the teapot and stirred the tea. "Will you have a biscuit, Norah?"

"No, thanks, Aunty Bridgie."

Bridgie took two cups and saucers down from the dresser and poured the tea. She handed a cup to Norah.

"You can sit in here for a while; I don't need you in the shop." She slowly eased herself onto the stool facing Norah.

"Well, perhaps I can go over the ledger while I'm sitting. There's an awful lot of people owe you money."

"Don't worry yourself about it. I need little enough for myself. You can collect all the debts when I'm gone and the shop is yours, if you wish. You'll be a wealthy woman then, Norah!" she joked.

The two women sat in comfortable silence drinking their tea until they heard the tinkle of the shop bell. Bridgie went to serve the customer, and Norah joined the children in the yard, searching the tangled hedges for eggs, as she did each morning. The chickens squawked their protest, but Norah was adept at avoiding their sharp beaks and soon had a bowlful of eggs. She washed them with water from the pump, carried them carefully into the shop, and placed them on the dairy shelf. From the large butter block she wielded the butter pats to shape small squares of butter. Norah wrapped them in greased paper and stored them beside the egg bowl. Her next chore in the rhythm of the morning was to tip tea and sugar into paper cones from the large tubs, then weigh them, write the price on the side, and stack them by the till for Bridgie's customers.

Norah had been helping her aunt in the shop for many years and expected to do so for many more. Every morning, except Sundays, Norah walked the three miles to Doonbeg. She had walked it alone, and then with one or more of her children. Michael was just the latest addition to join the small caravan.

Often, while Norah minded the shop, Bridget went to Mass or visited with friends in the village, but each day, come driving rain or summer dust, Norah returned to Glendarrig around noon. By then the children were cranky, and it was time for the long walk home.

1924

Norah

The cramp in her side had returned recently and was becoming more persistent. She'd been feeling nauseous for a few days, too. Perhaps I'm just pregnant again, she thought. With Michael now almost two years old and well able to walk, maybe it was time for another babe.

It was a beautiful spring day. Norah loved the walk home from the shop at this time of year. The sun climbed higher in the sky and warmed the air with the promise of summer. She smiled fondly at her three youngest children as they ran ahead searching the hedgerow for the pale lemon primroses they knew she loved. When they arrived home, she would put them in glass jars and tuck them into small spaces on the dresser and onto the dusty window ledges of the cottage. They would be little pockets of sunshine in the gloomy shade of their home.

Today the nausea was worse than before. Fine beads of perspiration formed on her forehead and upper lip. Michael got tired of walking and sat on the verge, waiting for his mother to scoop him up. She did, including him in her shawl, anchoring him securely on her hip, and continuing to walk homeward, one arm wrapped gently around his waist. He must be getting very heavy, she thought. It was hard to carry her youngest child.

"Walk a little more, Michael, please. Mammy has a stitch in her side."

Norah put him down, but her son knew when he'd walked enough. He sat in the rutted center of the road and cried until she relented and lifted him again.

Deep in her belly a pain burst in an angry explosion. She sank to her knees, gritting her teeth, breathing hard. Another stabbing pain made her double forward, still protecting Michael, her arm now gripped tightly around his waist.

Colm saw his mother on her knees, called to Sheelagh, and ran back.

"What's the matter, Mammy?"

"Nothing, son."

Norah took another jagged breath. It was easing. It was just the cramp in her side. Michael was getting heavy that was all. She remained still, afraid to move for fear the agonizing pain would return.

"Pick Mammy some more flowers, Colm, there's a good boy. Sure, you've hardly enough there for one jar yet. And you help him, Sheelagh darlin'. Let's make the biggest bunch in all the world."

She needed time to catch her breath, time to collect herself. Michael, quiet now, stared hard into his mother's face; his brown eyes watched her intently.

"It's all right child. Mammy had a cramp, and you're such a big boy now." She kissed him; "You're just too heavy for your Mammy."

Norah struggled upright, still clutching the boy. She brushed the dust from her skirt and stood motionless, waiting for the pain to return. It had subsided to a deep ache. She took a tentative step forward, then a few more, cautious, anticipating a return of the pain, but nothing happened. She took a deep breath, raised her head, and continued her walk. For the rest of the journey home she accepted handfuls of primroses from her children. She knew they wanted her to be all right, wanted to make her smile again. She had frightened them.

By the time Norah arrived home, the nausea and pain were worsening again. She filled the jars with the delicate spring flowers, and placed them on the windowsills. She also placed small bunches in two, blue-flowered mugs. She set them on the cluttered dresser, one in front of the statue of the Infant of Prague and another in front of the statue of the Blessed Virgin. She took her washing in from the line. She had hung it out to dry that morning, propped high, away from the pig, with a wooden pole. Her pain worsened as she stretched.

Norah prepared the evening meal, fed the children and, with Mary's help, put the three youngest to bed.

"Will you test me on my Catechism, Mammy?" begged Mary.

"Ask Pierce to help you like a good girleen."

The girl was to make her first Holy Communion a few months from now and must pass her Catechism exam with Father Mulcahy first. But Norah hurt too much. She went to stand at the half-door, breathing deeply, trying to control the pain. She wiped her damp forehead with the back of her hand. She was aware of her daughter watching her and tried to smile.

"Mary, call down to Annie, will you, alanna? Ask her to come up."

Norah clutched her belly, breathing in short staccatos, clenching her teeth against the pain, not wanting to frighten her eldest son who sat in the room behind her. What was it; was she losing another child?

"Pierce, where are ye, lad?" Brendan bellowed. "I've the horse unhitched already. Do I have to wait out here all night for you to give me a hand?"

Norah showed no recognition of Brendan's voice as she lay, pale and motionless on the settle, a basin on the floor beside her. Mary stood next to her mother, ready to fetch anything she or Annie might need.

Pierce stepped out of the children's bedroom, where Annie had banished him earlier.

She saw the boy standing at the top of the steps, and beckoned him down.

"Go and fetch your Daddy in, Pierce. Then stay with the horse, will you, lad?"

He hurried down the steps and out the front door, casting an anxious glance at his mother as he went. Brendan soon appeared. He dipped his finger in the small font on the doorjamb, and blessed himself. He was surprised to see Annie standing beside the fire. He couldn't see Norah, who was hidden by the high back of the settle.

"What is it, Annie? What are ye doing here? Is one of the childer sick?"

It was only as he stepped forward that he saw his wife. Her blouse was open at the neck, her ashen face beaded with perspiration, "Mother of God, what's wrong with her, Annie?"

"Brendan, ye'll have to take her to Ballyfin. She has to go to the hospital. She said she's had a terrible pain in her belly. She said it felt like it exploded today. I don't know what's wrong with her, but she's very sick, Brendan, very sick."

Brendan stared at Annie, then at his wife. It was nine miles to Ballyfin. He would have to take her on the cart.

"Mary, go and tell Pierce to hitch up the horse again, and tell him to wipe down the bed of the cart with straw. Be quick girl. Will you stay with the children, Annie?"

She nodded. "Fetch the coverlet from the bed, Brendan, and a pillow, that cart is awful hard."

Brendan took the eight steps two at a time, his heart racing. He ripped the coverlet from the bed, snatched the pillow, and returned. Annie took them from him.

"You'll have to carry her out, Brendan. She can't walk."

Brendan gently scooped his wife up in his arms, and followed Annie.

Pierce and Mary watched in silence as the two adults placed their mother on the cart, wrapped her close in the coverlet, and tucked the pillow under her head.

They remained where they were, unmoving, even when their father had driven out of the village, and out of sight.

As the twilight deepened, Annie took Mary's hand in hers. She put her other arm around Pierce's shoulder, and quietly shepherded the two youngsters back inside.

Brendan traveled the rutted road to the hospital as fast as the horse would allow. He chivvied the animal to go faster; then reined it back when he feared it would jostle the cart too much. He constantly glanced over his shoulder. He wanted to see if Norah was safe, if there was any change.

And he spoke to her.

"Please, Norah love. Please. We'll be there soon. Please don't leave us."

She didn't move, her eyes remained closed, her white face reflected the soft whiteness of the moon.

"Please, Norah. Think about the childer. They need you, Norah. Dammit, I need you."

His tears fell unchecked, the unfamiliar salt taste bitter in his mouth.

"You can't leave us, alanna. Not yet. Not like this."

He feared she was dead long before they arrived.

At the hospital he pulled the horse to a halt. He wiped his tear-streaked face with his sleeve and lifted Norah gently, so gently, from the cart. Looking down at her calm, peaceful face he thought she looked as if she was asleep. He kissed her softly. Her lips were cold.

His shoulders hunched, head bowed, Brendan carried his wife up the steps and into the hospital lobby. A porter hurried forward and helped him lay Norah on a gurney.

"Wait here, sir. I'll take her through."

The porter wheeled the trolley away, down a long, dimly-lit corridor. Brendan watched them go. He prayed to Saint Jude, the patron saint of hopeless cases. He prayed for a miracle, prayed that they would revive his wife.

A nun, dressed in a starched, white, nursing habit came up to him. She shook her head.

"There was nothing we could do. I'm sorry Mr. ...?"

Brendan stared at her, not wanting to hear what she said.

"Would you like to sit down?"

He shook his head.

"Could you tell me her name?" she asked softly.

"Norah."

"She's at peace now. Was she ill for long?"

He didn't want to talk to her. He didn't want to listen. He shook his head again.

She became more efficient. "There's no doctor on duty at the moment, he won't be here 'til the morning. He'll have to sign the certificate before we can release her to you.

"I'll wait."

"I'm afraid you won't be able to stay here all night, hospital rules. Do you have somewhere you can go?"

He nodded again.

"I have to get back now, I'm afraid. I'll send one of the nurses out to you. She will help you to fill out a few forms. I'm sorry for your loss, Mr. ...? I'll say a prayer for her."

He didn't respond.

She touched his arm briefly, in sympathy, before returning down the long corridor. The only sound Brendan heard was the quiet swish of her habit and the tap, tap of her heels on the tiled floor.

When the nurse came, and the form-filling was completed, he left the hospital. For the remainder of the night he sat, hunched and motionless, on his cart.

Long after dawn had broken the porter came out to tell Brendan that a nurse wanted to speak to him again. When he went in she told him that, according to the doctor, and based on the information that Brendan had been able to provide, Norah's appendix had probably ruptured. She said that unless he wanted the doctors to do an investigation, which might take a day or two, the hospital would put that down as the cause of death.

Brendan sensed it was of little consequence to them. And what did it matter to him? She was dead. He wanted to bring her back to Glendarrig as soon as he could. He agreed, and the nurse soon returned with the certificate. She told him he could now collect his wife from the hospital morgue.

Norah, lying in a rough wood casket, was placed on the back of the cart, and Brendan brought her home.

The Family

Annie was preparing food for the children when Brendan opened the cottage door. One glace at his haggard face told her what had happened. Mary, who had been telling the younger children a story by the fire, stood when she heard the click of the latch.

Annie moved towards the grieving man. "I'm so sorry, Brendan."

"I've brought her home."

"Will I fetch Peadar and some of the men?"

"I have to bring her in."

"Of course you do. I'll go and get them. I'll be back directly. Will you be all right, Brendan?"

"Is Mammy back?" asked Colm, climbing down from the settle.

"Keep the childer in here 'til I get back, Mary," said Annie sharply, catching Colm as he hurried towards the door. "Colm lad, go and fetch Pierce for me, will you? He's in the back yard, stacking turf." She turned her attention back to Brendan. "Will you talk to them Brendan, while I'm gone?"

He looked at her and she saw the anguish in his eyes.

"How Annie? How?"

"It has to be done, lad. And you are the one who should do it. I won't be long."

She left and Brendan realized that all the children were looking up at him. Even Michael, though still so young, seemed to sense that there was something wrong. He watched his father, silently, along with the others. Pierce and Colm stood just inside the back door.

Brendan sighed and walked towards his chair. He sat and beckoned to them. They came slowly and made a half circle around him. Mary held Michael's hand with Sheelagh beside him. Pierce stood slightly behind Colm, to keep him in place. Brendan looked at their solemn faces and squeezed his eyes tight against the tears. He opened them and spoke.

"Mammy was sick. She had a bad pain in her belly." He took a deep breath. "The doctors couldn't help her. So she has gone to God."

Colm frowned. "You said you brought her home."

Pierce caught his brother's arm and gripped it tightly. Colm looked around angrily.

"Well he did!"

Pierce dropped his head and said quietly, "Mammy's dead."

"But he said he brought her home." Colm insisted.

"Stop it, Colm. Be quiet." There was a catch in Pierce's voice.

"Pierce is right, Colm lad. I've brought her home for the last time, so that we can take her to the Church."

The latch clicked and the children turned to see Annie, her husband and two other men from the village standing in the doorway. Another neighbor, Kathleen Whelan, stood behind the men.

"Kathleen will take the childer up to Eileen Flynn at the Presbytery for a while, while we do what we must, Brendan. If that's all right with you?"

Brendan nodded. The woman stepped forward.

"Will you go with Mrs. Whelan, children? We'll have you back soon enough."

"Will I stay here, Da?' asked Pierce.

"I don't think so, lad," said Annie kindly, herding the children towards the door. "Your Da will be fine. Eileen will need your help with the younger ones."

They walked slowly out of the cottage. A neighbor was un-harnessing the horse. Mary and Pierce stared for a moment at the cart, and the long narrow box, before following the woman along the road.

Once the children were gone the men moved the table to the center of the room. They then carried in the coffin. Annie persuaded Brendan to rest for a while and once he was upstairs she prepared the body. She braided Norah's hair and dressed her in the blue bombazine dress she had worn for her wedding. When she was finished she took the spring flowers the children had picked for their mother only the day before and placed them at the corners of her coffin.

Later in the afternoon the children returned with Eileen. Brendan, unshaven and exhausted, ushered them to the table.

He lifted his youngest child and held him over the open casket.

"Kiss your Mammy goodbye, son."

Michael kissed her waxen face softly, and Brendan put him down. Pierce stepped forward, pulling Colm reluctantly behind him. Pierce, not tall enough to kiss his mother, reached to touch her hands wrapped round with rosary beads. He touched them gently, then kissed his fingers and touched her hands again. He retreated, dry-eyed, though his face was almost as pale as his mother's. Had anyone cared to look, they would have seen that his bottom lip was chewed raw. Brendan tried to lift Colm, who struggled in his arms, kicking and wailing loudly until his father put him down. Sheelagh stood close to Mary clinging tightly to her sister. Both were crying. Brendan lifted Mary then Sheelagh.

The box was sealed. Annie took the wildflowers from their containers and placed on the lid. Brendan, his brother, and two neighbors carried the coffin on their shoulders. They led the slow procession on the one and a half mile walk to the Church. Behind them, Aunty Bridgie and Eileen shepherded the grief-numbed children. Friends and villagers followed.

Norah Kelly was laid to rest in the cemetery beside the Church, her grave marked by a small granite rock.

Brendan

Walking back from the cemetery, surrounded by his children, Brendan thought about his wife. They had courted for two years before they married. Two years of shy courtship and wistful hopes. They walked out after Mass every Sunday. He even attended confessions on Saturday evenings for the opportunity to meet with her in the seclusion of the churchyard afterwards. He courted her between the graves and kissed her for the first time whilst they sat atop the carved marble tombstone of the Reverend Francis O'Toole. They talked of their future together while wandering between the rough granite rocks that marked the last resting place of many of the villagers. The difference between wealth and poverty was as clear in death as in life.

Brendan suggested they could go to America; maybe they could join his brothers and live in a grand house with slate roof and a separate kitchen. Or, maybe they could go to England, and Norah could get a job in service. They knew many young women who had done this and sent home good money. Brendan could work as a laborer. They would be rich.

But, his father was already ill, coughing blood-flecked phlegm into his rag of a handkerchief at any exertion. In truth, Brendan knew he would have to stay and mind him. Besides, the house would be theirs. No other brother had interest in claiming the family cottage.

After their wedding, the grinding reality of work and child rearing soon built a barrier of weariness between them. He became the provider and disciplinarian who controlled the household with terse words and swift retribution. She was the carer and comforter. Their private time was limited to a familiar and reassuring closeness as they slept together in the feather bed, or the urgent lovemaking that was often too hastily concluded. They seldom argued; Brendan was a good provider, and Norah was a good mother to their children. But, deep in his heart, he knew she was also a constant and abiding part of himself, his one true love.

Michael cried. Brendan lifted him and tried to sooth the confused child.

"Do you want me to take him, Brendan?"

Annie Quinn, her husband Peadar, and several of the villagers were also straggling homeward after the funeral.

"No, Annie, they are my children. I'll take care of them." He held Michael close and walked a little faster.

"Will you want people in tonight to keep you company?"

"I appreciate it, Annie, but I want some time to myself now."

"Can I help you with the childer?"

He was striding ahead of her, his four older children trotting to keep up. He struggled to control his anger, and the tears smarted in his eyes.

"Just leave us be, Annie. We'll be fine. Mary is well able to mind the little ones."

She fell back. She would wait. No man alone could rear five children and earn his living. Brendan Kelly was a proud man, but he would need help. She would be there when he needed her. For Norah and the children's sake, if not for his.

When they arrived back at the cottage, Brendan saw the neighbors had been busy. The table, now returned to the kitchen corner of the room, was laden with dishes filled with food, fresh bread, a small ham, and a basket of vegetables. He did not have to concern himself with finding food for his family for a day or two.

"Where's Mammy?" whimpered Sheelagh. "I want her back now."

Mary and Pierce looked up at their father, pale-faced and silently pleading.

"She's dead," said Colm, "That's why we put her in the box in the dirt."

Mary looked at her brother in horror and began to cry. Michael joined in.

Brendan stared helplessly at his children, then roared, "For the love of God, will you all give me some peace."

The silence was instant. He carried Michael to the chair beside the fire. Sitting his youngest son on one knee, he beckoned Sheelagh to sit on the other. She went forward cautiously, afraid he would shout again. He spoke quietly and gently.

"Mammy has gone to be with Holy God and the angels."

"Do angels live in the dirt, Da?"

"No, Colm son. It's Mammy's soul that has gone to Heaven. That's the most important part of Mammy."

"Will she be coming back?" asked Sheelagh staring up into the dark eyes and tired face of her father.

Brendan bowed his head and said nothing for a while. The children waited, expectantly. Without looking up, he shook his head.

"No, Sheelagh love, she won't." he took a deep breath and turned his attention to Mary. "You have to be the Mammy now, Mary. Will you mind these little ones for me while I see if I can get something to eat for us all? Pierce, get your father a jar from under the stairs, will you?"

"What can I do, Da?" asked Colm.

Brendan glanced around the cottage, trying to find a chore for his middle son. "Will you keep the turf basket filled from the pile outside the back door, son? We can't have wet turf on the fire, can we?"

"All right, Da." Colm hurried to fulfill his task.

The five children sat in a line along the settle, each with a bowl and spoon in hand, eating slowly. Brendan sat in his chair on the opposite side of the fire. Norah's chair stood empty between them. Five pairs of eyes watched him as he poured his fourth bottle of porter and raised the glass to his lips. He lowered the glass.

"Jaysus! Will you all stop staring at me! It's not my bloody fault she's dead. Oh, for God's sake, Mary, would you get some food into that child's mouth! He's shoveling it everywhere."

Mary hastily slid from the settle, put down her bowl and spoon, and took Michael's from him.

When they were finished eating, Mary prepared the two youngest for bed and remained upstairs with them. Pierce took Colm to fetch water, trying to keep him from aggravating his father any more. On their return, he persuaded his young brother to bed early with the promise of a story. Brendan was left alone. He fetched another bottle of porter, lit his pipe, and gazed morosely around the small cottage.

His father, Michael, built the place before *his* marriage many years ago. Since then three generations of Kellys had pounded the earthen floor to a dull shine. Brendan's mother died when he was still a boy, so it was his father who reared Brendan and his brothers, employing belt and fist to ensure his seven sons were brought up obedient and God-fearing.

"If he could do it, I can." He muttered, sipping his drink.

Brendan, the last to wed, brought Norah to the Kelly cottage as his bride. His siblings had long since gone their separate ways.

He puffed at his pipe and studied the sparsely furnished room dominated by the wide black hearth. Two small, dusty windows, deep-set on either side of the front door, let in a little light, but Norah's flowers were gone. The back door, a half-door that could open top or bottom, was open at the top, the only other source of natural light.

He and Norah inherited the meager furniture with the cottage, including the two rough-hewn beds and the feather mattresses that filled the two loft rooms under the thatch. Even Brendan's fireside chair once belonged to his father, the wooden arms polished smooth by fifty years of use. Brendan slowly rubbed them now in remembrance. The large high-backed, oak settle on the opposite side of the hearth had been a wedding gift from his mother's parents. The seat lifted to reveal a deep chest where extra blankets and the children's clothes were stored.

A ponderous black oak dresser, cluttered with an ill-assorted collection of china and family treasures, took pride of place on the wall opposite the hearth. Two plaster statues stood on either side of the top shelf, one of the Infant of Prague, the other of the Virgin Mary. A worn picture of the Sacred Heart rested up against a cup and a dusty Saint Bridget's Cross made from rushes leaned against an old whiskey bottle filled with holy water from the shrine at Knock. On the center shelf between a chipped glass and an old yarn shuttle was the wedding photograph.

He stared at the picture for a long time. Tears slid slowly down his whiskered face.

"What am I going to do without you, Norah love?"

Could he really care for the children himself? They were still so young. He didn't want to be beholden to the neighbors. They had enough children of their own anyway. Perhaps Bridgie could mind them. But she was an old lady. She wouldn't be able to do it for very long. He stared unseeing at the glowing embers of the dying fire and finally looked reluctantly back to the photograph.

"I'll have to wed again, Norah. The children need a Mammy. They're too young. But I'll have to ask your Aunty Bridgie to care for them in the meantime. While I look."

Once his decision was made, he acted promptly. The next morning, once the children were up and breakfasted, he hitched the horse to the cart and traveled to Doonbeg to Bridgie's shop. Mary sat beside him, Michael on her lap.

Colm sat behind with Sheelagh surrounded by four small bundles of clothes Brendan had gathered together earlier. They left Pierce behind in the cottage. Brendan decided he would keep him; the lad was good with the horse.

They traveled in silence, the children wondering where they were going, and Brendan deep in thought. He knew he didn't have time for a courtship; he needed a wife soon, but how to find one? There was no matchmaker in Glendarrig. He would talk to his brother; he would know.

Bridgie welcomed the children warmly and assured Brendan she would be happy to take them in until he was settled. With a brief farewell he left them in her safe charge.

Two weeks passed before Pat called to the cottage with news. He'd been making enquiries in several local villages and had finally heard of a young woman living in Rathfen. She was barely turned eighteen, and her family were seemingly anxious to see her to wed. Pat said he'd met her Uncle Johnjo in a local bar. The uncle was a bit of a matchmaker and would be happy to help Brendan "for a small consideration."

"The family probably has too many mouths to feed," said Pat. "Daughters are a terrible burden," he added. He had four of his own. "She's well enough looking by all accounts though I haven't seen her myself. Anyway, beggars can't be choosers, and you need a wife."

Less than a month after Norah's funeral, Brendan removed the heavy stubble from his chin with a well-stropped razor, washed and pasted down his unruly hair, and fought with his collar and studs. Without explanation to Pierce, he hitched the horse to his freshly scrubbed cart, climbed onto the narrow driver's bench, and urged the horse towards Rathfen.

He found the uncle's cottage located on the road into the village. The older man was standing at the side of the road waiting for him. He escorted Brendan to the ramshackle cottage. The thatch was neglected and holed, the interior dark and uncared for. Chickens strutted in and out of the open door, and Brendan saw a large sow heavy with litter lying on her side in the viscous mud of the back yard. Inside the cottage the smell of chicken droppings, soot, and stale food hung in the air. Two upright wooden chairs sat side by side in front of the fire, one occupied by a young girl. She stood as Brendan entered.

Her Uncle Johnjo introduced them, poured two small glasses of Madeira, and placed them on a stool near the chairs. He then excused himself saying he had to milk the cows. The meeting was awkward, the girl quiet, and Brendan acutely ill at ease.

She was as thin as Norah had been and barely reached to Brendan's shoulder. Her clothes were clean but worn, and she pulled her shawl tightly around her shoulders as if to protect herself. He saw her hands were red and raw. She was no stranger to hard work. The young woman seemed close to tears, but her jaw was clenched as tight as her fists, and she sat stiff-backed and silent as Brendan spoke.

"I'm not a man of words, woman. I have my own home and a horse and cart. I have five childer who are God-fearing and biddable, and I owe no man. If you have a mind to wed, I will ask your uncle Johnjo to post the Banns before I leave Rathfen today. We can be wed three weeks hence, God willing."

The girl nodded in silent agreement, staring down at her hands.

"I have no bad habits and will honor and respect my vows, no matter what," he said with more emphasis trying to convince her. "I have work and can provide."

He was struggling to find the words that would persuade this young woman of his good intentions. He watched her for a minute more, hoping for some other sign that his courtship had been successful. She said nothing.

"That's settled then," he said, reaching for the glass of Madeira and drinking the liquid in a single gulp. He grimaced at the sweetness, replaced the glass on the stool, and rose to leave.

"I doubt I can call again much before the day. I must visit my childer after late Mass on Sundays. My wife's aunt is minding them all, except for Pierce. I'll leave the arrangements to Johnjo. My brother Pat has business for his wife's father in Rosscar. He will be passing this way on Sunday week. He can meet with your Uncle and settle the details."

He paused, uncertain how to conclude his visit.

"It has been a pleasure to meet you, ma'am, and I thank you for your time."

Brendan left the cottage feeling uncomfortable at the subdued reception from his bride-to-be. But he was glad the marriage had been agreed to without too much fuss. He must pay the matchmaker a fee, but it was worth it to find himself a wife so quickly and easily. Bridget Clancy could not be asked to mind the children much longer.

Aunty Bridgie

"Fetch the eggs from the hens, and mind you don't startle them," said Bridgie handing Sheelagh the chipped mixing bowl. "And help Mary wash them before you bring them into the shop. There's a good child."

The little girl, tongue thrust firmly in her cheek in concentration, carefully took the bowl. She walked to where she knew the nests lay hidden in the tall grass and thick bramble hedge that marked the yard's perimeter. As she had seen her mother do so often, she flapped her smock to startle away a hen still sitting on its nest, then stretched her arm gingerly into the thorny undergrowth to find the still-warm eggs. There were two. She placed them gently in the bowl and continued her hunt.

Meanwhile, Colm collected a basket of turf from the lean-to where Bridgie stacked the sodden fuel to dry. It was his job to keep the wickerwork basket beside the hearth full. It seemed to the young boy that the fire was always burning too brightly and that Aunty Bridgie piled on the crumbling turf sods far too often, but he did as he was told. He worked slowly for he knew that as sure as he would finish one task she would find him another.

Mary washed the eggs her sister collected carefully removing dirt or a stray feather from the smooth brown shells.

"Mary, your brother has soiled himself," called Bridgie over the half-door. "Come and take him out there and wash him by the pump like a good girleen, and clean up in here when you're finished. I have to serve a customer in the shop."

Bridgie usually tried to escape the more distasteful aspects of caring for a small child, and Mary accepted the task that was so familiar to her. Fortunately the well and pump were close to Bridgie's back door, so there was no long trek for water.

She put down the cloth and egg, fetched Michael, and took him to the pump. She removed his shirt and pants and sluiced him down. The small boy gasped in shock at the coldness of the water, then stood obedient and quiet while his sister washed him. He watched her with the same sad, lonely expression that he watched everyone and everything these days. Since Norah's death he was silent, choosing not to use the few words Mary had so painstakingly taught him. He accepted his food when it was given, went to bed when he was told, and endured. He was equally unresponsive to Mary's ministrations and Bridgie's overpowering hugs as she clasped him to her ample bosom in spontaneous expressions of her grief.

Mary dried her brother with a rough towel, steered the shivering boy back to the cottage, and dressed him in warm clean clothes taken from the rack in front of the fire. She then sat him into the worn plush chair. He remained there, watching the flickering yellow and red flames lick up towards the chimney. He was content to sit, withdrawn in his own silent world.

When Mary had time, she sometimes sang him nursery rhymes and told him tales of fairies and enchantment, ancient kings and magical deeds. All the stories her grandfather had told to her, she now retold to her baby brother. He sat quietly in her small lap, watching her face animate the tales, but seldom smiled.

Michael was not the only one. All the children were subdued. Bridgie was kind and had not hesitated to take them in. She knew that Brendan must work and could not care for them on his own. No other family member could take on the burden of four extra mouths to feed, house, and clothe. Families were too large and resources scarce.

Pierce remained with Brendan. Though he said the boy was good with the horse and could help in the house, Bridgie thought Brendan also needed his son's company. Maybe it was a comfort to him to know there was still one of his children in the tiny cottage, now so quiet. The others would be going home soon, she reassured herself, as soon as he had a new wife.

When he came to visit them with his father on Sundays, she could see Pierce missed his siblings almost as much as he missed his mother, but the visits were strained, and there was little conversation. Bridget prepared a meal which they ate crowded together in the stuffy confines of the back room, the children even more quiet than usual in the presence of their stern father. He, in his turn, did not know what to say and ate in silence, watching his young family. They were surprised to see him drink milk instead of his usual bottle of porter. They didn't understand that Bridgie tolerated no alcohol in her house.

After the meal, while his father lit his pipe and Bridgie cleared the dishes, Pierce escaped to the back yard with his brothers and sisters. Even there, there was little laughter and less comfort amongst them as they tried in their different ways to adjust to the shock of losing their mother.

Colm seemed the least upset at their loss and tried to capture the attention of his older brother as he always had. He tried to show off to Pierce how grown up he was becoming, how he collected the turf, and how he sometimes fetched the water just like his older brother. But Pierce paid his bothersome brother little attention. He was more drawn to Michael. He would take his youngest brother by the hand and walk the yard with him, watching a bee fly from wildflower to wildflower, or a spider weaving a web, or a bird stealing tidbits from the pig's trough. The two had no conversation, just a quiet bond.

When father and son arrived at Bridgie's the Sunday after his visit to Rathfen, Brendan seemed more ill at ease than usual. He told the children to go and play in the backyard.

As soon as they were out of earshot, he addressed Norah's aunt.

"I've found a wife, Bridget." He fidgeted with the coins in his pocket. "We are to wed Saturday three weeks. She's a girl from above in Rathfen. Her family is agreeable to the match."

There was a brief silence while Bridget measured her response.

"I'm glad for you, Brendan. Norah would be glad too. The childer need to be in their own home, and they need a mother."

"Will you explain to them, Bridget? I wouldn't rightly know how."

"I will, of course. They will be fine;" the old woman said, patting his arm. "It will take them a while to get used to their new Mammy, but give them time, and they'll be grand."

"If you will keep them 'til after the wedding?"

She nodded. "Of course I will, lad."

"I'll take them home then."

She told them as gently as she could.

"She will love you just like your own Mammy," she promised, "and won't it be grand to go home again and not be shouted and roared at by your old Aunty Bridgie?"

Once they understood what would be happening, Mary was the first to react.

"I don't want to call her Mammy. She's not my Mammy," she said, beginning to cry.

"Now now, girleen, don't be upsetting your sister and brothers," said Bridget, drawing the girl to her, brushing away the child's tears, and trying hard to suppress her own. "Maybe you can call her Mrs. Kelly to begin with, then when you get to know her, you can ask her what she would like to be called," she suggested.

"I don't want to call her Mammy either," said Colm.

"I want my own Mammy," said Sheelagh, her lip trembling.

"Right, then ... why don't you *all* call her Mrs. Kelly to begin with," said Bridget, trying to fend off an impending scene.

It was agreed, but the tension continued to be high in the house. The children were on edge and nervous about meeting their new mother.

Pierce

On the day of his marriage, Brendan left at first light. It was to be a quiet ceremony. His brother Pat would stand for him, and Brendan thought it would be
better if none of the children were present. Pierce didn't mind. He was in no
hurry to meet the woman who was replacing his mother.

"You can feed the pig, fetch some water, then go over to Aunty Bridgie's,"
Brendan told him. "Stay there overnight, if she's willing. I'll collect you and the
other children tomorrow."

Pierce nodded his agreement. As soon as his father left, he hurried through
his chores and left for Doonbeg, getting there before Bridget's shop was open.

"Bless us, child, your brothers and sisters are barely out of the bed. You can
eat with them if you like. Will you have some porridge?"

Pierce nodded. He sat watching as his aunt prepared the breakfast. He spent
the day with the family, helping Mary and Colm with their chores and minding
the younger ones, while Bridget went visiting and Mary watched over the shop.
Aunty Bridgie said he was welcome to stay the night. She assembled a make-
shift bed on the floor in front of the fire.

When Pierce woke the next morning, his first thoughts were of his father,
and the new mother he would meet today. They would all be going home, and
the family would be together again. He stretched his limbs, stiff from sleeping
on the hard floor, and waited impatiently for his aunt and the others to be
ready.

Bridget hurried the children to first Mass, fidgeted through Father Mulcahy's long sermon, and briskly shepherded them homeward as soon as the
service was over. She was very curious to meet the new Mrs. Kelly and anxious
that the children should look their best. She prepared a hasty breakfast then

fussed about, readying the children and herself for the arrival of Brendan and his new wife.

"Would you look at the dirt of your face, Colm Kelly? Did any of your breakfast egg get inside you at all? Sheelagh, don't wipe your hands on your dress; how often must I tell you to use the cloth, child?"

Pierce wanted none of this. Since his mother's death, his father left him very much to himself. Excessive washing was not something he enjoyed.

"I'll walk out along the road to meet Da."

"But you'll be all dusty for your new Mammy," said Bridget.

"I'll be careful," he said. "Da won't mind."

Bridget was preoccupied with the younger children.

"All right, Pierce, we'll see you shortly, but mind your manners when you meet her."

He slowly walked the three miles homeward, expecting at any moment to see his father's horse and cart coming from Glendarrig. He kicked a small stone ahead of him, raising tiny dust clouds with his boot. Near the village he passed the horse that was still tethered at the side of the road. He was surprised his father had not yet set out. He petted the horse, gave him a few handfuls of sweet grass, and continued home.

The Children

"Will you hold still, child of grace."

Colm squirmed as Bridget soaped and scrubbed him.

"Now, out you get, lad." She helped Colm step out of the tub and wrapped him in a towel.

"Will you get Michael into the tub, Mary, while I dry Colm?"

Mary undressed her brother in front of the fire and lifted him into the now tepid and soap-scummed water. Meanwhile Bridget rubbed Colm dry with the rough towel until his skin glowed pink and warm. She poked the cloth into his ears, scoured his neck, and snipped at his nails with her tiny sewing scissors. When she was finished, she stepped back to admire her handiwork.

"Well you're as clean as I can make you lad; now sit still, and touch nothing 'til I finish Michael."

"When can I take out these rags?" pleaded Mary.

The previous evening Bridget decided to try to persuade Mary's long straight hair into ringlet curls, to match her younger sister's natural curls. She'd twisted and tied the reluctant hair into a dozen strips of damp cloth, and Mary patiently endured the laughter of her siblings when they saw what their great-aunt had done. Now, she wanted to see the results.

"I'll do it as soon as I've finished your brother," said Bridget snatching the damp towel from the chair and drying Michael vigorously. "Don't touch those scones, Sheelagh," she snapped, as she saw the little girl edge towards the table.

Bridget intended to welcome the new bride in style. She'd brought out her mother's best china the day before and washed it carefully. She also ironed her very best tablecloth, unused for many years. The china plates were now piled high with assorted scones and fruit bread. In the delicate flowered dishes there was homemade butter, two kinds of homemade jam, and fresh, thick cream.

"Can I taste the jam, please?" begged Colm, joining his sister.

"No, you can't, Colm Kelly. Look at you, you're a disgrace; you've not a stitch on you! Mary, get him into his clothes; there's a good girl. Your new Mammy will be here any minute. Do you want to make a holy show of me, Colm boy?"

Mary helped Colm into his knee-length trousers and his shirt. She buttoned it and tucked the long shirttails into his pants. She struggled with his suspenders, pulled on his thick wool socks, and tied his bootlaces in firm knots. Colm pulled faces at her the whole time. Bridget finished dressing Michael.

"Right then, Mary, let me get those rags out, and we can put in your new ribbon." She loosened and untwisted the rags, gathered the unsuccessful ringlets atop Mary's head, and tied them with a wide, red ribbon. "You look beautiful." She stood for a moment looking into the anxious face of the young girl, then cupping Mary's face between her hands; she kissed the child's forehead. "Your Mammy would be proud of you," she said. She remembered the reason for all this fuss, and hastily added, "and your new Mammy will be too." She turned to look at the other children. "Come here to me, Sheelagh, and I'll fix your ribbon. Now line up the lot of ye 'til I see how you are."

With Sheelagh tugging Michael into position, the four children lined up in front of the fire, all four standing stiff and straight facing their aunt and awaiting inspection.

"You are a sight for sore eyes," said Bridget. They broke line and surrounded her. Tense with nervousness and excitement, they bombarded their aunt with questions. What was she like? Would she really be like their own Mammy? Was she very old, like Aunty Bridgie?

Bridgie had no answers for them but laughed and replied, "Sure no one is as old as me." Then added, "have patience, we'll all know soon enough. Now sit down there, and Mary will tell you a story while I go and see if they're coming yet."

Mary sat in the armchair with Sheelagh tucked in beside her. Colm and Michael sat on stools on either side of the chair. She began to tell them the story of the Children of Lir.

"Not that one, Mary child. Not today," said her aunt sharply before walking through to the shop to look out of the window.

Four cloth bundles sat tied and waiting beside the shop door. They were all ready.

Pierce

When he arrived at the cottage, Pierce raised the latch and stepped in. Both of them looked up as he entered. His father sat in his chair beside the fire and a young woman busied herself at the table. They were not speaking. Pierce felt a tension in the house.

"Ah, Pierce, come in lad," Brendan beckoned the hesitant boy forward and turned to the young woman. "This is him; this is Pierce."

"Good morning, Ma'am," said Pierce, nodding his head.

The woman looked at him, nodded in return, and continued her work. The boy turned back to his father.

"Are you going to fetch them soon, Da? They're waiting for ye."

Brendan avoided Pierce's gaze, "I'll be going over soon enough boy." He stood, looked at the woman, and then turned to his son. "I've to go out for a while and then I'll be going over to Doonbeg."

Pierce was not sure if his father was talking to him or to the young woman, but as she made no response, he said, "I'll come with you, Da. I told Aunty Bridgie I'd ride back with you."

"You'll stay where you are lad," he father answered tersely. "Stay here 'til I get back. You can feed the pig and fetch some water. I'll be back before dark."

Again there was no response from the young woman. Brendan blessed himself at the font and left the cottage.

Pierce sat on the settle watching the woman wash the blue flowered bowls and china mugs. She was short, not much taller than himself. He was surprised at how young she looked, much younger than his mother.

She turned to look at him, "What are you staring at like a gob-daw?" She spat the words at him. "Didn't I hear him tell you to feed the pig and fetch water? There's none left in the bucket. Am I expected to clean this place with no water?"

Pierce jumped to his feet, startled by the hard voice and sharp words. He took the bucket of kitchen slops into the back yard and emptied the contents into the trough. As he re-entered the cottage, she thrust the water bucket at him.

"And when you get back, you can empty the privy; it's like a midden in that place. You're dirtier than pigs."

He snatched at the bucket, scurried past the angry woman, and hurried out of the front door.

The china was spread all over the table when he returned.

"You took your time," she said. "Pour some of that water in the kettle and set it over the fire. I can't clean the filth in here with cold water. And don't forget about the privy!"

He did as he was told, collected the stinking bucket of waste, and hurried out through the cottage again.

Once Pierce emptied the bucket at the pit, he decided to take his time going home. He didn't want to be on his own with the woman any more. He wanted to wait until his father came back with the rest of the family. As he walked, he realized that he didn't know how long Brendan would be. If *she* wanted to use the privy, and he didn't have the bucket back, he suspected he would get another tongue-lashing. He walked a little faster.

Arriving at the cottage door, he lifted the latch and stepped nervously into the room. She was drying the china and arranging it back on the dresser. The wedding photograph of his mother and father was gone. The picture of the Sacred Heart and the statue of the Infant of Prague were now in the center of the top shelf with a large, black crucifix between them.

She pointed at the bucket he was carrying; "You can take that thing out in the back yard and scour it with lye and hot water. I don't suppose anyone's ever done that before in this house. Then get back down to the pump and scour yourself. I won't have any foul-smelling little brats in my house."

Pearce did as he was told. He was confused and upset. Why was she so angry? What had he done? His mother never spoke to him like this. He was used to the belt from his father, but Brendan was a man of few words. If Pierce did something wrong then the belt was out, the beating painful, and the matter closed.

After scouring the bucket until his hands were as raw as the young woman's, the boy again set out to the village pump. He pumped the handle and thrust his sore hands into the stream of ice-cold water trying to clean all traces of dirt.

He took a thin twig from the hedge and dug at the dirt under his fingernails. He wanted no more scolding today.

Pierce decided to wait until he saw his father returning on the cart before he went home again. When the sun began to sink in the west, and there was still no sign of the horse and cart or his father, he set off to walk to Aunty Bridgie's in Doonbeg. He was over halfway there before remembering his father had told him to stay close to home. The boy turned and walked slowly back to Glendarrig. Still reluctant to return and face the woman, he ambled up and down the lane outside his home, aimlessly kicking stones.

The Children

Bridget expected Brendan to arrive in the early afternoon. Each time she thought she heard a horse and cart, she went through to the front of the shop. She leaned into the widow display of lucky bags, combs, ribbons, and soaps to peer up the road. Each time she returned to the small back room shaking her head at the expectant faces. She anxiously watched the clock on the mantle, constantly patted her wispy gray hair into place, and nervously smoothed her Sunday best black skirt.

The shadows lengthened across the yard, and still he did not arrive. Bridgie was becoming more and more anxious. The children had long since lost their neat and tidy appearance, though Sheelagh's ribbon was still held in place by her tight curls. Mary's tired, red, satin bow slid slowly down her increasingly lank hair. Bridget retied it a few times but finally gave up and tucked it into the girl's apron pocket. Colm, having removed his tight-laced boots, was rolling a large glass marble along tracks created with turf dust he'd taken from the bottom of the peat basket.

At teatime Bridget gave the children some of the scones. Sheelagh and Michael soon smeared the thick, sweet jam across their faces, hands, and clothes. Bridget seemed too distracted to notice. She must have made the journey to the shop window a dozen times, she thought. She even went outside the front door once or twice to get a better view of the road, but Brendan was not to be seen.

"Maybe your Da got some special work he had to do today," she told them reassuringly, "or someone is moving house and needs his horse and cart."

As dusk settled, she decided he would not be coming at all that day and told Mary to get the two youngest ready for bed. Then she again heard the clatter of horse's hooves on the road.

"Here they are; I'm sure that's them. They're coming," she said, hurrying yet again to the shop window. The children stiffened then followed her.

"It's him," she said turning and nearly tumbling over her charges. "Quick, go and tidy yourselves up."

They hurried into the back room, stumbling and bumping into each other in their haste.

"Colm, put your boots on and sweep up that dirt this minute. Mary, wipe the jam off their faces, child, and brush your hair! I'll tidy the table and fill the kettle."

Michael was tired and bewildered. He did not understand what was happening, but he sensed the tension. Alarmed by the fuss and bustle, and exhausted from the day's unusual activity, he began to cry. Bridget scooped him up in her arms and went to open the door for Brendan and his new wife.

Pierce

"What are you hanging about for, young Pierce; why aren't you at home at this hour?" Annie Quinn was standing in the doorway of her cottage, arms folded, watching the boy.

"I'm waiting for my Da. He's coming home with Colm and Mary and the others."

"That's good lad, it will be nice to have your brothers and sisters back. You've missed them, I'm sure. And is your new Mammy at home, Pierce? Wasn't your Da in Rathfen yesterday getting himself married?"

Pierce nodded.

"And how is she, lad? Do you think you'll like her?"

Pierce looked bleakly at his neighbor. Annie felt sorry for the boy. He looked so unhappy. "Come here to me, lad;" she beckoned the boy closer. Placing her hands on his shoulders, she bent to look into his face. "It's bound to be a bit hard to start with, son. She's married one day and has five childer the next. That's a lot for her to get used to, and from what I hear, she's only a young one herself. She's not ten years older than you lad, and now she has five to mind! Give her time Pierce; I'm sure she will be a great Mammy once she gets used to you all."

Pierce nodded again.

"Have you had your tea, son?"

He shook his head.

"Would you like a bite of bread and cheese while you wait? I'm sure your Da will be home soon."

Pierce nodded, he'd not eaten since breakfast in Aunty Bridgie's, and he was hungry. Putting her arm around his thin shoulders, Annie ushered the forlorn-looking boy into her cottage.

Brendan

Brendan arrived alone. Bridget and the children watched him descend unsteadily from the cart. He stood swaying slightly, his head down and shoulders slumped, not looking at the small group clustered in the doorway of the shop.

"Brendan, are you all right?"

He looked up and saw Bridget and the children. He took a deep breath, squared his shoulders, and stepped towards them. "I am, of course, Bridget. How are ye? Hello, Mary child."

Mary gave a half smile and stepped aside for him to enter the shop.

"Colm, it's quite the man you are now." He ruffled the boy's hair, dropped his hand to Colm's shoulder and let it rest there. Colm, standing tall, beamed up at his father. "And Sheelagh, would you look at that ribbon in your hair!" Brendan continued, "Aren't you a princess?" Sheelagh tucked herself shyly behind Bridget's skirt unsure of this attention from her father.

He looked at the small, now silent, boy Bridget held in her arms.

"How are you son?" said Brendan brushing a stray tear from the boy's face.

Michael stared unblinking at his father. There was no smile or glint of recognition for the large, whiskered man smiling down at him.

"Come in, Brendan, come in; we thought you'd forgotten us. Didn't we childer?"

As he passed, Bridget smelled the whiskey on his breath and pursed her lips. So, he'd stopped off at Daly's for a drink or two. That's what had him so late. She led the way into the back parlor.

"Sit down there 'til I make you a pot of tea. You must be parched with the thirst," she said with a hint of sarcasm. She put Michael down and placed the kettle back on the hearth to boil, though in truth she had been boiling it all day waiting for his arrival. "You didn't bring your new wife then, Brendan? We were all looking forward to meeting her, weren't we, children?"

The children continued to watch their father, not responding to Bridget's question.

"Have you seen young Pierce? He left here hours ago to meet you."

He nodded; "He's at home."

"Would you like a scone, Brendan? We made scones especially for you, didn't we children? And we have jam and cream."

Bridget was becoming nervous. Brendan seated himself in the chair before the fire and stared into the flames. She felt the need to fill the silence with chatter. "I have their bundles packed; there are a few damp pieces before the fire, but they'll be dry before you finish your tea. It will be ready in a minute, Brendan. Mary, get a scone for your Da."

He turned from the fire, "No, no scones." He took a deep breath. "Bridget, could the children sleep here tonight?"

"But I thought you came to take them."

She saw the pleading look in his eyes.

"Of course they can; it's late anyway, and it's time they were in bed. Mary was just going to take them up when we heard you coming. Weren't you, Mary darlin'? Would you take them up for me now like a good child? I'll be up in a minute to hear the prayers."

Mary took Michael and Sheelagh by the hand. Colm hung back, reluctant to leave his father. "I'm not tired, Da. I could go back with you tonight. We could come back for them tomorrow. I want to see the new Mammy. And I want to see Pierce. Where is he, Da? Is he with the new Mammy?"

Brendan cast a helpless glance at Bridget.

"Up to bed with you, Colm Kelly. Your Da and I want a cup of tea in peace and quiet. It's long past your bedtime. Tomorrow's another day."

Colm grudgingly followed his sisters and brother upstairs.

Bridget busied herself making the tea. She poured two cups and brought them to the hearth.

"Here, you need this, I think." She handed him a cup, pulled a chair to the other side of the fire, and sat facing Brendan. "What's wrong, lad?"

He stared at his worn boots, his hands wrapped around the cup as if he were cold. "I don't want the children home, Bridget."

"That's all right, Brendan; sure they're gone to bed now. Tomorrow is grand."

"I don't want them at all, Bridget."

"Brendan, don't be mad, man," she paused for a moment. "Did you not get wed, Brendan? Is that what it is?"

"Oh, I'm wed all right; made my vows before the altar and signed the register and all."

"Well, didn't you wed so the children could have a new Mammy? What ails you, man? Of course, you want your children."

"No, Bridget, I don't."

"But, Brendan, I can't look after them forever. This house is too small and I'm too old to be minding four small children. Sure I'm exhausted already, and I've only had them a few weeks. Anyway, they need to be in their own home. What on earth is possessing you to say you don't want your own children? What about Pierce? Where's he? What about him? Are you fevered, Brendan?"

He slumped disconsolately in the chair. "No, Bridget, I'm not fevered, and I know you can't care for them forever. I will be putting them in the Sacred Heart Orphanage above in Ballyfin. The nuns will take good care of them. I'll be keeping Pierce."

"Brendan Kelly, have you lost your head entirely? You can't pick and choose your children. They are *all* yours, Brendan, and you can't go dumping them in an orphanage just because you got yourself a new young wife. What would Father Mulcahy say if he heard you?"

"It's none of his business, Bridget, and it's none of yours either. They are my children, and I will do with them what I will." He stood and placed the still-full cup on the table. "It will take me a day or two to make arrangements. I would ask you to keep them 'til then. I'm very sorry about this, Bridget, but this is how it's going to be, and I'll thank you not to question me further."

"What about Norah, Brendan? The poor woman would turn in her grave if she knew what you were doing. I can't believe you mean this. What has gotten into you? What has your new wife to do with this?"

"You'll say nothing of my new wife, Bridget Clancy. This is my decision and mine alone." He walked towards the door. "I'll send a message when I have things done. I'm sorry Bridget, and I thank you for your kindness to the children. I will make arrangements as soon as I can."

Bridget followed him through the shop; "Who's going to tell them, Brendan?"

"If you would do that, Bridget, I would be grateful, but will you or no, they *will* be going to the Sacred Heart. Goodnight Bridget, and thank you again."

He left Bridget standing in the doorway of the shop, climbed clumsily onto the driver's seat of the cart and tapped the horse's rump with a stick. The horse moved forward. Another tap on his left rump, and the horse turned the cart to face the road out of Doonbeg and set off at a slow trot. Bridget watched until he was out of sight. Brendan never looked back. She returned to the parlor, sank into the armchair before the fire, and wept quietly.

Mary crept down the stairs, hesitated, and then went to her aunt. She put her arms around Bridget's shoulders. Tears welled in her eyes.

"I don't want to go to the Sacred Heart, Aunty Bridgie."

Pierce

His supper eaten, Pierce left Annie's cottage and again took up his vigil outside his home. It was night, and only a pale moon lit the narrow lane. At last he saw his father's horse and cart coming slowly towards him. He jumped up from the grass verge and ran forward to greet his siblings. The cart was empty. Only his father sat on the bench seat hunched over the slack reins, and letting the horse make his own way home along the familiar road. Pierce took the reins and led the horse to the grass patch beside the cottage.

Looking up at his father, he asked, "Where are they, Da?"

Brendan was startled by the voice. He'd not noticed his son. He stared down at him for a while.

"You look just like your Ma. Did you know that, son? You have her eyes, and you have her face."

He clambered down from the cart and stood unsteadily. Pierce caught the pungent smell of whiskey. Brendan rested his hands briefly on his son's head, stared at Pierce a moment longer, then dropped his hands and took a deep breath.

"They're not coming home. I told your Aunty Bridgie. They'll be staying with her for a short while longer and then we'll see. Don't look so worried lad. I'm keeping you here." He jerked his head in the direction of the cottage; "I told her you were staying, told her you worked with me and minded the horse. You'll be fine lad. You will stay put. Be a good lad and unhitch the horse and take him out to tether."

He patted Pierce on the head in an unaccustomed gesture of affection, took another deep breath, and walked purposefully to the door of the cottage. He staggered slightly as he went.

Bridgie

Main Street,
Doonbeg,
Co. Galway.
June 17th 1924

Dear Liam,

I am heart sore to have to trouble you again so soon after writing you the sad news about dear Norah, but I am at my wit's end.

As you know Brendan was set upon marrying again as quickly as he could to find another Mammy for the poor gosters. And find a wife he did. But Liam, the day after the wedding didn't he ride over here, the worse for drink I might add, and tell me he wanted nothing more to do with them, and that he was putting them with the nuns in the Sacred Heart in Ballyfin! The orphanage, Liam! I have no idea what has got into the man at all, and he with a healthy new wife. Though I have not met the girl, by all accounts she is God-fearing and a hard worker. But he has his mind made up.

I am keeping the children with me for now, all except Pierce; he is to stay with Brendan, but I can't go on forever keeping them. Young Mary knows what Brendan is about, but the others are just bewildered by it all. They still think they're going home, and I haven't the heart to tell them otherwise.

Mary made her First Communion a week ago, and though Brendan came, he said his new wife was sick and that was why she wasn't there. I made a grand breakfast for everyone afterwards, but he didn't stop. He gave Mary a few coins and left. Poor Norah would have been heartbroken.

I have asked him not to speak to the nuns for a while until I see if there is anything to be done, though I can think of nothing. His brother Pat is no help. He says he has a house full to the roof, and it's not his house either.

*I am sorry to burden you, Liam, but in the hopes you can find a miracle, I
remain—*

Your loving sister,

Bridget.

Bridget slowly folded the letter, put it into the envelope, addressed it, and
went to sit in her chair beside the fire. It was evening, the children were in bed,
and the house was peaceful. The crackle of the fire and the ticking of the clock
were the only sounds. She stared down at the letter in her lap. She would wait a
while longer; maybe she could manage, give it a little more time. Michael was
almost fully trained now. Colm would be starting school soon. Mary was trying hard to be helpful. She stood and tucked the envelope behind the clock.

When she saw Brendan at Mass the following Sunday, she asked him to wait
a while longer. There should be no more talk of the orphanage for the time
being.

Three more months passed. It was close to the end of September. Only
Sheelagh and Michael were with Bridgie all day. Colm had started school,
which should have helped, yet it seemed no easier. "I'm too old for all this," she
would mumble as she picked up discarded clothes. "Too tired," she sighed as
she scrubbed grimy collars and cuffs against the washboard; "too stiff," as she
kneaded dough and cleaned the range. She was exhausted with the care of the
children. They were becoming peevish and quarrelsome. When he was not in
school, Colm teased and tormented Michael and Sheelagh at every opportunity. Sheelagh, in her turn, was ill-tempered and tearful. She argued with her
brothers and sister and demanded Bridgie's attention to resolve every quarrel
and perceived hurt. Mary took on her father's role of disciplinarian. She boxed
Colm's ears when she caught him tormenting the younger children, and
shouted at Sheelagh to "stop whining and moaning like a baby." The girl was
even becoming short-tempered with the quiet Michael, tiring of her role as
minder and nursemaid.

Bridgie had little experience in coping with young children and the basic
chores of washing, cooking, and cleaning for so many. Minding the shop left
her little time. There was no time to give them the loving attention she knew
Norah would have provided. She was also beginning to realize the cost of feeding them, and she was too stubborn to ask Brendan to contribute, muttering to

herself, "If he doesn't know his duty to those children, I cannot teach him. I will not fight with his wife for his money."

"A flock of gannets, that's what ye are," she told them at tea when they yet again finished the entire loaf she'd made that morning, along with the soft boiled eggs which they mashed in their cups with spoonfuls of butter. "Don't cut the bread in such thick doorsteps, Mary; sure, they'll choke to death on those," she scolded. The children seemed undeterred by the large size of the chunks of bread and wolfed them down even more quickly as if fearful their aunt would take them back.

She could not cope, yet the thought of putting them into the orphanage still grieved her. She desperately needed a solution. She spoke to Father Mulcahy who assured her, "The children will get good care in the Sacred Heart, Bridget, and I am sure Brendan has good reason for his decision. Regrettable as it may be, it is not for me to interfere in the matter."

When she sought out Norah's friend, Eileen, she too was sympathetic.

"But I live in the Presbytery, Bridget. Wouldn't we be the grand family now: the Parish priest, his housekeeper, and four little ones? I would help you if I could, but I have to keep my position. I've nowhere else to live. Have you spoken to that chit of a wife of his? What ails them both that they'll not take the children back?"

Bridget wondered the same question herself. At every opportunity she continued to ask Brendan for a reason. He was steadfast in his silence on the subject.

"I have made my decision, Bridget. I will not have the children back in the house, save for Pierce. There is nothing more to be said."

He was clearly firm in his resolve, and she was afraid he would not even visit the children if she aggravated him further. As she still had not met his new wife, she tried a different line of questioning.

"Will I meet Mrs. Kelly soon, Brendan?"

Maybe at a meeting she could persuade the new bride to take on her rightful duties as stepmother as well as wife.

"In good time, Bridget; she is anxious to put the house in order and settle in. All in good time."

Annie and other neighbors from Glendarrig told Bridgie of the cleaning being done in the small cottage.

"*Both* feather beds were hanging on the line, and it blowing a gale! She's lucky they didn't land in the pig trough!" said one.

"Front and back door swinging wide open and every piece from the dresser on the table being washed and polished," said another.

"She has the lad worn out fetching water from the pump; sure his arms are growing longer by the day, poor mite," said a third.

"Too grand by half she is. Clearly thinks herself far too good for the likes of us!"

Tired of the children's squabbling and exhausted by the work, Bridget took the letter to her brother from behind the clock. She would have to mail it to Liam after all, though she had no idea how her brother would be able to help.

Within a month she received a reply.

22 Gloucester Road,
Brixton,
London.
October 28th 1924

Dear Bridget,

I am sorry it has taken me a while to reply, but I just might have some good news for you.

As you know, my supervisor, Mr. Fairburn, is a good man and many's the chat we'll have about this and that. Well, I was talking to him soon after getting your letter, and he says to me, "Isn't it a funny old world when you have four children in need of a good family, and wouldn't Mr. Sinclair and his good wife only love to have a family, but God hasn't blessed them? And now isn't Mrs. Sinclair getting on a bit for having babies?" And then he said, "Perhaps I'll mention it to Mr. Sinclair and maybe, as he might have sympathy for their plight and all, he might have a suggestion."

Well Bridget, doesn't God work in mysterious ways? The next thing I know, Mr. Sinclair is calling me into his office and asking me all about the childer, and what ages they are, and if they're healthy and all, and then he says to me, "I have always regretted I never had a son to take over the business when I'm gone Clancy. I always hoped to have a sign over the business that read, 'Sinclair and Son, Bespoke Tailors.' Unfortunately it seems it is not to be. However, Clancy, I have spoken with Mrs. Sinclair and she has said that if there were a boy available, preferably one ready for school—for she doesn't think she could cope with a child under foot all day—that she would certainly consider taking him in." Now doesn't that just fit Colm to the letter, Bridgie?

I know it was not the answer you would want, and it would be better if they were all together, but remember they would be separated in the orphanage anyway. And wouldn't it be a great opportunity for Colm?

That is not the end of it, Bridget. Mr. Sinclair may be able to find a home for Michael and Sheelagh too. It seems that an old friend of Mrs. Sinclair, who lives in Bristol and is also childless, may be willing to take the two youngsters. They have a haberdashery shop in a nice part of the city center. He says they are good people, and the children would have a fine life. The last, and best of the good news is that they are all Catholics, Bridget, so you need have no fear for the welfare of their souls.

At present I have no good news for Mary, but it may be that we have a small miracle here anyway. I hope you will reply with all speed, as the Sinclair's are anxious to know if they can begin to make plans. Mr. Sinclair says he will travel to Doonbeg himself to collect the children if you agree. By the way, he also asked if there was a photograph of them, so he could show his wife and her friend.

Mr. Sinclair says he will ensure the two youngsters are transported to Bristol safely if you and the other couple are willing.

Well, Bridget, what do you think? I look forward to your reply and hope you will not disappoint Mr. Sinclair who has always been very good to me.

Your loving brother,

Liam.

Bridgie folded the letter and returned it to the envelope. It was the fifth time she had read it since Mattie Byrne delivered the post that morning. She sighed. She knew she must decide. Things could not continue as they were. *Was* it the miracle she had been praying for? "God moves in mysterious ways," her brother had said. Well, maybe God *was* watching over the children. Maybe Liam was right. It was a grand prospect for Colm, and if the two youngest could stay together, wouldn't that be better than an orphanage?

She would speak to Brendan one last time on the subject and see what he had to say. Maybe the thought of losing his children altogether would bring him to his senses, though Norah always said Brendan was a willfully stubborn man once he made up his mind.

Maybe Mrs. Kelly could persuade him to soften his heart, thought Bridget. Perhaps it was time to pay her a visit. She decided she would have to try for the sake of the children, and the sooner the better. She decided she would go the next day. Mary could watch the shop. A day off school would do her no harm.

Mrs. Kelly

Though Bridget set out for Glendarrig at dawn, Brendan's cart was already gone from beside the cottage when she arrived. She took a deep breath and tapped on the door. There was no response. She stepped back and gathered her shawl tighter around her shoulders. She nervously patted her hair into place, brushed imaginary dust from her skirt, stepped forward, and rapped more firmly. The door opened slightly, but Bridget could not see into the shadowed interior.

"Mrs. Kelly?"

"Yes."

Bridget took another nervous breath.

"Mrs. Kelly, I'm pleased to meet you at last. I'm Bridget Clancy, the children's great aunt."

"Yes."

The door did not open any further.

"We haven't had a chance to meet, though I'd dearly like you to come over for a cup of tea. I know you have been busy, of course, what with your marriage and moving into your new home, but I thought I would take the liberty of making a call on you to welcome you to the family."

There was no response. Bridget felt uncomfortable. She was becoming acutely aware of the neighbors' curiosity.

"Would it be possible to have a word with you in private, Mrs. Kelly? I won't detain you long, just take a few minutes of your time."

The door opened wider, but still Bridget could not see the woman. She stepped down into the cottage, and the door closed behind her. She turned. Mrs. Kelly stood with her hand on the latch, watching her. Bridget was startled. She knew Brendan's wife was a young woman, but she was unprepared for what she saw. Mrs. Kelly was little more than a young girl. A painfully thin child with mouse-colored hair pulled into a loose bun at the nape of her neck. Ice-blue eyes were the only color in a tired, pale face. A much-darned dress, colorless from age and wear, hung from her frail shoulders, and she hugged her rough-woven shawl close.

"God Bless all here;" Bridget smiled gently at the young woman. "I am glad to make your acquaintance, Mrs. Kelly." She paused and glanced towards the settle. "May I take the weight off my feet for a moment? These old shoes are a little tight around my bunions, and 'tis a while since I walked a distance."

The young woman shrugged and gestured towards the settle.

"Thank you," said Bridget, as she slowly lowered herself onto the polished wooden seat. She glanced around the small cottage. "My, would you look at this place! I declare I never saw it gleam so. You've been working hard, my dear. Everything is sparkling. Brendan is a lucky man to have you to care to for his home."

"Forgive me, Ma'am, but I have a deal of things I must do ..."

"Of course, of course, I don't want to delay you. I just wanted to have a word with you about the childer."

"They are Mr. Kelly's children, Ma'am, and I suggest if you want to talk about them, it is he you should speak to. He will be home this evening; or indeed I can ask him to call on you if you wish."

"I have tried to talk to him several times, my dear, but he is determined to put the poor gosters into the Sacred Heart. I just can't believe that's what you would want. Sure haven't they a beautiful home right here with a Mammy and a Daddy to care for them?"

"I believe he has decided what he wishes to do with them, Ma'am, and I am not their Mammy."

"But, didn't you marry their Daddy? Didn't he marry you to have a Mammy for his children? I know Norah, God rest her soul, would be heartbroken at what he is doing. They are beautiful children, Mrs. Kelly. I know you'd love them once you saw them. And this is where they should be, in their own home. They miss their Daddy and their brother. Mary can turn her hand to anything, and Colm is getting so big now he can take on all kinds of chores. Sheelagh is a little dote, pretty as a picture, and young Michael would melt your heart with his big brown eyes. He's such a quiet child; sure you'd hardly know he was in the house. Mary can mind the little ones for you," she paused for breath, glanced around, and added, "She would make sure they didn't make a mess."

"Ma'am, I have no doubt what you say is true, but I must tell you again; this is Mr. Kelly's decision, and you must speak with him, if you will. Now, I must ask you to leave. I have things to do and time is passing."

"But you're barely above a child yourself. Can you not imagine how those poor children are feeling? First they lose their Mammy, and just when they thought they would have a new Mammy, they are told they must go to an orphanage. They're not orphans, child. They're four lonely, lost childer who want nothing more than to come home. Can you not imagine what it must be like for them with no Mammy and only this old lady to make a sorry hand of it?"

The young woman continued to stand erect before Bridget but turned her face away as if in impatience. After a moment, she turned back to face the older woman.

"Yes, I can imagine how hard it is, but there is nothing to be done. I would help if I could, but the final decision is not mine but his. I can do no more."

"But, how can you do this to them? You are fit and healthy, well able to mind them. What is the problem? Why won't he have them? Why won't you persuade him? Explain that to me. God knows there has to be a good reason. Just help me to understand what the reason is."

"Mr. Kelly will be in this evening. I will tell him you called."

She stood, unmoving, and eventually Bridget stood also.

"There is no swaying you then?" She tried to recover some of her composure. "I will take my leave of you, Mrs. Kelly. I must ask that you consider what I have said. I am too old to care for them myself, though God knows I wish I could. I must do something. I cannot see kin of mine go into an orphanage. That place is nothing more than a workhouse. We have never done that to our own in this family, and we'll not do it now. Would you ask Brendan to visit with me at his earliest convenience?"

A brief nod was the only response.

"Thank you for your time, Mrs. Kelly. I wish you well and still hope you may reconsider."

The young woman stood, stiff and silent, as Bridget walked to the door, dipped her finger in the font, blessed herself, and turned.

"Suffer little children, Mrs. Kelly. Isn't that what the Good Lord said? Suffer little children to come unto me!" She raised the latch and opened the door. "Good day to you, Mrs. Kelly." She pulled the door closed behind her.

Bridget walked the long road back to Doonbeg, angry and confused. Her feet ached, but anger fueled her quick steps, and her determination to take action sped her journey home. She didn't understand why, but it was clear there was no melting the heart of the new Mrs. Kelly, and Brendan had already closed his ears to any talk on the subject, so she must make the decisions herself.

Would she be able to give the care of the children to strangers, in England at that? Liam did say they were good people, and she trusted his judgment. What had he said? "A small miracle?" Well, maybe that's exactly what it was. Right, so … this Mr. Sinclair wanted a photograph. Well, she would get one taken, send it, and see what happened. Meanwhile she would talk to Brendan about her brother's letter. Maybe it would shake him into taking responsibility for his own.

Bridget didn't see the young woman she left behind in the small cottage fall to her knees, didn't see her bury her face in her hands, or hear the sobs that wracked the slight frame. Even if she had, she would not have understood.

Bridget

Bridget was surprised at how quickly things happened. Brendan called on her the evening of her visit to Mrs. Kelly. He was angry at her intrusion but as obstinate as ever about not taking his children back and about being prepared to place them in the orphanage. When Bridget showed him the letter from Liam, he shrugged his agreement, seemingly unfeeling to the care and welfare of his children. She arranged for a studio portrait of the five children to be taken and sent it, with a letter, to her brother.

Main Street,
Doonbeg,
Co. Galway.
November 13th 1924

My Dear Liam,

Here is the photograph Mr. Sinclair asked for. All the children are in the picture in case he might consider keeping the family together and give them all the same chance. I'm sure it's hardly likely, given that their own Da won't do it, but I will storm Heaven in case the Good Lord might help change his mind. At present it seems that if I do nothing, then nothing will be done. He seems content to let the younger childer go, though firm that Pierce will stay with him.

So, Liam, if Pierce is to stay with his Da, and the three small ones are to go to England, I have decided I will keep Mary with me. God love her, she is terrified of going to the orphanage, and rightly so. I couldn't do it to her, poor child. Anyway, I have grown very fond of her, and she is a great help around the house and shop. I can manage the one child, Liam, and I won't feel so badly that I have let poor Norah down.

So, now it is up to you. What must I do? They have very few clothes, but I will make sure they are as clean and tidy as I can make them. I have my button box beside me even as I write. Young Colm seems to lose shirt and trouser buttons as quickly as I can sew them on. He is growing so fast it is hard to keep him clothed, every stitch is stretched to the limit.

I hope to hear from you soon, Liam. Please tell your Mr. Sinclair how good the children are and how glad I am that my prayers have been answered through him.

God Bless you both,
Love,

Bridget.

The reply was prompt.

12 Victoria Ave.,
Finchley,
London,
November 27th 1924

Dear Miss Clancy,

I thank you for the delightful photograph of your grand-nephews and nieces. Colm looks like a very amiable young man, and I look forward to making his acquaintance in the near future. The two youngsters look charming, and I am sure Mr. and Mrs. Porter will be delighted with their new family.

Mrs. Sinclair sends her good wishes. She regrets she is unable to travel with me. However, I intend to bring your brother so that the children will not be too apprehensive on the journey.

I understand you are anxious to resolve their situation as soon as possible, so please let me know when it would be suitable to collect them. I have already made enquiries as to transportation. We are able to travel to Dublin on an evening ferry. We will travel by train to Ballyfin the following morning but trust you can arrange transportation to take us from there to Doonbeg. I also understand from Clancy that accommodation is hard to come by locally, so we will travel back to Ballyfin the same evening.

I trust these arrangements meet with your approval, and I will make the reserva-tions as soon as you provide me with a date. I look forward to our meeting,

Sincerely,

Edward Sinclair, Esq.

It was done. She had only to choose a date. But how was she going to tell them? How could she explain? Bridgie tucked the letter purposefully into her apron pocket. It would be Christmas soon. She could not send them away before then. No, she would write to Mr. Sinclair and ask if he would wait until after that. It would be time enough. She would have a few weeks. Bridget knew that Christmas Day usually differed very little from any other in the Kelly household. This year she would try to make it a special day, a day they would remember.

On receiving the letter from Edward Sinclair, Bridget quietly reassured Mary that neither she nor the rest of the children would be going to the orphanage.

"Are we to stay with you, Aunty Bridgie?" the girl asked hopefully.

Bridget was not ready to explain; she needed time, wanted to be sure she said the right thing.

"All in good time, alanna, not now. I have to think for a bit."

Mary badgered her aunt. Over the next few days she became increasingly upset and frustrated at Bridget's reluctance to give an answer. Finally, a week after she received the letter from Edward Sinclair, Bridget decided she was ready.

It was after supper, and the children were ready for bed. Their faces were washed, hair brushed, and nightgowns on. Evening came early at this time of year, and the warm yellow light from the oil lamp and the red glow of the turf fire gave the small room a cozy, safe feeling. Bridget gathered the small family around her as she sat by the fire. It was a time when, if she was not too tired, she would often tell them stories from the Good Book, or tales of Irish myths and legends, the feats of the brave Cuchulainn, or the battles of the High Kings.

This night with Michael nestled snugly into her lap, half asleep, she told them of their new lives. She tried to paint a picture of adventure: exciting train and boat journeys, great privilege, new friends, and wonderful opportunities. Colm was full of excitement; Sheelagh was nervous, but curious, and Michael understood little. Mary cautiously watched her aunt weave her tale. She only gave a grateful smile when Bridget said, "And I have to keep Mary with me. You have become my right arm, Mary," she said smiling at the young girl. "I could not imagine being without you."

The Children

As the small group left the church, Mary and Sheelagh pulled their shawls further over their heads and wrapped them across their chests. Mary tied hers in a firm knot at her back and then did the same for Sheelagh. The shawls gave some protection against the biting wind and the rain. Bridgie was also well wrapped in her black winter shawl. She held Michael close to her skirt to give him as much warmth and protection as she could. Colm seemed unaffected by the weather and scanned the exiting congregation looking for Pierce.

"There he is, Aunty Bridgie, and there's Da." He paused for a moment, squinting into the driving rain. "Is that her? Is that the one?"

Bridgie and the children looked to where Colm was pointing.

"Yes, Colm, that's her. That's Mrs. Kelly. Now all of you remember to mind your manners. Remember it's baby Jesus' birthday, and you have just been to Mass. And don't point, Colm!"

Brendan, his wife, and Pierce joined them. The four children stared in silence at the woman standing beside their father. She stood, head bowed, hands hidden in her shawl.

"Good morning, Bridget." He indicated the young woman beside him, "You have met Mrs. Kelly, I believe."

"I have. Good day to you, Ma'am. Good morning, Pierce. How are you, lad? Will you be coming back to the house with us? I know your brothers and sisters would like that."

Pierce glanced sideways up at his father who gave a slight nod.

"Yes, please, Aunty Bridgie."

"Hello, Da."

"Hello, Colm son. How are ye?"

"I'm fine, Da. Me and Michael and Sheelagh are going to England."

"Yes, son, I know."

Brendan's voice was unusually gentle.

"And we're going on a boat, and Uncle Liam is coming over to fetch us."

"Yes, son, I know that too." Brendan brushed rain from his face. "It is a grand chance for you, son. You be sure to make me proud of you. All of you."

He looked at Sheelagh, then Michael. "You're all growing very fast! You're no baby any more, young Michael!" He turned to his eldest daughter; "I'm glad you are staying with your Aunty Bridgie, Mary. Your mother would be happy to know that."

There was an awkward silence. Mary stared hard at her father, anger and hatred burning in her eyes. She said nothing.

Bridget cleared her throat.

"Right, so! I'm sure you have things to attend to, Brendan, so I'll not keep you. Come on children; we are going to visit your Mammy before we go home for a grand big breakfast."

She gave Brendan and his wife a curt nod. Then, putting one arm around Michael's shoulder, and grasping Sheelagh's hand tightly, she guided them all to the small mound of earth and the granite stone that marked Norah's grave. Once there Bridget led the family in a subdued decade of the rosary. She led the prayers, feeding the small glass beads through her fingers:

> "Hail Mary, full of grace,
> The Lord is with thee.
> Blessed art thou amongst women;
> Blessed is the fruit of thy womb, Jesus."

Here Bridget and the children bowed their heads for a moment in reverence before the children chorused the second half of the prayer:

> "Holy Mary, mother of God,
> Pray for us sinners,
> Now, and at the hour of our death.
> Amen."

Ten times they repeated the prayer while the rain soaked into their wool clothing and the wind whipped their hair against their solemn faces. Bridget finished the prayers, and the children blessed themselves. They stood in silence, the two youngest visibly shivering.

"Come on then, children! Your Mammy would not be happy if I let you all get drowned in the rain. And on Jesus' birthday! I'm sure you're all famished. If we don't get home soon, we won't have time to put the dinner in the oven, and then what would we have for our feast later? Mary, why don't you tell Pierce what he has to look forward to. Colm, mind your small sister doesn't fall in the puddles. Come on, young Michael; let's get you home for some warm milk."

They left the churchyard, Bridget chattering to fill the silence and to distract the serious little group.

A white linen cloth covered the table set for six with all of Bridget's best cutlery and china. She bustled around making a pot of tea and warming milk in a small pan for Michael. She laid several thick slices of bacon on the griddle, and the rich salty smell soon filled the room. When the bacon was almost ready, she cracked six eggs, tipped them into the hot grease, and added generous slices of bread to sizzle and fry, soaking up the fat.

The children were standing in a half circle watching their aunt.

"Mary child, pass me the plates one at a time, and we'll feed these gannets before they take it right out of the pan." She smiled at Pierce. "You're our special visitor today, so I think we will give him the first plate, Mary."

She put two slices of the crisp bacon, an egg, and a wedge of fried bread on the boy's plate. "There you are, lad. That will fatten you up; you look all skin and bone. Doesn't that woman feed you at all? Right, Mary, I think Sheelagh is next. Will you cut hers up for her?"

She was laughing at Colm who all the while was busy trying to stand closest to her where he could best be seen.

"All right, Colm, I'm getting to you. Stop jiggling around so, or you'll knock somebody over."

When they were all sitting at the table, Bridget said grace. They quickly chorused their Amen's and attacked the food.

"You would think I never fed you," she said, smiling proudly at them.

There was silence as the children busied themselves eating. Intent on their meal, they did not see the stray tears that escaped Bridget's eyes, or hear the quiet sob that escaped her tightened throat. She quickly squared her stooped shoulders. This would not do, she told herself. They *would* have this special day, and she would not spoil it with tears.

"Keep some room for later. We have a big dinner to eat as well with roast chicken!" she said, and hugged Sheelagh.

It was a happy day. Mary played Hide-the-Thimble with her brothers and sisters. Pierce taught them to play Dominoes with an old set Bridget found at the back of the dresser, a remnant from her childhood. They played I Spy and, when the rain stopped for a short while, they went for a walk, all of them sucking on the barley sugar sticks their Aunt gave them from the large glass jar in the shop.

When dinner was over and the dishes washed, dried, and put back on the dresser, she told them she had one more surprise.

"All of you sit there by the fire. I've to go upstairs and get something. When I tell you to, close your eyes for me. Will you do that?"

All the children nodded, the younger ones squirming with excitement. Bridget climbed the narrow stairs to her bedroom. She gathered up the different packages wrapped in brown paper and tied with string. She tugged them from under the bed, uncovered them in her tiny cupboard, and burrowed for them amongst her clothes in the chest of drawers. When all the packages were gathered, she called out, "Close your eyes," and carefully descended the stairs.

"You can open them now."

She handed out the gifts to her surprised charges: a new shirt each for the boys, and new smocks for Mary and Sheelagh. The boys also received a pair of socks each. "Your sister Mary and I nearly went blind knitting those for you, lads. Didn't we, dear? So, try not to put holes in them too soon."

She gave the girls two small peg dolls dressed in scraps of material from her sewing basket. She also gave the girls new ribbons for their hair. There was blue for Sheelagh. "To go with your eyes my darlin' girl," she said, kissing Sheelagh's forehead, "and pink for you, Mary, to show off your beautiful brown hair."

Soon after the gift-giving, Pierce said it was getting late, and he would have to leave. Bridget gave him a slice of fruit cake to eat on his walk home.

"Walk carefully. There's precious little moon to light your way. Will you be over to say goodbye to the childer on the Sunday before they go?"

"I will, of course, Aunty Bridgie."

"Good, we'll see you then. Take care, lad. You know you're always welcome here, Pierce. Mary will be happy to see you, too. I'm sure she's going to miss the little ones dreadfully."

After Pierce left, Bridget and Mary put the younger children to bed, washed the dishes, and tidied the room. At last Bridget sank exhausted into her chair and Mary sat on the stool beside her.

"What a day. Didn't we do well, lass? I don't think they will have a better Christmas anywhere. They'll look very grand in their new clothes when they meet Mr. Sinclair."

She looked down at Mary's pensive face.

"Don't fret yourself, child. We'll manage, alanna. Somehow we'll manage. And I promise you, they will be well minded."

1925

The Children

Three days, that was all she had left, three days. She bustled around her tiny home gathering the children's belongings together. She darned and patched, washed and ironed. She polished their scuffed boots and shoes until the worn leather shone. She trimmed hair and nails and drilled them endlessly on manners, prayers, and behavior. Mary ran the errands, prepared the meals, and minded the shop. By the day of Mr. Sinclair's arrival, Bridget and Mary were exhausted, and the younger children were in a high state of excitement and apprehension.

Bridget had convinced Brendan that the least he could do was meet Mr. Sinclair and Liam at the station in Ballyfin and bring them to Doonbeg. He eventually agreed, with reluctance. During the ride, all of Sinclair's attempts at engaging the children's father in conversation were greeted with morose grunts. The smell of whiskey on Brendan's breath did little to encourage Sinclair to persevere. They made most of the six mile journey in silence.

When the horse and cart arrived outside the shop, the four young Kellys stood quietly inside the doorway while Bridget hurried out to greet her brother and the smartly dressed stranger. Liam jumped down from the back of the cart and gave her a quick hug. They waited patiently while Mr. Sinclair stepped down from the bench seat and brushed down his immaculately tailored overcoat. Liam introduced Bridget to him.

Sinclair removed his glove and extended his hand. "I'm delighted to meet you, Miss Clancy."

Bridget subconsciously wiped her hand on her skirt before proffering it.

"Mr. Sinclair, sir, thank you for coming and for bringing Liam. I don't see half enough of him."

She bit her lip.

"I mean, being the only brother I have left, it's always nice when I get to see him, and I'm sure the children will be happier traveling with him."

Her hands flew to her face, which suddenly felt very warm. Why couldn't she say what she meant?

"I mean, this being the first time they have met you, and you being British."

His accent would be unfamiliar, that is what she had meant to say. She hadn't meant to criticize the fact that he was British. Though, Bridget thought, Lord knows didn't we have the right to criticize the British after all they've done to us? She shook her head, took a deep breath, and spoke again.

"I mean, the strange accent would be hard for the little ones to understand …" Her voice trailed off.

"Won't you come in, Mr. Sinclair? I have tea in the pot."

He smiled reassuringly at her.

"Forgive me, Miss Clancy, but it took longer to get here than I expected. I have arranged overnight accommodation in the hotel in Ballyfin and would like to make it back there before dark. Mr. Kelly has assured me we can do it if we leave with all haste. I know this must be a difficult time for you. But, if the children are ready, I would like to leave immediately."

"Yes, sir, of course."

Liam watched the awkward meeting between his sister and his employer.

"Mr. Sinclair is a very busy man, you know, Bridget."

She turned her attention to her brother. She could feel tears burning her eyes. She would have no time with her brother after all. They were going to leave now, right away. She closed her eyes, struggling hard to stem the tears and tried to compose herself. Oh, Norah, I'm so sorry, she thought. I should have tried to keep them with me. I should have made Brendan help me. I should have tried harder. She took another deep breath, opened her eyes, and tried to smile at her brother's employer.

"Let me introduce you to the children, sir."

Colm quickly stepped around his older sister and hurried forward. His hair was slicked into order with water, his face scrubbed to a pink glow. His new shirt was neatly buttoned, and his knee-length wool pants were held up by sturdy gray suspenders. He was wearing the new socks Bridget and Mary knitted for him and tugged at them before grinning up at the man. Mr. Sinclair smiled down at him and extended his hand.

"From the photograph, I'm guessing you must be Colm."

"Yes, sir."

"I'm pleased to meet you."

Mary led Sheelagh and Michael out, both clutching her hands tightly.

"And, you must be Sheelagh and Michael."

Sheelagh glanced at her aunt for reassurance, then nodded. The large blue bow tied high in her red curls bobbed as she did so. Michael stared up agape at the stranger. He, too, wore a collarless shirt buttoned neatly to the top but frayed and faded with age. Bridget had cautiously decided to pack his new shirt for his arrival in England. His hand-me-down pants, though hauled high under his arms by his suspenders, still reached below his knees, and his wool socks, also hand-me-downs from Pierce and Colm, were worn thin and well darned. Bridget put her hand on Mary's shoulder.

"This is Mary, their older sister. She is the one who has made it possible for me to mind them for as long as I have. She's a great girl and a credit to her Mammy."

Bridget gave Brendan a hard look, and he shuffled uncomfortably under her critical gaze. Liam again intervened.

"And, she'll be great company for you, Bridget, with Norah and the little 'uns gone. I would be worrying about you if I was thinking of you on your own all the time."

He gave Mary a warm smile. Bridget had not tried to torture her hair into curls again. It was in a short bob with a thick, dark fringe cut scissor-straight across her pale forehead.

"You will take good care of your Aunty Bridgie, won't you, Mary?"

The girl nodded. There was a brief silence.

"Will we put the children's things on the cart, Mr. Kelly?" said Mr. Sinclair. "Do you children think you can climb up on the back?"

"I can. I'm nearly as big as Pierce now," said Colm, "and I can carry water like him, and fetch in the turf."

"Well, I doubt we'll have need of those talents when we get you home, son, but I'm glad you have been of help to your aunt. Right, then, I think it's time we were going."

He turned again to Bridget.

"We will take good care of them, Miss Clancy. Mrs. Sinclair is most anxious to meet young Colm, and Mr. and Mrs. Porter are traveling to our home to collect the two little ones. Mrs. Porter is just as excited as my wife. I don't doubt they will be waiting for us on the front doorstep when we get home. I will write and give you news of the children once they are settled in."

He turned to the group standing beside the cart.

"Well, are we all ready?"

Colm had already clambered up and settled himself on the cart immediately behind Brendan's seat. Brendan placed the children's three small bundles beside his son. Mary lifted Sheelagh, held her close, and began to cry. Bridget put her arms around them both, making reassuring noises, but she too was crying.

"You be a good girl now, Sheelagh, and mind your young brother," she said wiping the tears from the child's face with her shawl. "Mind your manners, too, and don't be looking for attention all the time."

She held the little girl's freckled face between both hands.

"Don't forget your old Aunty Bridgie. Will you, child? You'll be in my prayers every day." She kissed Sheelagh, as Mary, still weeping silently, lifted her young sister onto the cart.

"You mind her, Colm," she scolded her younger brother. "Be sure she doesn't tumble over when the horse starts up."

Colm nodded unconcerned.

She turned and lifted Michael. Bridget kissed him too, and Mary sat him up beside Sheelagh. She tucked the bundles around the two of them to help them keep upright and to protect them from the harsh cold of the January afternoon.

"Don't forget to say your prayers before you go to bed, Sheelagh, like I taught you. Teach Michael his prayers too, and be sure he says them each night. And, don't forget, 'God Bless Mammy.'"

Brendan was now sitting hunched on the driver's bench, and Sinclair climbed up beside him. Liam gave Bridget a hug.

"Sorry we can't stay, Bridgie, but it's just as well. He has to get back to his business, and I have to get back to work. Don't be worrying yourself about the children. They will be fine. They're going to good homes. You know it's for the best."

Liam hoisted himself onto the rear of the cart, his feet swinging over the back. "I'll write to you as soon as I can and let you know how the journey went. You start praying for a smooth crossing on the boat. I never knew such a rough sea as we had on the way over. We don't want them getting sick on their nice clean clothes, now, do we? I'll be back before too long, lass; mind yourself."

As Brendan tapped the horse, Bridget suddenly remembered the envelope in her pocket.

"Wait, wait, I must give you this, sir."

She groped in the depths of her pocket, retrieved the envelope, and handed it up to Sinclair.

"It's their baptismal certificates, sir, from the parish records. Father Mulcahy thought you would be needing them. It shows they are all baptized and Catholic, sir. It has the birth dates as well. It will give you all the details you will be needing, sir."

Sinclair thanked her and tucked the envelope into his inside pocket.

They set off towards Ballyfin, the jingle of the harness and the rhythmic clop of the hooves sounding clearly on the late afternoon air. Colm knelt up behind his father and Mr. Sinclair, peering between them to see the road ahead. Sheelagh and Michael sat among the bundles, tear-stained but quiet, looking solemnly back at their sister and elderly aunt. Liam waved to Bridget and Mary until the cart followed a bend in the road and they were lost to his sight.

The elderly woman and the young girl stood side by side for several more moments, staring at the empty road, until Bridget put her arm around Mary's shoulder, and they slowly walked into the empty shop.

Pierce

Pierce sat beside the fire, staring angrily into the flames.

"I don't see why I couldn't have gone with my Da."

"He told you. There was not enough room on the cart. And anyway, don't I need you here to fetch in the turf and get the water? God knows your father's never around to do it."

"But I wanted to say goodbye. I wanted to see them before they went."

"And haven't you been over there every Sunday? You see your sister every day at school. She's going nowhere. You can see her whenever you like."

"But, I wanted to see the others before they went away to England. I will never see them again. It's all your fault anyway. Why couldn't they stay here? Everyone says it's your fault. We were all fine before you came along. A real Mammy wouldn't make them go away. I hate you. You made them go away, and I'll never see them again, and it will be your fault."

Despite the tears welling in his eyes, he stared straight at the woman.

"Get out of my sight, you little brat. You know nothing. It's not my fault they're gone; ask your precious father. I'm sick of you looking at me like that. Get up those stairs, and don't bother coming down again this night. I'll give no supper to an ungrateful little brat like you. And you needn't think I'll forget this, Pierce Kelly. Hate me, do you? Well, I hate you too, so you keep out of my way from now on, or it'll be the back of my hand for you. I'll get your father to send *you* to the Sacred Heart if you don't mind your step. Then you won't see your sister or your precious Aunty Bridgie either. If you're not doing work around here, just keep out of my sight. Do you hear me, Pierce Kelly?"

Pierce stormed up the short flight of stairs. At the top he turned and glared at the woman.

"I do, and I don't care. I hate you. You're not my Mammy. You'll never be my Mammy. I'm not scared of you. You'll burn in hell."

Sheelagh and Michael

Despite Bridget's attempts to prepare them, the two-day journey by boat and train was a terrifying experience for the two younger children. The Irish Sea crossing was mercifully calm, but the thunderous throb of the boat's engines, and the intermingling of a hundred different sights, sounds, and smells overwhelmed them. Edward Sinclair and Liam Clancy tried to reassure the frightened pair, but the accents of the two men made them almost incomprehensible to Sheelagh and Michael. While they could understand Liam when he remembered to speak slowly, his native Irish accent was overlaid with a cockney twang that often left the children mystified. Their older brother had no such difficulty and patently enjoyed the whole adventure.

At the end of the second day, the exhausted youngsters were petrified when Edward led them towards the shiny black automobile at the railway station in London. Only the gentle urging of their Uncle Liam, and the enthusiasm of their older brother, convinced them to climb into the forbidding, leather-perfumed interior of the strange metal monster. When the engine started with a loud bang from the exhaust, they both screamed and cried for several minutes until Mr. Sinclair and Liam soothed and reassured them. Colm laughed at their fright and begged Mr. Sinclair to allow him to sit in the front seat. Edward laughingly agreed, and once the two youngsters were calmed and settled in the back with their great-uncle, they set off.

Colm sat on the edge of his seat for the whole journey, alternating between examining the interior of the car with its polished wood dashboard, clocks, dials, knobs and levers, and craning to see where they were going as they drove through the leafy London suburbs. Liam sat in the back seat with Michael sitting on his lap and Sheelagh tucked in tightly beside him.

The children stood in the center of the room like sheep in a pen surrounded by adults. Liam Clancy waited by the door, their bundles in his hands.

"Well, my dear, here they are, our little orphans, in from the cold so to speak. Jim, it's good to see you."

Sinclair shook the man's hand.

"And you, Edith dear."

He kissed the thin woman lightly on the cheek. "Now, I'm sure you are anxious to meet your new charges."

He beckoned to Colm who came to stand beside him.

"May, my dear, here is our new son, Colm. Colm, come and say how d'you do to your new mother."

Colm extended his hand to the tall woman smiling down at him.

"How d'you do …" he hesitated, unsure how to continue, "Ma'am, I mean, Mammy."

"I think if you call me, Mother, it would be nice, Colm."

She wore a slim, knee-length green dress, low-waisted as was the fashion. A long, double string of pearls hung from her neck, and she twisted them nervously as she spoke. She had blond hair cut short and coaxed into tight Marcel waves. The fine dusting of her pale face powder highlighted the delicate tracery of lines around her eyes and mouth.

"Yes, Mother," Colm gave her his most winsome smile.

"Come on over here, you two."

Mr. Sinclair beckoned to the younger children who came shyly to him.

"Now then, this is Mr. and Mrs. Porter. They have been kind enough to agree to take you into their home and be your new mother and father. Say hello, children."

Sheelagh and Michael turned from Mr. Sinclair to look at the imposing dark-suited man who stood, thumbs tucked into his waistcoat pockets, staring down at them. His face was flushed, as if the starched white collar of his shirt was too tight. He leaned down towards Sheelagh.

"Good afternoon, young lady. What's your name?"

She stepped back quickly, bumping into Edward Sinclair's legs. "Sheelagh," she said quietly.

She had lost her blue bow somewhere on the journey. Her wool dress and smock were crumpled and stained, but her tousled curls and freckled face gave her such an appearance of sweet innocence that Jim Porter smiled despite himself.

"Is it indeed?" He turned his attention to Michael. "And what about you, young man, can you talk yet? What's your name?"

"That's Michael," said Colm. "He doesn't talk much, but he doesn't cry much either."

"Is that so? Well, I'm sure he knows his own name. Don't you, young man?"

Michael stared up at the red-faced man with the bristling white mustache, but he said nothing.

"Well, speak up. What's your name, lad?" The man frowned.

Sheelagh gave Michael a dig in the side with her elbow and whispered, "Say Michael."

Michael continued to stare up at the large intimidating man who reminded him vaguely of his father.

Colm spoke scornfully to his younger brother, "Michael, say 'Michael,' you amadan."

The small boy finally spoke his name.

"Good boy. Now, say good afternoon to Mrs. Porter."

He turned to his wife, a timid-looking woman in a floral print dress trimmed at collar and cuffs with cream lace. She wore small, wire-framed spectacles and squinted down at the children. Michael looked up at her but said nothing.

"Good God, is he a simpleton, Sinclair? Is the boy half-witted?"

"He's just tired after the journey, Jim. All this must be very confusing for him. Give him time. He's very young."

"I didn't bargain on any simpleton, or indeed any babies either."

"He's not a baby sir. He's nearly three. He can use the privy, and he doesn't wet the bed any more either," said Colm, feeling he should stand up for his younger brother.

"I'm very pleased to hear it."

"I think they're probably tired and hungry. Do we have some food for them, May?"

"Yes, of course." She hesitated, "Will I feed them in the kitchen or the dining room, Edward?"

"The kitchen will be fine, May dear."

His wife put her hands on the heads of the two smallest children and guided them to the door, calling to Colm to follow her. It was then that Edward noticed Liam still standing by the door, bundles in hand.

"Ah, Clancy! May dear, these are the children's belongings. Should I get Clancy to leave them in the hallway?"

May looked with some distaste at the three small cloth bundles.

"You can leave Colm's under the stairs, dear. I will see to it later. Give the other two to Edith."

"I'll show you where, Clancy. We can do it on the way out anyway. I don't suppose you want us to detain you any longer. Would you like to say goodbye to the children before you go?"

Liam nodded and turned to the children.

"Right then, little 'uns, I'll be off. You mind you behave yourselves, and don't give any trouble to these kind people."

He turned to the Porters and offered them two of the bundles. Jim Porter impatiently signaled his wife to take them.

"My sister, Bridget, and I are very grateful to you both for your Christian goodness. The thought of these poor mites in an orphanage all but broke her heart. I'm sure they will be very happy with you."

He turned to Edward Sinclair.

"And I thank you too, sir, and your good wife. I hope he never gives you an instant of trouble. You make them proud of you. Do you hear me, young Colm?"

Colm nodded.

"I'll be off then."

He stood for a moment, not knowing what else he should say, then turned and stepped into the hall followed by Mr. Sinclair. Mrs. Sinclair guided the children down the long hallway and through the door to the kitchen. Her husband watched them go and then turned to Liam.

"I've been thinking about it, Clancy. It would probably be best if you didn't see Colm after today. A bit confusing for him, don't you know, when he's settling into his new family and everything. Probably best for all concerned if he gets used to us as his family now. I'm sure you understand."

Sinclair hesitated.

"Of course, we'll let your sister know how he gets on. I'm sure the two youngsters will be very happy with the Porters, too. They'll want for nothing, you know. Jim Porter is a wealthy man. They'll get a good education, and I know his wife will be kindness itself."

"I have no doubt, sir. Thank you, sir. I know they are in good hands, and I quite understand."

As he was about to shake hands, he realized he was still carrying Colm's bundle.

"Just throw it under there, like a good man," said Sinclair, indicating a small door under the stairs. "My wife will deal with it later."

Liam placed the bundle under the stairs as Mr. Sinclair opened the front door.

"Good man, Clancy, and thank you again for your help." He held out his hand and gave Liam a brief handshake. "Take care."

He watched Liam descend the four steps to the footpath, then closed the door and returned to the sitting room.

"So, here we are. Can you believe it? Three children! And a month ago we didn't have one between us. Quite extraordinary!"

He sank into a large armchair beside the fireplace.

"I must say, I'm pretty tired myself after that journey. I'm sure they must be exhausted. What are your plans, Jim? Are you going to stay with us for a few more days?"

The older man snorted, "Indeed I'm not. I have a business to run, Edward, and I've lost two days as it is. No, we'll be getting the train first thing in the morning. Ramsey is a good man, but you can't trust anyone these days. Nobody runs your business like you run it yourself. You have to keep an eye on them all the time. No, we'll be off first thing."

Colm sat quietly at the table with his sister and brother while May Sinclair poured three glasses of milk, then carved several pieces of ham. She placed them with thin slices of bread and butter cut into triangles onto three plates and put them in front of the children. To May's horror Colm snatched up a slice of ham and stuffed it into his mouth.

"Colm, your knife and fork are there by your plate and so is your napkin."

She took the linen napkin, unfolded it, and laid it over his lap. She cut his ham into small pieces, speared a piece on the fork, and handed it to the young boy. He took the fork and put the meat into his mouth.

"There, isn't that better?" she asked.

She did the same for the other children, cutting up their food and showing them how to coax bite sized pieces onto the back of the fork, then she sat at the end of the table to watch them eat.

Sheelagh looked with curiosity at the triangles of bread and butter. She was only familiar with the thick slices of the brown bread her mother and Aunty Bridgie baked. She didn't recognize these pale, soft, slices as bread. But she was hungry, and her older brother seemed to be enjoying his, so she chose the smallest piece and nibbled tentatively.

"Is that good, child?" asked May. Sheelagh nodded and continued eating.

Michael watched his brother and sister and the tall, smiling woman, but he did not eat.

"Are you not hungry, baby? Will you try a little of the bread and butter? See, your sister likes it, don't you?"

Sheelagh nodded again, her mouth full of the spongy white bread. May held up a small triangle for Michael, which he cautiously took and ate.

When they were finished, May wiped their hands and faces with a damp cloth and brought them back to the sitting room.

"Here we are. I think they are probably feeling a lot better now," she said.

Making a slight grimace at her husband, she added, "I think Irish eating habits are a little different to ours, but I'm sure they will learn."

"Manners maketh man. That's the first thing you must teach a child, is manners," said Jim Porter staring hard at his wife. "It's what separates us from the animals."

"I'm sure they will have to get used to a lot of new things." Sinclair laughed, "Their accent had me foxed for a while. I could hardly understand them at the start of the journey. I'm glad Clancy was there to translate. But they're getting better already. Colm can say 'thank you' now instead of 'tank you'. Can't you, Colm?" Sinclair laughed, and Colm nodded. "They'll get used to speaking the King's English soon enough."

"I think I should take them upstairs now, dear. We only came in to say goodnight. They are very tired, and I want to bathe them before they get into bed. Say goodnight, children."

"Good night, Colm, sleep well, son. I'll see you in the morning."

Colm smiled, "Goodnight, sir."

Jim Porter leaned forward in his chair, "Goodnight, children. We have an early start in the morning, so get a good night's sleep. Say goodnight to the children, Edith, and stop grinning at them like an idiot."

Edith continued to smile gently. "Goodnight, my dears. Can I give you some help, May?"

"You'll have your hands full after tonight, Edith. I think I can manage for one night, though I wish I hadn't given Ella the evening off."

"I'll see you in the morning, children," called Edith, and she blew them a fluttery kiss as May ushered them out of the room.

Sheelagh and Michael

Amid a great deal of bustle and fuss, Jim Porter and his wife said their good-byes to May and settled themselves into the back of Edward Sinclair's car. Ella carried out their bags and crammed them into the trunk while May Sinclair helped Sheelagh and Michael. Colm stood at the door watching them. He did not seem upset at the departure of his brother and sister or at being left alone with his new mother. In truth he was already anxious for them to be gone so that he could explore his new home and the intriguing back garden he'd seen earlier from the bedroom window.

Edward kissed his wife. "I'll go straight to the office from the station, dear. You'll be able to manage the lad for the day, won't you?"

"Of course, my sweet, and Ella is here to help. I'm anxious to get to know him before he is whisked off to school."

"Don't forget! Father John will be over for dinner this evening. We'll sort all that out then." He glanced round at his passengers. "Is everyone ready?"

He started the engine and with a final wave to his wife drove away down Victoria Avenue to the main road.

Sheelagh and Michael sat on either side of Mrs. Porter for this, their second trip in a motor car. They were still terrified, though this time their confusion and distress were so profound they did not scream or cry. They sat in mute fear between the formidable man with the red face and the nervous, gentle lady wearing a severe black coat with a fearsome fox fur around her neck. The fur had been the cause of another bout of hysterics earlier that morning when Sheelagh first saw the brown furry animal with the amber glass eyes staring at her from the hall table. It took some time, patience, and explanations to calm and reassure her. She was still wary of the fashionable accessory and continued to watch it closely for signs of life.

They had lost everything and everyone familiar to them, even their Uncle Liam. There was no Aunty Bridgie to chivy and scold them, no big sister to feed or dress them, and now their brother Colm had been left behind with the smiling lady in the big house.

The Porters' attempts at engaging the children in conversation were met with blank stares. Jim Porter finally confined his conversation to Edward, while Edith nervously polished her glasses, occasionally smiled at Sheelagh, and watched the road ahead for fear of an accident.

The journey was uneventful. When Sinclair left them at the station, Jim Porter barked his orders to the railway porter, his wife, and the children. They all did as they were bid. They sat in select isolation in their first class railway carriage, the windows tightly closed against the black smut and smoke of the engine. On the two-hour journey to Bristol, Michael and Sheelagh watched fields and houses, factories and churches speed by in silence and were eventually rocked to sleep by the regular rhythm of the train. Mr. Porter isolated himself behind his copy of *The Times,* and his wife took out her crochet hook and fine thread and set to work on more of the lace trim they were to find on every pillowcase, sheet, feminine collar, hem, and handkerchief in the Porter home.

Arriving in Bristol, Jim Porter again marshaled his small group and with the help of a willing taxi driver loaded them and their bags into a cab. Within another half hour, they arrived at the austere, gray-stoned, three-storey house in Cornwallis Grove, Clifton.

Edith gently held each child by a hand and led them indoors.

"Here we are, dears. Welcome home."

The quiet-spoken woman and the two small children stood in the long, high-ceilinged hallway made oppressive by the dark, floral wallpaper. Having paid the taxi driver, Jim Porter strode into the house past his wife and the children shouting, "Martha! Martha! Dammit, where are you girl? There's bags out here that need bringing in."

A young woman opened a door at the rear of the hallway. She wore a black dress with a starched white apron, black stockings, and shoes. A neat white cap bobbed precariously on her dark curls as she hurried forward. "Sorry sir, I didn't hear you. I was in the pantry getting out some things for dinner. Welcome back, sir, Ma'am."

"Good, damned railway food's a disgrace; can't even get a decent sandwich. Get the bags in, girl, and then you can help Mrs. Porter with these two." He waved his arm vaguely in the direction of the children.

Martha hurried past the small group and out to where the taxi driver left the bags.

"Come on, Edith, stop cluttering up the hallway. Why don't you take those two up to their room. They're probably tired after the journey. Clean them up a bit before we eat."

Edith led Sheelagh and Michael up the steep carpeted stairs to a large room at the rear of the house. "Here you are, dears." She indicated the two beds set on either side of the room. "I thought you might like to stay together until you get used to everything."

Both beds had floral chintz covers and white starched pillows edged in thick, cream-colored crocheted lace. There was a neat pile of clothing at the foot of each bed.

"I wasn't sure of your sizes, so I got Mr. Porter to bring home a selection of clothes from his shop, just in case. He has a very big shop in town, you know. Perhaps one day I'll take you in and show you." She turned to Sheelagh, "And he has all kinds of ribbons and laces and pretty buttons. I know you'll love it, my dear."

The two looked fearfully around them. Apart from the beds, a highly-polished mahogany wardrobe filled one corner of the room with a long thin mirror set in its center panel. A mahogany dressing table stood in front of the tall, lace-covered window, and a chintz-covered stool sat neatly in front of the dressing table.

Edith walked to the door. "I'll go and see if Martha's free and we can get you ready for dinner." She hesitated, "Will you be all right for a minute? I'll be back directly."

She smiled and left. When she returned accompanied by Martha the children had not moved.

"Oh, you poor darlings, you look so frightened. There's nothing to be afraid of. Now, this is Martha. She is going to wash you and get you ready for dinner." She spoke to the maid.

"Somewhere in the bags there are two sad little bundles of clothing that their old aunt sent, but I don't think we'll use them." She wrinkled her nose in distaste. "Just put them away for the moment, and use the things on the bed. I hope they will fit reasonably well."

She spoke to the children, "I'll be back soon, dears, and don't be afraid. We're very happy you're here, and we're going to make you happy too. Aren't we, Martha?"

Martha nodded, and Edith left. "Come on then you little waifs. Let's get you cleaned up before his lordship starts barking for his dinner. What are your names, then?"

Martha gently coaxed the children out of their clothes, chattering to them all the while. She washed them and dressed them in the simple clothes Jim Porter had provided.

"You'll have to wear your own shoes. Mr. High-and-Mighty forgot all about those, probably 'cos he doesn't sell them in his own shop, mean bugger. Come on then, let's take you down and show you off. And give us a smile. I'm not going to kill you, and neither will they." She playfully tickled both children in their tummies and when they finally giggled quietly, she said, "That's a bit better. Let's go."

She carefully led them down the steep stairs.

After dinner, it was Martha who took them back upstairs, got them ready for bed, and tucked them in.

"Do you say your prayers, little one?" she asked Sheelagh. The child nodded, "Go on then," she said with an encouraging smile.

Sheelagh began haltingly to repeat the short prayer her sister had taught her. When she finished, she remembered the litany of relatives she must ask God to bless and finished with "God Bless Mammy." Martha looked surprised. "Where is your Ma then, little girl?"

"Aunty Bridgie says she's gone to Heaven," Sheelagh replied.

The maid sat quietly on the edge of the bed for a few moments longer. She tucked the bedclothes snugly around her new charge.

"Well, God Bless you too, little one. We'll mind you, don't you worry. Good night, both of you. I'll see you in the morning."

Jim Porter retired to the front parlor, settled himself into the comfortable wing-backed chair beside the fire, and lit his pipe. Once the children were securely in bed, Edith joined him.

"Well, Edith dear, I hope you're satisfied. You're going to be kept busy with those two. I can't imagine how Edward talked me into this. 'Son and heir' indeed! I'm beginning to think we would have managed very well without those two little people cluttering up the house."

"I think they're delightful, Jim. The little girl is pretty as a picture with that auburn hair and those freckles. Did you ever see such curls?"

"I just hope that boy isn't going to be a handful. Boys need discipline you know, Edith. Boys are a lot harder to handle."

"I'm sure he'll be just fine, and Edward's right; I'm sure he'll be a great help in the business when he's older. 'Porter and Son', doesn't that sound wonderful, Jim?"

"Don't count your chickens before they're hatched, woman. We've a long way to go before we're at that stage, a lot of bridges to cross. Let's see if we can civilize them first. If their accents are anything like their older brother's that will be quite a challenge on its own. I could hardly understand a word he said."

"I thought it was quite charming, dear, and I'm sure we can get them elocution lessons."

"There you go, extra expense right away, and they're not in the door a day. I've already outfitted them from head to foot. Now, you want them to have elocution lessons. Elocution lessons be damned; they will learn by example, woman, learn by example."

Mary

Bridgie sat at the fire, a bundle of cloth scraps on her lap, and her sewing box at her feet. Mary sat beside her on the stool. The aunt chose a square.

"This is a piece of my mother's favorite dress. She would be your great-grandmother," she explained. "You see the tiny flowers? Periwinkles, that's what they are. Father always said they were the same color as her eyes. They were too." Bridget grew thoughtful and distant for a moment.

"Blue like Sheelagh's," said Mary fingering the soft cotton fabric gently.

"That's right, Mary, I hadn't thought of that. Maybe your sister inherited her eyes from your great-grandmother. Will we put it in the middle of this group? And we can put a square from this smock of Sheelagh's beside it. Would you like that?"

Mary nodded. It had been several weeks since her brothers and sister left for England. Apart from a brief letter from Liam telling of their safe arrival, and another from May Sinclair saying how happy she was to have Colm, they heard nothing. No news of Sheelagh or Michael, and no word from the Porters ...

"There's nothing to worry about, child." Bridget assured her. "Your Uncle Liam would not let anything bad happen to them. It's just taking a while for them to settle in, that's all. Didn't that nice Mr. Sinclair say that the Porters were good people? Give them time. We'll hear from them eventually."

But Mary was hard to console, and eventually Bridget had the idea of the quilt. She rummaged in the small trunk at the foot of her bed. She found old dresses of her mother's, some well-worn shirts which had belonged to her father and Liam, and even a dark red skirt Bridget herself had worn in the days before she took to wearing all black. She cut a large collection of squares from the old clothes. She also cut a few small patches rescued from some of the children's clothes—the ones she had thought too shabby to put in the bundles for England. Bridget even persuaded Pierce to find a piece of clothing belonging to

Norah. The boy found her second best blouse, which Mrs. Kelly was using as a cleaning rag, and brought it over to Doonbeg.

"The material has seen better days, but I think we can get a few patches out of it," said Aunty Bridgie. "So then you will have a piece of your Mammy with you always."

She gave the sad-faced little girl a hug. Mary was barely nine years old, but Bridget had been so used to relying on her when the children were all there she had forgotten how young she was, poor child.

"You help me decide where we're going to put all these pieces. Will we put your mother's patches beside the children's?"

Mary nodded again, and then said shyly, "Can I put a piece of me in the quilt as well, Aunty Bridgie?"

"Good idea; of course we can. We have to have all of you in it, don't we? What about that old red ribbon? We never could get it to stay in your hair, could we? A bright piece of red satin would be very cheerful."

"No, I don't want it. I hate that ribbon."

It was the one she wore the night she heard Brendan tell Bridget about the orphanage. "Can I have a different piece?"

"Certainly, child," said Bridgie, surprised at the child's vehemence. "I'm sure we'll find something you've grown out of. You grow taller every day, Mary. You're like a sunflower, a beautiful tall sunflower. Let's get sewing, shall we? We'll have this quilt made in no time."

The old woman and the young girl bent over the small patches, sewing the precious memory quilt by the light of the fire.

Michael

"I have been giving the matter a great deal of thought, Edith. I'm not at all sure about the lad. I think maybe we were a bit hasty when Edward and May contacted us."

Jim settled himself in his chair. Dinner was over, and Martha was putting the children to bed as usual. Edith fidgeted through her sewing box seeking the crochet hook she needed for her latest project.

"But they've only been here a short time, Jim, and everything is so new to them. Imagine, they had never seen a flush toilet before. Can you believe that?"

"That doesn't surprise me one bit, woman." He reached for his pipe and tobacco pouch on the side table. "That's just the sort of thing I mean. It's no excuse, you know, for wetting the bed. The little girl isn't too bad, I'll grant you. It's all very well having that pretty little thing in the house for you to dress up and play with. But a boy is a different matter. And another thing—we can't have him climbing into his sister's bed every night. He's not a baby."

He filled the pipe, tamping down the thick threads of tobacco.

"He only does that occasionally. And the bed wetting was our fault. Martha and I forgot to show him where to go. It was only one night."

"Once too much for my liking, thank you. I didn't bargain for that."

"He's a very quiet little boy, Jim. You'd hardly know he was here."

"Precisely!"

Holding a lit match to the pipe bowl, he puffed clouds of aromatic blue smoke at his wife.

"He hasn't said a damned word since he got here. Nearly three years old and barely able to talk. He just doesn't seem to be too bright to me. No, if he was all there, I'm sure Edward would have kept him. I think we may have been landed with an idiot."

"We can hardly claim to know him yet. I'm sure it will take time."

"What's to know? It doesn't matter too much if a woman is slow-witted, Edith. As long as she can cook and clean and run a household, most husbands won't give a tuppenny damn if she's bright or not. I ask you, who wants to be married to an Emily Pankhurst-type anyway? But if a man is slow-witted, he's good for nothing, nothing particularly useful anyway."

"I'm sure he's quite a bright little boy; we just need to give him a chance."

"And what if we've made a mistake? Too late then, isn't it? We can't just cast him adrift in ten years time when we discover he's a complete fool."

Edith looked surprised.

"I always thought you wanted a son and heir as much as Edward did."

"And I did, Edith, I did. But I don't want to be landed with a pig in a poke. We have no idea what we're getting here."

Edith put down her crochet. She was not used to disputing matters with her husband but felt she should speak up on the boy's behalf.

"Well, he's ours now, Jim. He's here. We can't just throw him away. He's not a toy."

"I'm well aware of that, Edith dear. I don't need *you* to tell me. Anyway, I have thought it through. We won't be throwing him out, quite the contrary. I have an excellent plan for the lad."

Her brow furrowed as Edith tried to understand what her husband was saying. He was always a very forceful man, and she knew she could do little to change his mind once it was made up. She felt great sympathy for the small child as she anxiously awaited her husband's pronouncement.

"Wyn can have him."

Edith looked startled, immediately recalling the formidable image of her sister-in-law. Edith had little in common with Wyn, whose sharp tongue and brusque manner so intimidated her.

"But she's not married, Jim. She can't look after a small boy."

"Of course she can. It's the perfect solution. She can raise him. I will help financially, of course, and when she can't do all that dressmaking and mending stuff any more, then he will be grown enough to provide for her. In her old age, as it were. *She* looks after him now, and *he* looks after her later, a perfect arrangement. He should be able to do that even if he's not too bright."

Edith gripped her hands tightly together in her lap.

"Your sister doesn't even like children."

"She doesn't have to like him; she just has to rear him. It's an investment, Edith. She's always worried about who will mind her when she gets old. You see! That's always a problem when you don't have a husband to provide for you, my dear. I've always said marriage is a most important institution, especially for women."

"Do you think she'll want him?"

"Of course she will. Common sense, she'll see that. After all, who else has she got?"

Edith searched her mind frantically for some way of preventing her husband's plan.

"What will we tell Edward and May?"

"We don't have to tell them anything. *They* didn't want him, did they? Quite happy to pawn him off on us."

Despite her discomfort, she was still anxious to defend the boy.

"But we *did* say we wanted them both. That's why he brought them to England, because we said we wanted both of them."

He angrily tapped his pipe out on the fender.

"*You* wanted them! Leastways you wanted a little girl. The lad was always an extra. We got carried away with the 'son and heir thing', didn't give it enough thought."

He shook the dottle from his pipe bowl into the grate.

"We don't have to say anything about the new arrangement, Edith. Let's face it; we are doing everyone a favor, and I'll still be paying for his upkeep."

Edith, afraid she was going to cry, stood.

"I'm going upstairs to say goodnight to them."

1926

Colm

May wasted no time in disposing of the "sad little bundle of rags" Bridgie had packed for Colm. On the same morning that the Porters left with Michael and Sheelagh, she took Colm into London and bought him a complete new wardrobe of clothes. She took him from shop to shop along Regent Street discarding his old clothes in fitting rooms and waste containers as they were replaced.

By mid-afternoon the transformation was complete, and the boy could not be persuaded to try on another shirt or pair of boots. With May's arms full of packages and parcels, they made a final stop in Hamley's Toy Shop. There she told him he could choose five items from the vast array of toys, books, and games on display. This unexpected reward immediately revived the bewildered and exhausted Colm who had never seen such wonders. Back in Glendarrig, Mickey Dunne had a wooden spinning top his father bought for him on a trip to Dublin, but toys were not a familiar sight in Colm's old home. He looked in wonder at the armies of lead soldiers, miniature landscapes full of train sets, and a seemingly endless selection of clockwork toys, stuffed animals, and jigsaw puzzles. After more than an hour of awed exploration and investigation, he finally chose a rubber ball which could bounce almost as high as his head, a box of tin soldiers, a clockwork mouse, a picture book, and a packet of coloring pencils.

Colm soon endeared himself to the Sinclairs. He was eager to please, and as May told her friends, "He has such a sunny disposition that you just *have* to love him."

Within a few weeks of his arrival in London, Edward and May enrolled him as a boarder in The Priory, a preparatory school located in the quiet Suffolk countryside. Edward and May drove up to the school to see him every weekend. Once a month they brought him back to Victoria Avenue where he was pampered and petted and shown off to friends and dinner guests. On other weekends May or Edward took him on visits to the City, parks, or museums. On their trips into London, they would finish the outing at Simpson's, the Savoy, or Fortnum's where they treated him to a lavish high tea before returning him to school.

A few months after his arrival in the school, the Sinclairs met with Father John, the school principal. He told them Colm was doing very well. He said that almost all traces of the boy's Irish accent were gone, and his manners were improving daily. As for his academic studies, Father John said Colm was proving a willing student, learning to read and write. He was also excelling at sports.

"You made a good choice, Edward. I think we can mold this lad into someone you can be proud of, and we look forward to the challenge."

1927

Colm

It had been a year since the young boy arrived at Victoria Avenue. He quickly settled into his new home and his new way of life. His memories of Glendarrig and Doonbeg were fading. He felt very much at home in the affluent household, despite only occasional visits there during term time. He learned quickly, both at school and at home. He watched and listened carefully to his new parents, classmates, and teachers. He mimicked their accents, manners, and behavior. He rapidly discovered how far he could go with each member of the household before a sharp reprimand or a furrowed brow told him he'd overstepped himself. He learned well.

"I don't think your mother would be happy to see you throw stones at the cat like that, Master Colm," said Ella when she saw him taking aim with a small pebble from the gravel path. He dropped the stone quietly at his side.

"I wasn't really going to do it, Ella. I was just practicing my aim for when I'm a big game hunter."

"And don't lie either! I've been watching you from the kitchen window."

Colm colored, suddenly remembering his father's lecture about lying.

"Sorry, Ella."

He ensured she never caught him stoning the cat again.

"Master Colm, I shall have to ask Mr. Sinclair if he wants you playing in his rose beds like that."

Gabriel, the Sinclair's gardener, had caught him using a bamboo cane to behead the rose bushes of their prize blooms.

"I was practicing my sword fighting. He wouldn't mind anyway."

"I think you're wrong there, Master Colm. He's very fond of his roses. Let's go and ask him, shall we?"

"No, he's busy ... I think ... and I won't do it again, Gabriel."

And he didn't, though afterwards Colm delighted in disconnecting the garden hose or trampling a plant or two when he knew Gabriel was working elsewhere in the garden.

At school he was popular with his classmates. A natural mimic, he imitated the teachers' and students' mannerisms and speech with accuracy and humor. He also impressed his friends with his ability to escape detection, and the possible subsequent retribution, for his pranks.

"I'm sorry, sir. I was having a nightmare about my mother, the one that died. I thought a glass of milk would help me get back to sleep," he sobbed when caught foraging in the pantry one night.

He did not like "the strap," which was a favored form of punishment at The Priory, and he was adept at avoiding it.

"I didn't know I could throw that far," he claimed when he "accidentally" hit a particularly disliked teacher with a cricket ball. "I never owned a ball at home."

Father John mentioned this "wayward tendency" to Edward and May, but they put it down to high spirits and learning new ways. Father John did not necessarily agree, but reserved judgment. He felt sure that judicious application of "the strap" would improve his behavior eventually.

"Can I have a friend to visit next weekend, Mother?"

"*May* I, Colm, not '*can* I.' Whom do you want to invite?"

"David Gough; he's in my House at school, and we share a dorm."

"Do I know him, dear? Have we met his family at all?"

"Father was talking to his father when he took me back after half term. He's my best friend, and he has a real leather football, and he says his mother has met the King, and he said they have two houses and the other one is beside the sea, and I can go there with him sometime, and we can swim and make sand castles."

"Well, I'm sure he's a very nice boy, darling, but we will ask Father when he returns this evening. Does this mean you are dreadfully fed up being here with me?"

"No, Mother! I like it, but it would be nice to have a friend come and stay too. The holidays are boring."

"Boring indeed? Ella says you get up to enough mischief for five little boys when I leave you with her. You know Father and I have to go out sometimes, dear. We can't possibly forfeit all our friends just because we have one very special little boy in our lives now."

Colm grinned mischievously at May.

"Ella let me make scones the last time I was home."

"Yes, I know, and she told me there was flour all over the kitchen floor."

"I wanted to leave tracks like the wild animals do, so that hunters can follow them."

"Yes, so she told me. But using the flour shaker to spread flour all over her clean kitchen floor was not a good idea dear. She has enough work to do without cleaning the kitchen floor twice in one morning. The poor woman said she only turned her back on you for five minutes while she answered the door."

"It was a great trail. I will be a hunter when I grow up. I will hunt lions and tigers and put their heads on my wall like David's grandfather does. He says his grandfather has all kinds of animals on his walls, and they all have glass eyes, but they look like real ones, and they follow you round the room and watch you all the time."

May smiled, "Do they indeed? Well, I'm sure that's very interesting, but that still doesn't excuse your spreading flour all over the kitchen floor. You must be a bit more thoughtful, Colm. Do your hunting out in the back garden where you can't make such a mess."

"Yes, mother."

May sat at the small desk in the drawing room reading that morning's mail. Colm was playing with a Meccano construction set Edward bought for him two days before. Red and green parts were strewn around the hearthrug, and Colm was deep in concentration with screwdriver, nuts, bolts, and various pieces of drilled metal plates as he tried to construct a small crane. He glanced up at May who was watching him, smiling indulgently. She gestured for him to come close. He stood in front of her, and she caught his hand in hers.

"I have a surprise for you, darling," she said. "I know you've been bored, and I'm sorry your friend David was unable to visit. I know the school holidays have been long, and I'm quite sure we are not as good company as your school chums. So, I arranged a little surprise. Guess who's coming for a visit?"

Colm waited expectantly.

"Your brother and sister!" she said with delight. "Now, what do you think? Won't that be nice?"

Colm stared at May unsure of his feelings, unsure of his response. He'd put such distance between his old family and his new. He didn't miss them, had barely thought of them since his arrival at Victoria Avenue over a year ago. He enjoyed being an only child and the center of attention. The news that two of his siblings were about to intrude into his special world was not altogether welcome.

But, it would be nice to show Pierce all his new toys and his very own bedroom with the wash-hand basin in the corner and running water so there was no need for trips to the pump. He could show him the big garden full of hiding places *and* the red and green crane he was building, too. Pierce would be impressed. Colm would be able to show his big brother how grown up he was and all of the things he had. Yes, it would be nice to see Pierce again. He didn't much care about Mary.

Colm smiled at May, "When are they coming? Is Aunty Bridgie coming, too?" He wondered for a moment if his father would also be coming, but it was impossible to imagine Brendan in this grand house.

May looked puzzled, then realized his mistake.

"Oh no, dear, I didn't mean the Irish ones. I meant Sheelagh and Michael. I've invited Mr. and Mrs. Porter to come and visit for a few days. It's been so long. I've hardly heard from them since you all arrived. I expect they've been very busy with their new family. So, I thought it would be nice for you to see your brother and sister again. I'm sure they've grown up a great deal since you last saw them. It's hard to believe it's nearly a year and a half," she squeezed his hands and smiled. "They will be here on Friday. Now, isn't that a nice surprise?"

It took Colm a few moments to adjust. Sheelagh and Michael, the two babies! He had no interest in Sheelagh. His memories of her were blurred, but he seemed to remember she was always whining or crying. Whenever he'd teased or played with her, it seemed to end in tears. She was a crybaby, and he'd no interest in a crybaby. Michael was still a baby in Colm's mind, unable to talk very much and clinging to Mary or Pierce whenever Colm was around.

What kind of a surprise was that? *They* would be no fun. *They* wouldn't care about his toys or his bedroom. He didn't want to show *them* his hiding places in the garden, or his Meccano set. He looked at May's expectant face and gave a weak smile.

"That will be nice."

She was disappointed at his muted reaction.

"We can go to the park and maybe up to Hamley's while they're here. I don't think they have a shop like that in Bristol. Wouldn't that be good? We could buy them a nice toy, or Sheelagh would probably like a pretty doll. We could have ice cream at Forte's. What do you think, Colm?"

Parks were no novelty to Colm, and dolls were of no interest, but Hamley's and Forte's were always good, so his smile broadened, and he gave his mother's hand a return squeeze.

"That will be super, Mother."

He leaned forward and gave her a soft kiss on her cheek. She was happy. She kissed his hand in return, "Good. Now off you go and play. I have to make some household arrangements before they arrive."

Colm went back to his Meccano, but his thoughts were not on the crane nor on Sheelagh and Michael. He was thinking of his big brother. He thought, for the first time in a long while, about how they fetched water from the pump together, trotted along the country lane on the back of the bony, dirt-caked horse, and how they shared whispered secrets lying side by side in the warm chaos of the children's bed.

Pierce

It was a house of silence. Each morning Mrs. Kelly opened the back half-door to let light into the dark, smoky cottage, and then busied herself sweeping the hearth and the earthen floor. She raked the ashes, added turf to the fire, and filled the blackened kettle with water. Having cleaned and chopped the vegetables, she tossed them into the pot for the evening meal and put the scrapings into the slops bucket under the table. After adding a few lumps of fat to the pot, she hung it over the fire. When all this was done, she set out to the pump with the two water buckets. Meanwhile, Brendan roused Pierce. The boy stumbled out of bed bleary-eyed, dressed hastily, and headed out to fetch the horse. Brendan let the pig out of its pen, tipped the food slops from the bucket into the trough, and made tea for his son and himself. Not a word was spoken between them. The only sounds heard in the cottage every morning were the swish of the broom, the spitting of the damp turf on the fire, and the click of the latch.

Father and son left at first light, often before Mrs. Kelly returned. Whether it was the soft early-morning warmth of a summer's day or the biting cold of mid-winter, it made little difference. Man and boy sat side by side on the rickety cart, each hunched in private thought and silent resignation. It was their life and their livelihood undertaken without comment or complaint.

Some days their work involved collecting the still-steaming manure from the barns and yards of local cattle farmers. They shoveled the stinking cargo onto the cart until it was fully laden. The strong stench of ammonia caught Pierce's breath and made his eyes sting, and the slimy cargo stuck to everything. They hauled the straw-matted waste to neighboring farms where Brendan and Pierce labored again to pitch it onto the margins of the fields. It was left there to rot down before the farmer used it to fertilize the land. Pierce hated those loads, and their consequences. If every trace of the manure was not removed from his hands and clothes he would receive a tongue-lashing from his stepmother when he returned home. It was an impossible task.

On other more rewarding days father and son scrubbed the cart clean and hauled farmers' produce to town. The sacks of cabbages, potatoes, or onions were heavy and the young boy's back and shoulders ached unmercifully by the end of the day. Nonetheless, Pierce preferred these days and the diversions at the market.

He enjoyed the hustle and bustle of the Ballyfin Market Day: the sights, the smells, and the sounds. While his father slaked his thirst in one of the several bars, Pierce was happy to watch the lively commotion happening all around him: the haggling of the cattle dealers who could, and often did, argue for hours before finally spitting into their palms and shaking hands to close a deal; the noisy vendors trying to out-shout each other as they sold their trinkets and ribbons, holy pictures, and sugary treats; the tinkers mending pots with their round-headed hammers, hot irons, and thin plates of tin. He delighted in the sparks that flew in bright starry arcs from the knife grinder's wheels as they sharpened scissors, knives, and small farm tools, and he laughed at the antics of the drunken farmers as they celebrated a good sale, danced spontaneous jigs, or chased barefoot urchins with mock ferocity.

Pierce especially liked watching the horse-peddlers show off their fast-trotting animals. They gripped the coarse rope bits with muscled fists to hold the horses' heads high and proud. They showed the nags' sturdy backs, lifted their legs to reveal well-pared hooves, and folded back lips to expose strong teeth to prospective buyers. Pierce listened to their patter, learned about horses, and remembered what he learned.

A fight was part of the day begun over a supposed insult, an old grudge, or a new grievance. Whatever the cause, it was the signal for a circle of onlookers to create a cheering and shouting human ring around the combatants, egging them on and wagering on the outcome.

Once, as he watched an impromptu cockfight, he looked up to see his stepmother walking quickly through the market, her shawl covering her head, hiding her from prying eyes. He was surprised, but not interested enough to watch where she went or to wonder why. Even at fourteen he was wise enough not to mention it to his father. He wanted no more cause for arguing or fighting in the house.

Despite his great enjoyment of the market, Pierce's favorite trips were when they fetched sand or seaweed from the beach. Both were in demand from farmers whose thick clay soil was impossible to plough or plant. Pierce loved the sharp, salty, smell of the sea and the often-blustery weather on the shore. Even in the wintertime when the harsh salt winds blew in from the Atlantic and the sea spray caused his hands to chap and bleed, his eyes to smart, and his face to sting, he still felt invigorated and alive.

Every day they traveled either from the seashore and manure-filled farm-yards to the fields or from neighbor's barns to market. They hauled anything in pursuit of their meager livelihood, straining the horse and themselves to the limit. Occasionally it was necessary for Pierce to sit on the rear of the cart to ensure the cargo remained in place, but usually father and son traveled in their long-familiar silence side by side on the driver's bench.

At the end of the day, they returned to the cottage. Pierce freed the horse from its traces and led it out to graze on the roadside. Brendan took the heavy leather harness inside where he hung it on a large wooden peg beside the door. His wife made it clear she would not have the stench of manure fill her home or any "filthy, manure-covered hands" touch the bread or any food she pre-pared. Though father and son sluiced their hands and boots at the pump before returning to the cottage, it was not enough. A jug of hot water along with a chipped enamel bowl, a lump of green lye soap, and a bristle brush sat waiting on the oilcloth-covered table. Brendan washed while she took a dish from the dresser and ladled in a helping of stew or broth from the pot over the fire. When his hands were washed and dried, she handed him the dish and a thick slice of brown bread. He took both to his chair beside the fire. Still, no words were spoken.

On Pierce's return he also used the hard soap, coarse-bristled brush, and the same water now cooled and murky. He discarded the water over the half-door into the back yard before cutting his own bread and helping himself to a ladle-full of stew. He sat on the wooden settle opposite his father and ate. The woman sat in the patched old wicker chair knitting, darning, or sewing.

Each evening after his meal, Brendan reached into the deep pocket of his trousers and removed the fistful of coins he had earned that day. He put the money in the old cracked Toby jug that stood on the mantle. On good days he slipped a few of the coins back into his pocket, took his pipe from the mantle, and left. He returned long after the woman and boy were asleep, stumbling noisily into the cottage and cursing to himself as he negotiated the shallow flight of steps to the loft. If there were only a few coins from the day's work, he dropped them all into the china jug, fetched himself a bottle of stout from the wooden crate under the stairs, and drank in morose silence. This was a danger-ous time for woman and boy. Any source of irritation—a smoky fire, a stray burning ember, even the too-loud clacking of knitting needles—was enough to rouse him to a blind fury of angry words and threats.

Pierce retreated to his room as soon as he could after his meal. If his father remained at home, it was a safer place to be. But even if his father left, the woman would find chores for him to do or a reason to complain about his smell, the state of their home, or the lack of money. He said nothing during these outbursts, but his silence only seemed to anger her more. His room was a safe haven.

He visited Mary and Aunty Bridgie almost every Sunday after Mass. His stepmother left early on Sunday mornings saying she was visiting friends in Ballyfin. She was gone for most of the day. Brendan took the opportunity to spend the time in the snug in Daly's Bar. All three returned in the evening, none seeming to relish the cold comfort of the cottage.

At fourteen Pierce was old enough not to have to attend school any more, though Aunty Bridgie told him it was important to complete his education.

"Without reading and writing, lad, you will never better yourself. You know your mother put great store by you doing the learning. I know your Da needs you to help him on the cart, but go to school when you can, lad, and read the books at night. You won't be sorry. It will stand to you, I promise."

He didn't like school, being shut in a classroom all day reciting spellings, tables and catechism in seemingly endless chants. He was glad when his father said it was time for Pierce to work full-time with him. Aunty Bridgie persevered and arranged with Master Keogh that Mary would bring home schoolbooks and a little homework for her brother. Pierce, in boredom, spent the evenings in his room reading by the light of a smoky hurricane lamp. He completed the sums the Master set for him in his jotter, carefully writing the answers under the ruled lines. Without the discipline of the classroom, he found he especially enjoyed sums. He found the concentration required to puzzle out the answers kept his mind busy, stopped him thinking too much about his life and, for a while, helped keep the loneliness at bay. He sorely missed his brothers and sisters and thought often of his mother and how things might have been.

Sheelagh

Edith brushed Sheelagh's wild curls into neat orderly ringlets, coaxing each lock around her finger then gently drawing her finger away. Sheelagh stood quite still, cuddling the newest doll Edith had bought for her. When the ringlets were completed, Edith gathered a few into a pink satin ribbon atop the child's head and tied a large bow.

"You see! The ribbon matches your dress exactly. You look just as beautiful as your little dolly."

Edith leaned forward so that her face was beside Sheelagh's. They gazed into the dressing table mirror together. She adjusted the two smaller side mirrors so that Sheelagh could view her finished appearance from all angles.

"You are the most beautiful little girl in all the world." She hugged her gently. "I am so proud of you. I am going to miss you so much when it's time for you to go to school."

"I don't want to go to school, Mummy." Sheelagh's bottom lip trembled. "I hate school. I want to stay here with you, always."

"I know, my little darling. I don't want to lose you either, but you must go to school when the time comes, then you can grow up to be a clever and beautiful lady. All the boys will fall in love with you because you are so beautiful and clever, and you never make silly mistakes."

"I won't make silly mistakes, I promise. Please don't send me to school, Mummy. I love you."

"There, there, my pet, don't upset yourself. We have lots of precious time before that. Now, we really must go. The car will be here soon, and you know how Daddy hates to be kept waiting."

Jim Porter arrived at the bedroom door.

"Good God, Edith, what's she sniveling about now? I never knew anyone snivel so much. Oh, never mind, I'm sure it's something quite trivial." He drew his watch from his fob pocket, "Are you ready? The car will be here directly. We don't want to miss the train."

He left the room followed by Edith and Sheelagh who had stopped crying, her final tears sliding slowly down her pale, freckled cheeks.

Reaching the hallway, Jim Porter bellowed, "Martha! Martha! Where are you, girl? Damned girl is never around when she's needed. It's time to take these bags out, girl," he shouted towards the kitchen, "The car will be here soon." He peered through the leaded glass of the front door, then turned back to glare at Edith with exasperation. "Where is that damn girl? Martha!"

The young maid scurried from the kitchen.

"I'm here, sir. I was just packing a little lunch for Miss Sheelagh. I'll take the bags out right away, sir."

"Lunch? Lunch? Anyone would think we starved the child. An apple should be enough for her. We're only traveling to London not the North Pole."

He stepped aside as the maid lifted the two polished-leather suitcases and carried them to the door. "We'll be there in a couple of hours." He opened the door for her. "I'm sure the Sinclairs will be quite happy to provide us with lunch when we arrive, don't you think so, Edith?"

"*I* asked Martha to pack a snack for the child, dear, just in case."

"In case? Stuff and nonsense!" He glanced through the open door, "Here we are. I can see the taxi. Come along both of you. Stop dawdling."

He ushered the woman and girl out of the house and down the path and chivvied them into the back of the taxi. Martha put the bags into the trunk, helped by the driver.

"Are you done?" snapped Porter impatiently from the curb.

"Yes, sir," said the driver, giving the young maid a quick wink. "All packed in and ready to go sir."

"Good, so I should think. We don't have all day."

He turned to Martha and barked orders like a drill sergeant.

"No entertaining any gentlemen in my absence, young lady, or you will be out on the street without a reference before you know it."

He closed the back door of the taxi and continued, "I've told the neighbors to keep an eye on you, so don't think you can get away with anything."

He opened the front passenger door. "I've had a good look in the pantry so don't think you can eat me out of house and home while we're away either."

He sat into the car but continued to harangue the maid.

"I trust Mrs. Porter has given you enough chores to keep you busy 'til we return on Monday."

She nodded.

He slammed the door closed and turned to the driver. "Right, let's go, and no taking a tour around the city. I know the way to the station. I'll not pay a single penny over the correct fare."

"Aye, Aye, sir."

They departed with Jim Porter sitting as stiff as one of his store mannequins in the front seat. A relieved Martha waved briefly at the retreating vehicle before sauntering back into the house.

Colm and Sheelagh

When the Porters arrived at Victoria Road, Edward and May were surprised that Michael was not with them. Edith had made no mention of the change in her monthly letters to May, and the Sinclairs had no idea that charge of the boy had been handed to Jim's maiden sister, Wynifred.

"Discovered he was not quite as bright as the one you got," Jim confided to Edward when he asked about the child, "a little slow, don't you know. But Wyn will sort him out. Plenty of time on her hands has Wyn, no-nonsense type of a woman, far better for him than my Edith. She'd be too soft with him, and he wouldn't have learned anything that way."

The Sinclairs deferred more questioning whilst they made their guests welcome. Ella took their bags to their rooms, and the Porters accepted May's invitation to "freshen up before lunch."

Edward again took up the subject at the dining table.

"I must say, I am a little surprised, Jim."

He passed the tureen of vegetables to his friend.

"I had actually promised the aunt that the two youngsters would be staying together. Does she know about this?"

"They will see plenty of each other, Edward. It's not as if I gave him away to the gypsies or anything." Jim gave a derisory snort. "Far too much of a handful for Edith really. I should have realized earlier. She couldn't possibly have managed two. She's not the healthiest of ladies, are you, dear?"

Edith blushed and dabbed at the corner of her mouth with her napkin.

"But, have you told the aunt?" Sinclair persisted.

"Dammit, Edward, no I have not! I wasn't sure if the woman could even read. She didn't want them anyway from what I gather. I thought it should be a clean break, new life, all that. No point in trying to bring them up properly if they're still in touch with the old ways, is there?"

"Well, how is he doing?" asked May, trying to calm her guest. "Is he happy? He seemed like such a sweet little boy. I almost wish we had kept him as a companion for Colm."

"I'm sure he is quite happy. He's still very quiet, though Wyn tells me she has him saying his prayers, and she's taught him his 'please' and 'thank-yous'." Jim glanced at Sheelagh, sitting at the other end of the table, and lowered his voice a little. "We don't see too much of him for the time being. Want him to settle in, grow up a bit first, don't you know. And we don't want to upset the little one too much. She wouldn't stop crying when he first left; thought I'd go out of my mind with the noise. When they are a bit older, I'm sure it will be fine."

"But he is all right, isn't he?" pressed Edward. "I do feel a little responsible for them under the circumstances."

"Right as rain, Edward, right as rain. Wyn is a good woman. He'll be fine with her."

"Perhaps I'd better let the aunt know, just to be on the safe side."

"Whatever you think best, dear boy, so long as she doesn't start interfering. None of her business now, is it, really? She was quite happy to hand them away to complete strangers last year. She can hardly show concern now, can she?"

There was an awkward silence. Colm watched the four adults. When May rang the small silver bell set beside her place, Ella cleared away the meat platter, tureens, plates, and cutlery. She returned with an apple pie and a bowl of thick, whipped cream. Colm glanced sideways at his sister. The pink satin dress and pink bow in her red curls looked comical to him. Sitting prim and upright in her chair, she looked a bit like a wooden puppet. He reached under the table and pinched her leg. She jumped and gave a small cry. All eyes turned to her.

Edith reached out her hand. "What's wrong, darling? Are you all right dear?"

Sheelagh blushed, glanced sideways at her brother and nodded. May had a suspicion that Colm was the cause of the little girl's cry.

"How would you like some apple pie and cream, darling?" she said.

Tears spilling readily from her eyes, the child nodded again, and everyone spoke at once to cover the small incident.

"I'm sure she would love that; it's your favorite. Isn't it, sweetheart," gushed Edith.

"May made it herself," said Sinclair beaming at his wife. "Didn't even let Ella pick the apples, did you, dear? From the garden, you know."

"Oh, Edward, don't embarrass me."

"Don't fuss with the child, Edith," growled Porter. "Of course she likes it. Why wouldn't she?"

Lunch finished in a hubbub of chatter, and Michael was forgotten.

"Do you have your own bedroom?"

The children had been sent to play in the garden after lunch while the grown-ups "had a little rest." Colm was reluctant to spend any time with his sister but knew he must do as he was told on this occasion after his misbehavior at lunch. They wandered out onto the lawn where Sheelagh, having made quite sure there was no dirt to soil her dress, sat primly on a wrought iron garden seat. Colm threw himself on the grass in front of the seat and idly watched an ant crawl over his fingers.

She nodded, "And I have a special chair in the kitchen too, and only I can sit on it. Daddy has his own special chair in the dining room, and so has Mummy." She smoothed her dress down over her knees. "He has a special chair in the sitting room too, but Mummy and I don't."

He lay on his stomach on the grass looking up at his sister.

"Mummy and Daddy!" he jeered. "I call mine Mother and Father. Only girls say Mummy. Michael doesn't live with you at all then?"

"No. Daddy said he was stupid and that he didn't agree to have any stupid boy in his house, so he sent him to Aunty Wyn."

"What's she like?"

Sheelagh shrugged, "I only see her at Christmas, and sometimes after church. She's a big lady with a cross face. Daddy goes to see her every Sunday while Mummy is watching Martha prepare lunch. He calls it his brotherly duty."

The ant darted over Colm's hand and tried to escape back onto the grass, but he continued to block its path, and it scurried over his fingers again.

"So, you are on your own too. It's good isn't it? You get lots of toys and things and you can eat anything you like. I don't have to do any chores, except keep my room tidy, but Ella does it even if I don't, so that doesn't matter really."

"I have lots of pretty clothes and a big dolly with a beautiful dress, and she closes her eyes when she lies down." She paused and frowned, "But next year I have to go to school, and I don't want to. Mummy says she will be very sad when I go."

"Are you going to a boarding school?"

"What's that?"

"It's a school where you sleep as well as have your dinner and come home at weekends for treats or visiting."

"No, I'm going to a girl's school with nuns. Mummy says they will make me clever, and you have to be clever so that when you get married your husband will like you."

Colm squashed the ant between finger and thumb.

"Do you miss the others in Ireland?"

"No, I don't think so. I am a very, very, lucky girl to be out of that house. Daddy says so. Sometimes I miss Mary; she was nice, and Aunty Bridgie. But Martha is nice too."

"Who's Martha?

"The maid."

Colm thought for a moment, studying the remains of the ant. "Sometimes I miss Pierce. He was fun." He said wiping his fingers on the grass. "I'm going to write him a letter and tell him about school and my bedroom and everything."

"I can't write."

"That's why you go to school."

"When you write, Colm, will you tell Mary I remember to say 'God Bless Mammy' every night?"

May opened the French doors. "Children, come along! We're going for a walk in the park."

Mary

"Aunty Bridgie, look! It's a letter from London."

Mary ran from the shop into the back room where Bridget was brewing her midday pot of tea.

"Well, give it to me, dear. Let's see who it's from."

Letters from London were rare. Bridget's brother Liam was not a great letter-writer and after the first note from the Sinclairs telling of the children's safe arrival, there had only been one other brief letter to say Colm had started school and was settling in well.

Bridget continued to write to Colm once a month, telling him the small pieces of news about Doonbeg, Glendarrig, and his sister and brother, but she was not sure he received them. As for Sheelagh and Michael, she never heard from the Porters. After six months silence, she wrote to Liam telling him of this. Her brother's response, at the time, upset Bridget greatly,

22 Gloucester Road,
Brixton,
London.
July 3rd 1925

Dear Bridget,

Do stop distressing yourself so. You have to understand that these people are very grand, Bridge. They don't like to mix with the likes of us. Mr. Sinclair explained to me early on that it would be better for Colm if he didn't get confused as to who his family is now. He said it would be better not to upset the lad by reminding him of his old family and the old ways.

He's right Bridget, and I expect the Porters feel the same way. As I told you, I met them the day we delivered the children. I know they are good people.

- 121 -

Sheelagh and Michael will be fine. These people just want to give them both a whole new life, and isn't that what you wanted for them? Don't fret yourself about the little ones. You just mind yourself and Mary and young Pierce,

Love,

Liam

Bridget found her brother's advice difficult to accept and continued to worry about the two youngest Kellys. Maybe this new letter brought news of them at last.

As she opened the envelope, she smelled a faint whisper of perfume. She wafted the envelope under Mary's nose and pulled a wry face.

"There's a grand smell now, Mary child." She smiled as she unfolded the single sheet of notepaper. A second, smaller scrap of paper folded into a tight square fell out onto the floor. Mary picked it up as Bridget read the letter.

"What does it say, Aunty Bridgie? Is it about Sheelagh and Michael? Is it about Colm?"

"Will you give me a minute, Mary? Amin't I trying to read it? I'll tell you in a minute."

Mary looked down at the small parcel of paper she held in her hand.

"Look, Aunty Bridgie, it's for Pierce. Can I open it?"

Bridget looked from the letter in her hand to the folded scrap Mary was holding up.

"Wait now; wait now; let me sit down and read this properly, then we'll look at that one. Go and see if there's anyone in the shop first."

"But, I didn't hear the bell."

"Go anyway," said the aunt distractedly.

Mary hurried out to the shop then back in again.

"There's no one there. What does it say?"

Bridget was frowning at the letter in her hand.

"It's from Mrs. Sinclair."

She took a breath and scanned the contents.

"Right then! I'll read it to you. Stop fidgeting.

Dear Miss Clancy,

I trust this letter finds you well. It has been some time since I last wrote, but felt I should apprise you of a little news.

"What's 'apprise' mean?"

"Letting me know; now, don't interrupt again or I won't read it to you." She continued:

"*As a surprise for Colm I arranged a weekend visit with our friends the Porters. I think my husband mentioned to you that Edith Porter is an old school friend of mine. We had not seen them for some time, indeed since the arrival of the children, but I knew they would be very busy with their new charges. Even one little boy is quite a handful, as I have discovered.*

Anyway, Miss Clancy, I just thought you should know that Mr. Porter, after a great deal of deliberation and consultation with his wife, decided that the very best care Michael could get would be with Mr. Porter's sister. He felt she would be better able to give him the individual attention he needs and deserves. Though she is unmarried, I understand she has her own home and is an excellent guardian for the boy. Mr. Porter visits his sister on a regular basis and assures us that Michael is in the very best of health. Mr. Porter continues to take an active role in his upbringing and still hopes Michael may one day inherit the business.

I have taken the liberty of informing you of this change, as I am acutely aware of the fact that we are the ones who encouraged you to part with the children. I suspect that Mrs. Porter may not have been in touch with you on this matter, so hope this will reassure you as to the little boy's well-being.

As for Sheelagh, she is the most darling little girl. Both the Porters are charmed by her, and she is the prettiest little thing. I so enjoyed meeting her last weekend. She has grown up a great deal in the last year and a half and is beautifully well-mannered too. I understand she begins school in September just before her sixth birthday. Edith is reluctant to part with her, even for a few hours, but Mr. Porter is anxious that she start soon.

So, Miss Clancy, I trust this puts your mind at ease. Both children are in good homes and have excellent prospects. I must also assure you that Colm is a wonderful little boy who has brought great happiness into our lives. I cannot thank you enough for your generosity in parting with him. Enclosed is a short note he wrote to his brother Pierce. I hope you will ensure he receives it.

We extend our good wishes to you and hope you remain in good health.

Sincerely,

May Sinclair

Bridget folded the letter. "So, there you are, my dear." She smiled at Mary. "All our worrying was for naught; they are all well and happy."

"Now, can we read the letter that Colm sent to Pierce?"

"No, we cannot!"

Bridgie took the note from Mary and tucked it behind the clock. "We will give it to him when he comes on Sunday."

And, with that Mary had to be content though she could hardly wait for Sunday to arrive.

Pierce

"There's a letter for you, Pierce. It's from Colm, and Aunty Bridgie has it behind the clock. Hurry up, Pierce, and we can open it."

Mary was so anxious to meet with her brother and give him the news as soon as possible that she had earned her Aunt's disapproval by fidgeting all the way through Mass. Now she tugged at Pierce's arm, urging him to "hurry up" as they walked from the church towards Doonbeg and the shop. He was smiling at his sister and Bridgie, happy to be out of his own house. He was almost as excited as his sister at the prospect of his very first letter, but as a big brother he tried to appear unconcerned.

"*We* can open it?" He teased, "I thought you said it was for me. Who says *you* can read it?"

He walked a little faster, nonetheless.

They covered the mile and a half speedily, Bridget puffing and panting as she tried to keep up with the youngsters. She wondered why she hadn't thought to bring the note to church. She could have saved herself all this rushing and fussing; but she too was laughing and in high spirits as they hurried homeward.

When they arrived Bridget reached behind the clock and handed the note to Pierce. He unfolded it carefully and laid it on the table so that he could smooth out the creases. Mary circled the table trying to get a glimpse, but her brother shielded it with his arm until she finally gave up in exasperation.

"What does it say? *Please* tell me what it says, Pierce. Is it really from Colm?"

Bridget stood expectantly beside him, and Mary tried to peek as her brother read the short note. When he finished, he handed it to her saying, "He wrote a message for you too," then turned to Bridget. "Can I have something to eat, Aunty Bridgie?"

"Well, what did he say, lad? Yes, of course, you can. Wait now, and I'll cook up some sausages for you."

Pierce remained silent, and Bridget busied herself with cooking. Fasting from midnight so that they could receive Communion meant they were all hungry.

"Can I read it out loud to her, Pierce?" asked Mary.

He nodded.

"Pierce, he spelled your name wrong, look." Mary showed it to Bridgie. "P-E-R-C-E," she continued reading slowly,

"I have my own bedroom and a lot of toys. I have toy soldiers and a football and a Meccano set and I can make all kinds of things with it. It is good fun here. Tell Mary that Sheelagh says she remembers to say "God Bless Mammy" at night, ..."

Mary looked up at Bridgie and smiled then continued reading,

"... so do I. I don't fetch water. It is in the tap. How are you? You can write to me if you like. Colm."

"Toy soldiers indeed!" Bridget gave a short laugh, "And I wonder what a Meccano set is." She laughed again, "It's nice to know he's missing us all so much, isn't it?"

She bustled about the small room fetching cups and plates from the dresser, brewing tea in the brown china pot, poking the sausages in the pan. As she worked, she quietly watched Pierce take the note from Mary, fold it, and put it carefully in his pocket before he sat at the table.

Mary also took her place at the table.

"I'm glad that Sheelagh remembers Mammy."

For a long time afterwards Pierce kept the note, reading it occasionally. The paper became soft and aged with fine creases and the penciled words became increasingly difficult to read. It mattered little—Pierce knew them by heart. He wanted to write back; he thought about it often, but didn't know what to say. Many times he began writing in his school copy:

Dear Colm ...

Then what? Many nights he lay in bed chewing the end of the pencil stub, trying to find words for his younger brother. He didn't want to ask Colm what "Meccano" was or "a tap." He thought it might be like an inside pump. He was the older brother; he should know about these things. He didn't want to write about his father or Mrs. Kelly either. What could he say anyway? That his father was spending more and more time in Daly's bar? That often, in his father's absence, he went without food because his stepmother refused to feed him? He didn't want Colm laughing at him. It was his own fault he was so stupid, that he'd been left behind, that he was so useless that no one wanted to adopt him. He didn't want his young brother's pity. He tore the pages out of the copy and screwed them up. He would write when he had something to say.

After three years, Pierce finally threw the worn and tattered remnants of his brother's note into the fire, but he did not forget it. As he grew into a young man, he increasingly took on his father's work. When Brendan did not or could not get out of bed, Pierce fetched the horse, harnessed it to the cart himself, and went about his father's business. Despite his father's unreliability, farmers continued to send word when they needed a haulage service, and word passed easily in the small community. They trusted Pierce to get the work done even if his father was unable to. A child would call to the door, or he would meet a neighbor out on the road.

"Mattie Dolan needs manure for the top field. He says will you bring some in next week?"

"The Finns want seaweed and sand. Will you make a trip to the beach?"

Though it took longer on his own, and his young body suffered under the heavy workload, he did not complain. When he worked alone, it was he who received the payment. Pierce felt no guilt when he kept one or two coins, tucking them into a worn sock he hid under his mattress. He put the remainder in the Toby jug as his father did.

A quiet bitterness replaced even the occasional angry outbursts in the household as the years went by. It seemed to Pierce that an unspoken truce grew between Brendan and his wife, and they spoke civilly enough when speech was necessary. She continued to make Pierce's life miserable. Some days Brendan worked with his son, and most evenings he spent in Daly's snug. His wife spun and knitted her yarn, cooked and tended the cottage, and went visiting every Sunday. Pierce worked or kept to his room.

Brendan took more and more money from the jar for his increasingly frequent visits to Daly's. Mrs. Kelly used what money was left to buy provisions. Pierce watched. He kept an accounting of the charges made for hauling the different loads in his small copybook, and he began to plan. The memory of Colm's note goaded him on. He *would* write to Colm.

Dear Colm, I want to have enough money to get a horse of my own …

He tore out the piece of paper and screwed it into a ball. He would write when he had a horse.

1930

Pierce

The village grew. The main street was paved, and a draper's and a general store now stood alongside the older businesses like Daly's bar, Kathleen Byrne's dairy, and Biddy Egan's fruit and vegetable shop. Anxious to share in the new prosperity, a few women in the village started a cooperative. Mrs. Kelly was approached to see if she would be part of the group. Her husband's horse and cart were useful assets.

Crofters grazed sheep on the stony, inhospitable slopes of the Knockglas Mountains above Doonbeg. Journeymen clipped the sheep in late spring, and for years haulers, like Brendan and Pierce, took the wool to the market in Ballyfin. But things were changing. Now, at the spring shearing the women from Glendarrig bought large quantities of the matted, oily wool direct from the crofters. Brendan or Pierce carted it to the village. Each in her own home, the women worked to pick out the twigs, dead insects, and debris tangled in the fleece. They washed, carded, and spun the cleaned yarn. Some, fastened in thick skein twists, they sold to other local women. The rest they knitted into sweaters, cardigans, and shawls for sale in the larger towns. Later, father or son took Mrs. Kelly to Ballyfin to negotiate and to sell the yarn and the knitted garments to the bigger shops. The family was prospering despite Brendan's drinking.

It was Pierce's seventeenth birthday, though neither Pierce nor his father remembered. They were traveling to Ballyfin in the mean cold of a February morning, father and son huddled under old sacks for extra protection against the biting wind. A fine dusting of snow lay over the fields, and the dark sky threatened more snow to soak them and their load. They were delivering a load of beets to the market and were to bring back bolts of cloth for Niall Mahon who owned the new draper's shop in Glendarrig.

"Da, can I have some money?"

"What in the name of all that's holy do you want money for? Haven't you got a home, and aren't you fed and clothed? What more do you want?"

"I want a horse."

"Do you indeed?" Brendan turned to look at his son. "And what would you be doing with a horse? Don't we have a horse already? You can't hitch two horses to the one cart, you know."

"I know that, Da, but I could hire him out. There're never enough horses for the plowing, or harvesting. Everyone wants it done at the same time. And there's many an old cart that folk could harness it to if they wanted to do a bit of muck spreading or that."

Brendan turned back to watch the road. "Doing me out of business—is that what you want?"

"No, Da, but there *is* more work here now. We could be hauling more if we had another horse and cart. Having my own horse would be a good start."

"We'll see. Would you have any money saved up by any chance?"

The question caught Pierce by surprise. "How could I, Da?"

He felt nervous. His father was always unpredictable, though he'd not struck Pierce for some time. Still, the young man remembered his father's angry outbursts from the past and was anxious not to aggravate him.

"I'm not a fool, Pierce. I know you don't put all the money in the jug. I know what should go in there after a job. The drink hasn't addled my brains entirely."

Pierce stared straight ahead at the road, afraid to catch his father's eye.

"Is that what you've been taking it for? To buy a horse?"

Pierce nodded.

"Did it not occur to you, son, that I'd know where you got the money?"

Pierce bowed his head. No, he hadn't thought that far. He only knew he wanted to be able to write to Colm to tell him he had a horse, to show his younger brother he was successful. But he'd not thought about how he would explain the purchase of a new horse to his father.

"Do you think you can look after another horse as well as do your work and chores?" asked Brendan.

Pierce gave a quick sideways glance at his father. "I do, Da."

Brendan tapped the horse's rump with his stick and shook the reins. "Gedup there!"

They traveled in silence for a while. The threatened snow began falling from a leaden sky, blanketing their heads and shoulders and settling in Brendan's thick moustache and bushy eyebrows.

"Maybe we'll have a look at some nags in Ballyfin. The tinkers always have a few for sale, robbers though they are." He glanced at his son. "Did I ever tell you you look very like your mother, lad?"

Pierce nodded. He could have a horse! They were going to look at horses *today*! He could rent it out. He could ride it whenever he wanted. He could earn money for himself. He could write to Colm.

Colm

Dear Colm,

I have a horse. We bought it in Ballyfin last week. It is only five years old and has a bit of a sway back, but Da says that will be fine as it's a horse for pulling not riding. But I'll be able ride it sometimes on Sundays to go over to Aunty Bridgie's and to see Mary, and I'll be able to ride it over to whoever wants to hire it.

Paddy Flynn has already said he'll pay me to use it for pulling rocks off land he wants to clear up by his top field, and John Dooly wants it for hauling logs.

Da says I can keep the money, but I have to give some to Mrs. Kelly for my board and lodging, as that's what a man is supposed to do.

Mary works in the shop a lot now as Aunty Bridgie has the rumatism and gets very stiff if she goes too far from the fire. Mary will finish school for good this summer and then Aunty Bridgie says she can work in the shop all the time. I think Mary likes that.

When I told Mary I was going to write to you about the horse, she said to ask you how are Sheelagh and Michael? I would like to know too. Mary says Aunty Bridgie and her have no address for them and didn't want to bother the Sinclairs.

Mary also says to give you her love, if you remember her, and says, do you still say your prayers and did you make your First Communion, and did Sheelagh as well?

I have no more paper so will end here. I can write again. I can get more paper from Aunty Bridgie. I am fine and hope you are fine.

Pierce

"What are you reading, darling?"

Colm stood in the front hallway, Pierce's letter in his hand.

"It's a letter from my brother, Pierce."

May was startled. "Where did you get that?"

"The postman just delivered it."

"I didn't know that you were out of bed. How are you feeling? Oh, Colm darling, you don't even have your slippers on. Come on, little man, let me tuck you back into bed, and I'll bring you some warm milk. It's very cold in this hallway."

"I was tired of being on my own, then I heard the postman, and I was going to bring you the letters, but this one was for me."

He showed her the small white envelope, its flap torn open.

"So I see." She put her arm on his shoulder, "Come on, dear, back to bed with you before you catch your death of cold."

May followed her son back up the stairs and into his bedroom.

The letters from the Aunt Bridgie had stopped a long time ago, ever since May asked Edward to speak to Liam Clancy again. She had asked her husband to explain to him how it would be better if they left Colm alone. He had a new family now; it wasn't necessary to remind him about the old Irish one. It had worked, and after that she thought there was no need to monitor the mail to intercept the monthly letters from the aunt. May was not expecting another one after all this time.

"I hope it hasn't upset you, darling. We don't want you getting ill again, do we?"

Colm was recovering from the mumps. An outbreak in the school had prompted Edward to drive up to Suffolk to fetch his son before he caught the infection. He had caught it anyway, but May was happier to nurse him at home, and Colm was delighted with the unexpected holiday. He felt fine. In fact, apart from the swelling in his neck, there was no sign of any debilitation, but he was happy to be fussed over and pampered. Even Ella was solicitous.

"He has a horse," said Colm, as he climbed into bed.

"Really, darling? I didn't imagine your brother going out riding."

Colm laughed at his mother's stupidity. "It's not a horse for riding Mother, not like for hunting or anything like that. It's for hauling. It's going to haul logs and help pull rocks out of the ground. And Pierce will get money for it. But he can ride it sometimes."

May sat on the bed beside her son. She'd hoped he'd forgotten all about these people, yet now he seemed quite at home speaking of his brother owning a *carthorse* and plying it for *trade*.

"Colm, dear, I'm not sure your friends in school would be very impressed if you told them about this. I'm sure if they mentioned it to their mothers or fathers you might not be asked to visit any more. Working class people are very necessary, of course," she reassured him, "But you're taking your entrance examination to Kings College this summer, and that's not a school for working class people. I think maybe we should keep this as our little secret. What do you think?"

Colm understood. His mother didn't approve of Pierce.

"Mary wants to know about Sheelagh and Michael too," he said, watching his mother's reaction carefully.

"Oh dear, this really is most difficult, Colm. I don't think the Porters have any inclination to contact the Kelly family."

"Should I ask father when he gets home?"

May was anxious to minimize the fuss.

"She asked if Sheelagh made her First Communion yet," Colm persisted.

May, a devout Catholic herself, suddenly felt embarrassed.

"Dear me," she repeated, "This is very awkward. Yes, of course they want to know."

She remembered wondering at the time if Edith had sent a photograph or a note to the old aunt. It seemed she had not.

The year before, Edward, May, and Colm had been invited to Bristol for Sheelagh's First Communion. May thought Sheelagh looked like a young bride in her white satin dress and French lace veil—maybe even a little over-dressed for the occasion, but then Edith was always inclined to over-embellish. After the service they met Jim Porter's sister, Wyn. She had the little boy Michael with her, Sheelagh's brother. Of course he was Colm's brother too, but May preferred to think of Colm as an only child. It was the first time May had seen Michael since their arrival at her house over four years before. He looked as if he was doing well, she thought. Wyn told her the boy was nearly eight years old now and due to make his own First Communion the following year. Jim over-heard the comment and said that it was lucky a boy wouldn't need the same kind of fuss and expense as a little girl.

"Boys don't care so much about all the dressing up and everything," he explained. "I think it will be a far quieter affair. I certainly don't think it will be worth you and Edward traveling all this distance again."

May was surprised at his comment. Colm was a little boy, and *his* Communion had been a very special event for him and his classmates, celebrated in the school Chapel. And Father John had presided over a rather splendid Communion breakfast for the students and their families afterwards in the Great Hall. She and Edward gave Colm a beautiful embossed prayer book and a watch for the occasion.

At Sheelagh's lavish Communion breakfast that the Porters hosted at the Grand Hotel, May had the opportunity to compare the two boys. She conceded that Michael was a handsome child, fine boned where Colm was inclined to be stocky. Michael's hair was dark and curly like Sheelagh's, whereas Colm's was mouse-colored and straight, and required a great deal of pomade to fix it in position. She admired Michael's dark brown eyes, and she found herself entranced by the young boy who stayed so close to his Aunt Wyn and said very little.

May felt Colm's hand tugging at her sleeve, trying to regain her attention.

"Can I write back to him, Mother, to Pierce? Please, can I?"

"Do you *really* want to, darling?"

May wrinkled her nose very slightly, a sign which Colm recognized as disapproval, but he wanted to know more about the horse.

"Yes, please."

"Very well then, dear, but don't mention it to anyone except Father and me. All right, my sweet?"

He nodded.

"Perhaps I could enclose some photographs for the aunt. I have some of Sheelagh's Communion pictures. And I think I took one of Michael. I could even send one of you, dear. Do you think they would like that?"

Again, Colm nodded.

"I'm sure I don't have to write, that's really up to Edith, but at least they will know that we are true to our word. She will know that you are all well and being brought up properly."

May was pleased with her decision. She would be doing the right thing without having to write personally. It was a most satisfactory resolution.

Colm asked her for pen and paper.

Mary

Bridgie sat in her chair in front of the fire. Mary sat on the stool beside her.

"Doesn't she look beautiful?" She asked yet again, as she looked at the photograph of Sheelagh in her Communion dress.

"She does, alanna, but you'll have those pictures worn out if you look at them much more." Bridget smiled at her grand-niece. "I think we had better get some nice frames for them and put them on the mantelpiece. Wouldn't that be a good idea?"

Mary nodded. "Hasn't Michael grown up? He looks a bit like Pierce, doesn't he?"

She was reluctant to give up the pictures.

"I don't think that hair is red like Pierce's, but he certainly is as skinny as his big brother, not like that chubby young man."

Bridget pointed at the picture of Colm, standing ramrod straight in his school uniform with a large Communion rosette pinned to his jacket lapel. His straight hair was slicked down and shiny.

"He doesn't look like he's being starved anyway, does he? And look at that grin. I'd say he's a handful that young brother of yours. He looks like he could charm the birds off the trees."

Mary smiled and returned to studying the picture of Sheelagh.

"She does look happy though, doesn't she, Aunty Bridgie?"

"Yes, she does, and I'm sure she is." She put her arm around Mary's shoulder. "You have to stop worrying about them, child, after all this time. They all look well, and I'm sure they are very happy with their new families."

"Michael doesn't look happy though, does he?" The young girl persisted.

"Michael always did have a serious face; God Bless him. Stop worrying, Mary. I did the best I could, child. We have to trust in God that He will take care of them and us. Now, let's get some supper before your poor Aunty Bridgie fades away from lack of nourishment."

She smiled at Mary and raised herself painfully from her chair.

The young woman and the old lady had become very close over the last few years. Mary, who was now nearly fifteen, took Norah's place in the shop and in the gentle care she took of her aunt. Bridgie grew to love the plain, awkward girl with the serious face and loving nature more and more.

"You'll make a wonderful mother one day, Mary."

"And I won't die and leave them either," the girl replied vehemently.

"Your Mammy didn't do it on purpose, child. We're all in God's hands. She loved you very much."

"Da didn't care about us though, did he? He still doesn't."

Bridget paused before she answered. Mary was bitter and unforgiving about her father. When the younger children first went to England, he would sometimes call in to the shop on his way to Ballyfin, but Mary always retreated to the back room and refused to see him. Eventually he stopped calling. They would see each other at Mass, occasionally, and Bridget would stop for a brief word, but Mary always walked away, visiting her mother's grave, or walking slowly homeward until her aunt caught up with her. Bridget tried to heal the rift.

"I can't begin to know what got into that man's head, child. But I do know he is paying dearly for his mistakes. There's no love in that house by all accounts. Annie says his new wife is a hard woman. That's part of the price he's paid. And no children have taken your place. That's God's curse on him, child, for rejecting you. He's not been blessed with more children." She smiled sadly and shook her head. "He was happy with your mother, though heaven knows they had a hard enough life. Now the demon drink is eating him up. Don't be so hard on him, alanna. I have a feeling he's hard enough on himself."

"I hate him, Aunty Bridgie; he was going to put us in the Sacred Heart. It's his fault we are all split up."

"I know, child, I know. I don't know why it happened, but I'm sure he's very sorry. Can you not find it in your heart to forgive him?"

"Never," Mary responded.

But anger, like any strong passion, is difficult to sustain. As the years passed, her anger turned to bitterness and then contempt for the big man she saw often unshaven and reeking of drink at Mass or passing by the shop on his horse and cart.

She persuaded her aunt to let her take the pictures to her room that night. The small front bedroom was hers, her narrow bed tucked in tightly beside the upright piano, a discard from the front parlor when the shop was created. She propped the photographs on the lid so that she could still see them as she lay in bed. She placed Sheelagh in the middle with Colm and Michael on either side. Still gazing at the pictures, she climbed into bed and tugged the patchwork quilt up under her chin. She fingered the patches from her mother's blouse, then those from her brothers' and sister's pieces. "I haven't forgotten you," she whispered, "and I won't. I promise."

She studied the pictures, trying to imagine their lives, what their new homes and families were like, how Michael was coping being on his own. She and her aunt were distressed when they learned that Michael and Sheelagh had been separated; they couldn't understand why.

"But they're still close," Bridgie reassured her at the time. "It's not like it's a completely different family or a different town. I'm sure they see each other quite regularly."

"We will be back together one day. I know we will," Mary told the three young faces in the pictures. She wanted it to happen so much she felt she could will it.

She stared at the photographs for a long time, and as she did so her resolve hardened. She vowed to herself that she would, somehow, keep the family in touch with each other. She didn't know how, but she would do it; she would not let those people keep them apart. They were a family—her family.

Sheelagh

Jim Porter paced the room, tapping his pipe stem impatiently on his teeth.

"Well, I don't like the idea, Edith. I thought we'd made a clean break."

"But the child is very polite. It's a charming note, and they are sisters after all."

"It took her a while to think of that! For four years we hear nothing, and now this. How did she get the damned address anyway?"

"May forwarded her little note. The girl has given her word not to overdo it, Jim, look," Edith drew her husband's attention to the line as she read aloud:

"I do not want to be a nuisance and promise not to write all the time."

She looked pleadingly at her husband. "It's very touching, Jim. She sounds so lonely. I'm sure Sheelagh would love to have a little note from her sister on her birthday and at Christmas. I don't think it will upset her one bit. She's very happy here, Jim. I don't think she would dream of going back to those primitive conditions."

"What about Wyn?"

"You know if you tell your sister that you have allowed it, she will agree." She smiled encouragingly at her husband. "Just try it, dear. If they get upset then we can stop it right away. May says Edward has agreed to letters for Colm." She paused and frowned, "Of course, there was that little mishap of him getting the brother's letter anyway. But Colm doesn't seem any the worse for it, according to May."

"Very well then, but the first sign of the water-works or that little one getting upset and that will be the end of it."

Edith smiled. "Oh, thank you, dear! I'll write back immediately. It's Sheelagh's birthday next month. Won't she be surprised when she gets a letter from her sister? She still remembers her in her prayers, you know."

"Come along, Miss Sheelagh, all your guests are waiting. Let me fix your collar."

Martha adjusted the delicate crocheted lace collar on Sheelagh's dress and stepped back to admire the little girl.

"My, but don't you look grown up. Give me a twirl."

Sheelagh pirouetted and gave Martha her best ballet curtsy.

"Very elegant, Miss Sheelagh, you look beautiful. Come on then, time to go downstairs. You don't want to be late for your own birthday party, do you?"

As Martha opened the door, Edith entered.

"Well, my little birthday girl, show me how you look."

Sheelagh gave another twirl and curtsy.

"You look lovely. Doesn't she, Martha?"

"She certainly does, Mrs. Porter. If you don't mind, Ma'am, I'll go on downstairs. I'm sure the guests will be arriving soon, and I want to make sure the table is set out properly."

"Yes, yes, off you go, Martha."

Martha left closing the door behind her. Edith sat on Sheelagh's bed and patted the space beside her. Sheelagh joined her mother.

"I know you received our gifts earlier, darling, but this is just a little surprise I was saving for you until we were on our own." She held out the envelope. "Daddy was afraid it would upset you, but I thought you would be happy to get it."

Sheelagh took the envelope, inserted her finger into the small gap at the edge of the flap, and carefully opened it. She began to read the letter, then looked up at her mother, perplexed. "It's from Mary, my sister Mary."

"I know, dear."

Sheelagh flushed and returned to the letter. Downstairs the doorbell rang. Sheelagh continued to read. There was a knock on the bedroom door. Edith Porter called, "Come in."

Martha stuck her head around the door.

"Sorry, Ma'am, but two of Miss Sheelagh's guests have arrived."

Sheelagh looked up from her letter.

"Oh dear!" said Edith standing up from the bed. "We can't keep our guests waiting, can we? Have you finished your letter, darling?"

She had not. Excited and flustered at receiving this unexpected note, she was having difficulty concentrating on the words. But it was her birthday; she had friends arriving, and there was a table laden with delicious party food downstairs.

"Yes, I have, Mummy."

She tucked it under her pillow. "I'm ready. Can we go down now?"

Edith put out her hand, Sheelagh grasped it, and they went downstairs together to greet their guests.

During the hubbub of little girls' squeals and shrieks, Edith managed to snatch a brief moment with her husband.

"You see, I told you. She was fine about the letter, not a bit upset."

"Good, glad to hear it. Now I'm going to the study to get away from the infernal noise. Let me know when they've all gone."

1936

Mary

For five years Mary wrote to Colm, Sheelagh, and Michael on their birthdays and at Christmas. She told them about Aunty Bridgie, Pierce, and herself. She wrote about friends and neighbors, births, weddings, and deaths. She tried to keep alive their memories of Glendarrig and Doonbeg, of relatives and old school friends. She knew Sheelagh and Michael were probably too young when they left Ireland to remember much, but she wanted them to know about their home and their heritage. Just as she had related their grandfather's fairy tales to them when they were young, she now wove stories of real people they did not know and places they would not remember.

> ... *Father Mulcahy was moved to a new parish and we have Canon Finnegan now and he's a terrible man at confession. He gives two decades of the rosary if you say you were late for Mass, and we saw Colm Brady do the Stations of the Cross* <u>twice</u> *just after he came back from a visit to Dublin and everyone was talking about it ...*

> ... *Pierce has another cart now, so he drives one and Da drives the other, but Pierce says Da's horse is getting old, so Pierce is saving his money to buy one of them lorries. That's what he wants next ...*

> *Pierce and Da have built another room on the side of the cottage where they used to keep the cart, and there's talk of running water being put into the village, so they might be having a water closet one day soon, then Pierce won't have to keep the privy clean. He hates that job, so did I. Aunty Bridgie and me have had a water closet for nearly a year now, outside by the turf shed.*
> *They keep the carts now on a piece of land Pierce is renting from Shay Rafferty, the squint-eyed farmer on the Ballyfin Road that has the two woefully ugly daughters. When Pierce told Aunty Bridgie, she said she hoped the rent wouldn't be to marry one of them, but I don't think Pierce would be that daft, even for a chance at getting the farm ...*

… We don't keep a pig any more. Aunty Bridgie said it was too much just for the two of us and she's getting too old to be doing all that work. We buy the bit of meat we need from Gabriel Dooley who has a grand butcher shop in Doonbeg. He used to be the one that butchered the pigs for everyone, even Da took our pigs to him, but now there are all kinds of rules and regulations for slaughtering and Mr. Dooley says he can't be bothered with all the paperwork the government says they want, so he opened the shop and lets the big slaughterhouse in Ballyfin do all the dirty work …

… Aunty Bridgie is very bad with the rheumatism, and sometimes she can't get upstairs, and so she sleeps in her chair. She can't walk to Mass any more, and Canon Finnegan brings her Communion on a Sunday …

… Kathleen Murphy was married this year, and she is two years younger than me. It makes me feel very old. She married Mick Mahon whose father owns the draper's shop in Glendarrig and she is expecting her first child soon. Aunty Bridgie says Mammy was married when she was 18 too …

… The shop is doing well, and I run it on my own now, though Aunty Bridgie keeps an eye on me. We got rid of most of the chickens. Do you remember how you used to chase them, Sheelagh, until one pecked you? We just keep enough for ourselves and buy in the eggs from the co-op for the shop …

There is a great scandal over in Glendarrig. It is said that Breda Rafferty is with child, and she not wed! She is gone from the village of course. Her mammy says she has gone into service in Dublin, but no one believes it. Aunty Bridgie says the whole family is shamed, and Breda will never be able to show her face here again. I'm only glad I was never friendly with her.

… Master Keogh, the school teacher, died in January. He taught you Colm. They said he had the influenza bad, but Aunty Bridgie says he was always very frail anyway and didn't eat properly. She said the big bag of broken biscuits he bought from us nearly every day was what he had for his dinner, if he didn't share them with the children. Terrible sweet tooth she said he had, and no wife …

… Do you remember the Quinn's? Annie Quinn is a midwife. She delivered us all. She lays people out too. They live in the cottage close by the Da's in Glendarrig. Well, Pierce is courting her daughter Freda now. They have been an item for a year, but Pierce says he's not thinking of getting married for a while yet …

… They are building a picture house here in Doonbeg. Can you believe it? We will be able to see all the famous film stars that I've read about in the paper.

They are not going to have an organ because they will be showing the talking pictures. Isn't that very grand? Canon Finnegan says it will be an occasion of sin …

… I have been walking out with Joseph Daly for a while now. He's the one whose father owns the bar in Glendarrig. I met him at Mass. He was with Pierce. Aunty Bridgie does not like him because of his father owning the bar but Joe doesn't drink and he doesn't even work with his Da in the bar, his older brother does that. Joe has a job working in the meat-packing factory that was built on the Rathfen Road. He looks after the machines …

For five years Mary wrote her letters. In five years she heard nothing. No one replied, but Bridget was reluctant to discourage her.

"Maybe they aren't very good at letter writing," she'd say, or, "I'm sure they're far too busy to be replying to the likes of us," or "they are young, alanna, they don't know the value of a letter yet. I'm sure they'll write eventually." But they never did.

Then one day Mary came downstairs to open the shop and bring in the milk delivered by Sean Reagan, and she knew it was a different day. The house was quieter. Apart for the ticking of the clock in the back parlor, there was no sound. There was no crackle from the fire which was almost out, and no gentle snoring from Bridget sitting in her red plush chair wrapped in her crocheted shawl. There was no heavy breathing—no breathing at all. Mary put her hand on her Aunt's arm and shook her gently, very gently. But she knew.

Main Street,
Doonbeg,
Co. Galway.
October 21st 1936

Dear Colm,

I know it is not your birthday, or Christmas, but I had to write to tell you that Aunty Bridgie died a week last Tuesday. It was very peaceful. Dr Taaffe said it was her heart and that her rheumatism was so bad it was probably a blessed relief anyway. She was buried beside her mother and father and is near Mammy.

There were a lot of people at the wake and at the funeral. Even Mrs. Kelly came, though I didn't speak to her. Canon Finnegan gave a lovely sermon on how good Aunty Bridgie was, and kind and generous, and didn't press people for money when they didn't have it. I told him that bit.

A lot of people offered to carry her coffin, but Da and Pierce and Uncle Pat and his two sons and Joe did it. There is no one left from her family. Uncle Liam could not get back in time, though I sent him a telegram the same day she died.

Aunty Bridgie's solicitor, a Mr. Maguire, wrote and told me to come and see him after the funeral, and when I did, he told me that the house was now mine. Her and Uncle Liam decided that that was for the best, and anyway he said he will not come back and live here now that she is gone.

It is very quiet in the house, and it feels strange to be here on my own. Joe says if I want to get wed we can, and then I would not be on my own, and we have somewhere to live so that's not a problem. I might.

I'm sorry to give you this sad news. She loved you very much and hoped you were happy in England. I hope to hear from you soon,

Love,

Mary

She wrote the same letter to Sheelagh and to Michael. Sheelagh was the first to reply.

17 Cornwallis Grove,
Clifton,
Bristol.
November 2nd 1936

Dear Mary,

I was very sorry to hear about Aunty Bridgie. I don't remember her very well, though I think I remember she always wore black. I remember the sweet little shop and the dark stairs up to the bedroom and how we all squashed into a tiny bed next to a piano. I suppose I was very young when we were there.

Thank you for all of your letters, I'm sorry I didn't write back, but I didn't have much to tell you really.

I finish school this year. I go to a Catholic convent school, full of French nuns with impossible accents, and I'm sure you know what nuns are like! I will be glad to be finished, though I don't know what I will do then. Mummy and Daddy are taking me for a holiday to Scotland. Daddy says he will not go to Europe as he does not like this Herr Hitler in Germany and thinks he is a dangerous man. I kept explaining to him that I wanted to go to France, not Germany, but he said it's too close, so he decided we are going to Scotland, so Scotland it is. Mummy says it is beautiful up there.

Can you imagine, you are thinking of getting married! Is he very handsome? Will you have a beautiful dress? I don't have a picture of you, so I can't imagine you in your wedding dress. Please send me one when you can. It seems very strange to have a sister you can hardly remember, but I think you looked after me a lot, didn't you?

It must be nice to have your own house, especially when it is a shop as well. Is it very hard work?

Mummy told me you said you would only write on my birthdays and Christmas, but I think I am old enough to get letters whenever I like now, so do let me know if you get married. And don't forget the picture!

I don't know if Michael will write to you. We don't talk too much. He lives with Aunty Wyn, and she is SUCH a dragon. I think Mummy is afraid of her too, but she can't say that to me of course. I see him at Mass on Sundays. He is an altar boy you know. I have to admit my friends think he looks divine. We all went to the pictures for my friend Cicely's birthday and afterwards they said Michael is just like Little Lord Fauntleroy with his curly hair and big eyes. It was a very sad picture, and we all cried.

I must tell you about my name. I'm going to change my second name legally. Everyone calls me Sheelagh Porter but Mummy said it wasn't changed properly, because it was an informal adoption, which means there were no papers. It has always been a bit awkward filling out forms and things. But anyway I have said I would like to change it legally now that I'm old enough. It's only fair really.

I must stop now, Martha says tea is ready. Don't forget to write.

Love,

Sheelagh (soon to be) Porter

Mary read and reread the letter. Sheelagh said that Aunty Wyn was a dragon, which upset Mary, but maybe Sheelagh was exaggerating. She always was inclined to make a fuss. Changing her second name was strange. She would be doing it anyway when she married, so why bother now? When Mary told Joe about the letter, she said she thought her sister had turned out "a bit giddy," but Joe said Brits were nasty work, and hadn't it taken over seven hundred years to get them out of Ireland? And here they were stealing Irish children and trying to make them into Brits. Mary tried to explain, but Joe would hear nothing good about the British people. For the sake of peace, she decided to say as little as possible about her sister and brothers in England.

Then she received a letter from Colm.

> *12 Victoria Ave.,*
> *Finchley,*
> *London.*
> *November 10th 1936*

Dear Mary,

I was sorry to hear about Aunty Bridgie. I think she was a good lady, and she was certainly good to you, leaving you the shop, though I seem to remember it was quite a small one. Was Uncle Liam the one who brought us to England? He seemed very nice too. It's funny; I don't think I've ever seen him since, though I think he works for father. Just as well really, it would seem a bit strange bumping into him, wouldn't it? I wouldn't even recognize him now.

Father wants me to take over the business when I'm older, but he wants me to finish my studies and go to University first. We are thinking of Oxford or Cambridge. I do my entrance exams next year, so I have to decide soon.

I have not heard from Pierce for ages. He sent me a letter or two then stopped. You said in one of your letters (thanks for them by the way, I love all of your funny stories) he was going to buy a lorry. Does he have it yet? Tell him to write and let me know what he is doing.

I am getting a car for Christmas. Father says I have to pass my test first, but that will be easy. He has let me try driving his car, but I want something a bit racier like an Alvis or an MG, but I have to tread a bit carefully with mother. She's a worrier.

Sorry about the Aunt. Do keep writing. It all sounds so "other world." There are quite a lot of Irish here, but they are all working people, so we don't exactly chat a great deal, don't you know.

Hope your wedding goes well. Do you have to hand over the shop to him then?

Yours sincerely,

Colm

Yet again, Mary studied the letter. Like a detective she sifted through the information to learn what she could of Colm's life, his family, and how he fared in the years since he left Doonbeg. He, like Sheelagh, sounded very happy, and if he was still not working then she supposed his family must be very rich.

Joe was always talking about the machines in the factory, so she understood that Colm was interested in the same things, but she wondered why he didn't just get a job in a factory if he wanted to learn about cars and engines. What would he study at a university? Universities were usually for Protestants anyway. She knew Catholics were not allowed to go to Trinity College in Dublin, and *that* was a university, wasn't it? Canon Finnegan had gone on about it from the pulpit one Sunday when there was talk of Liam Rattigan's son going there.

Colm made no mention of going to Mass; Mary hoped he was still practicing his faith. Joe said the Brits were a godless bunch who divorced at the drop of a hat and only went to church for weddings and funerals. She would have to ask Colm in her next letter. She knew he made his Confirmation; she had the photograph framed and sitting on the mantelpiece beside the other pictures May sent, but that was several years ago.

Mary didn't understand what he meant by "the funny stories." She couldn't remember telling him any funny stories. Maybe he misunderstood something she said. She tucked the letter behind the clock beside Sheelagh's. She would show it to Pierce the next time he came over. He could write to Colm himself and tell him about the lorry and the cottage.

She didn't hear from Michael.

Pierce

It took Brendan a long time to agree to Pierce's arguments on the benefits of a motorized vehicle. He kept finding new excuses. "Frightens the horses, and you can't tell it what to do! A lorry won't fetch its way home at the end of a day either."

"We can get more work, and we can haul heavier loads, Da. With the new hard roads they're putting in, we can go all the way to Dublin in a day if we want to."

"Who's going to pay for it?" Brendan roared one evening as Pierce badgered him yet again. Money was always a source of argument in the house. Pierce worked hard, and often alone, while Brendan met with his friends in Daly's, or slept off his excesses in the loft bedroom. The horse Pierce bought with his father's help was rented out on a regular basis, but Mrs. Kelly claimed most of that income for his "keep." Pierce saved the few coins left over until after four years he bought the old cart that had sat neglected and unused at the rear of Rafferty's barn since Shay Rafferty bought himself a shiny blue lorry. Pierce increased his profit from renting out the second horse *and* cart, and continued to put aside his savings, though now he kept his money in the Bank of Ireland in Ballyfin, not in the old sock.

The money Pierce earned driving Brendan's cart he continued to put in the jug. Mrs. Kelly frequently prompted her husband to ensure the full sum was deposited. Brendan took what money he wanted, and his wife managed the rest of the finances. She bought provisions and removed the remainder to what she called "a safer place." She never spent money on clothes for herself or her husband unless it was absolutely necessary, and Brendan never questioned her housekeeping, as long as there was enough money for the drink. Pierce was expected to provide for himself. Expanding the business and filling in the columns of figures in his notebook were far more important to him than clothes. He wanted a lorry.

"All right! All right!" Brendan bellowed at his son as they shoveled sand onto the cart. "If you earn the down payment, we'll talk about it. I've had enough of listening to you going on about that damned lorry. You just better know what you're doing! And you're the one who is going to do the driving. I'll stick to what I know with the horse and cart."

Pierce was elated. He had most of the deposit already saved and now worked harder, even on Sundays if he could get the work. He made sure to work well away from Glendarrig and Doonbeg to avoid the wrath of God via the anger of Canon Finnegan.

Years before, Mrs. Kelly had persuaded her husband to clear out the additional room on the side of the cottage which had become cluttered with horse tack and empty crates and allow her to use it. "I need space for my spinning wheel and somewhere to store the wool and yarn," she told him. Brendan agreed. Now she announced to her husband that she wanted a *real* second floor *and* a slate roof on the cottage. Brendan flew into a rage.

"Where do you think I would get the money for that?" he roared. "Is this place not good enough for you now?"

Pierce was eating his supper but rose from his seat at his father's angry voice.

"It's glad enough you were to take it when we first wed, woman." Brendan continued, "Bad cess on you for the day I ever met you."

Pierce had not seen his father this angry for some time. He'd forgotten.

"I've kept the vows I took before God and have kept you as my wife though it has cost me dear. It's cold comfort you've been to me all these years, Ma'am. And now you tell me my home is not good enough for you! I should throw you out on the street where you belong."

"Don't you threaten me, Brendan Kelly! You've had use enough of me in your bed, and little enough I got in return, as well you know. You'll drink yourself to an early grave, and good riddance to you, say I. And what will I have then? Precious little except this pigsty! A house is what I want, and it's what I'll have, Brendan Kelly, for all the years I've spent taking care of you," she turned and pointed an angry finger at Pierce, "and your brat."

Though he was a grown man, easily the height of his father, Pierce still did not like the harsh sound of angry voices and wanted no part in this fight which had been simmering in icy silence and hard words for so many years. He tried to edge towards the loft steps.

"... And no thanks I got for it, but a few coins and a sullen hate," she continued.

"Thanks? Thanks? He's all that I have left woman, thanks to you."

Brendan thrust Pierce behind him, as if to protect him from the woman's venomous wrath.

"I have lost all my children but him, and you gave me no more. No child wanted shelter in your belly or succor from your breasts."

"Don't you dare say that to me, Brendan Kelly! Don't you dare! You *chose* to give away your own children, old man. That was you. Don't put your sins on my soul."

"That's not true. You know that's not true. It's why I wed you. Everyone can testify to that. I wed a lying bitch." Brendan's face was livid red.

"You didn't want them enough though, did you? Your own children! And you didn't want them!" she yelled.

He moved towards her, his hand going to the buckle of his belt.

"Hit me, would you?"

The small woman took a step closer to her husband. She was as angry as him, her pale blue eyes flashing. She paused and said more quietly, "Have a care, old man. I will harm you yet."

She turned, snatched her shawl from the chair, and left the cottage. Brendan watched her leave, speechless in his anger. As the door slammed closed and the latch clicked into place, he turned to glare at Pierce.

"What are you looking at? Get out of my way, and keep out!"

He pushed Pierce to one side, snatched down the jug, and emptied the coins into his calloused hand, spilling some on the floor in his anger and haste. Thrusting the money into his pocket, he too left the cottage.

Pierce stood in silence before the fire, yet again facing the question of why his family had been separated. Was the woman telling the truth? Was it his father who had changed his mind, decided he didn't want to keep his children? Why was he the only one not sent away? Pierce had always blamed *her*; *she* was the one who poisoned his father against the children; *she* wanted the house to herself. Was he wrong?

He bent slowly, collected the spilled coins and put them in his pocket.

Pierce did not see his father for two days. Since the argument, he and his stepmother continued to share their home but did not speak. Communication had always been brief, limited to necessary exchanges—passing on messages about jobs or her demands for chores to be done. Even these were now abandoned as each ignored the other.

On the third morning, Pierce rose early as usual, anxious to avoid his stepmother and determined to leave the house before she was out of bed. When he descended the loft steps into the smoky darkness of the room below, he saw his father sitting hunched in his chair. Pierce filled the kettle with water, hung it over the fire, and opened the top of the half-door to let in the first pale light from the morning sky.

He was taken aback by Brendan's haggard appearance. His father's shoulders, always so broad and square, were now stooped; his head bowed, showing his thin, graying hair. His craggy face was etched with deep and mournful lines. Pierce knew the change had not actually happened in two days. He realized he'd hardly noticed his father for years, despite working alongside him and seeing him every day. Was this the strong man who had once ruled his young family with voice, belt, and fist? Was this the man who intimidated Colm until he wet himself? The man whose arguments with his wife at home and his friends in the bar were the source of gossip and scandal throughout the village?

Brendan looked up. Pierce saw the bloodshot eyes, heard the heavy breathing, and smelled the stale alcohol, cigarette smoke, and urine. "Do you want a cup of tea, Da?"

His father nodded. Pierce brewed the tea, poured a cup for himself and his father, and sat to drink.

"I'll build the house."

Pierce looked up from his cup. "What? Why? Just because she says she wants it?"

"I'll not share my bed with that woman another night. We will take the roof off and build the walls higher, and we'll build over the side room. We'll have three rooms up there then. We can put in windows," he looked up the loft steps towards the room where his wife lay and shouted, "and bloody doors."

"Where are we going to get money to do that? We don't know how to put on a slate roof; we can't do that ourselves."

"There are men that will help us. I've been talking to them in Daly's. We can do it. That woman has been hiding money away for years; yours, mine, and hers. She's been fighting for this for a long time. Well, she can give up that money now if this is what she wants."

He raised his voice again.

"She will give up every penny she has if she wants a house that badly."

"Then there will be no lorry," said Pierce quietly.

Brendan looked back at his son and sighed, "Yes, you will have the lorry. I gave you my word. You will have the lorry as soon as the house is built."

Brendan eased himself back in the chair and closed his eyes. Pierce took the cup from his father's hand, set it on the floor beside him, and left for his day's work.

"Freda doesn't understand, Mary. We can't get married yet. I have to finish the house with Da. Then we're getting the lorry. *Then* we can find somewhere to live and wed."

"Why can't you live with Da?"

"I'm not living with that woman. I want a place of my own. I'll not bring Freda to that house. The woman is hardly civil to her as it is."

They were sitting in the back room of the shop. When Pierce came to visit his sister on a Wednesday evening, Mary knew something was wrong. Pierce worked every daylight hour. Mary hardly ever saw him these days, not even on Sundays. But this was a Wednesday, and it was still daylight, so what Pierce had to say must be important. She turned the white card sign hanging on the window to CLOSED and pulled down the blind. In the back room she brewed a pot of tea and sat listening attentively while her brother tried to explain.

"She says we've been courting for nearly five years, and she'll die an old maid if we don't wed soon. But I can't right now, Mary. Will *you* try and explain it to her, please? All she does is cry and says she'll go off to Dublin and find a husband, or some such nonsense, if I don't make up my mind soon."

"And what do you think I can do? She's right, Pierce. You have your own room. She could easily move in."

"Not while *she's* living there."

"So, why didn't you move out, instead of starting to build? Da could have had your room. You didn't have to build for her at all. And he wouldn't be sleeping in that chair every night."

"Then he wouldn't get us the lorry. I know he wouldn't. Anyway, he doesn't sleep in the chair all the time; he sometimes sleeps in with me. I'm just glad he's not drinking right now. I don't want him pissing in my bed."

Mary wrinkled her nose in disgust. She shared her late aunt's distaste for drink and what it did to people. Every story Pierce told about her father's drinking, the arguments, the oppressive silences, and the inability to work, all convinced her she was right. She could imagine from all that her brother said what life must be like in the cottage. She never had visited and was firm in her resolve that she never would visit her old home, despite occasional journeys to Glendarrig. She could never bring herself to reconcile with her father or to speak to her stepmother.

When Aunty Bridgie had died, she'd offered Pierce a room with her, but he seemed reluctant to leave his father. When Pierce told Mary about the most recent argument and how Mrs. Kelly again placed the blame on Brendan, Mary believed it. Pierce could not believe it, and continued to blame Mrs. Kelly for the breaking up of the family and for their father's excessive drinking. Mary found it impossible to understand her brother's apparent sympathy for their father.

"So, when will the house be finished?" she asked.

"I need to collect about two more loads of stone, and we'll have enough to complete the side wall, that will be all the walls finished. The men are ready to help us with the roof. The windows frames are in place already. Another month will see it mostly done if Da stays sober and the weather stays fine."

"Where is her ladyship for all this?"

"She's staying with a friend in the village, though with the oilskins over the roof, we are doing fine. Even the fire stays lit. She brings us our meals regularly."

"So I should think. Anyway, I don't want to talk about her. Are you going to marry Freda, Pierce?"

"I don't know."

"Does she have any family you can live with?"

"No. Her Ma and Da still have a houseful of children, and her grandmother lives with them too. There's no room."

"Well, if you don't know whether you want to wed her or not, I can't help you. Be sure you don't lose her, Pierce, 'cause then you might end up living with Da and that woman for the rest of your life."

Pierce sat quietly for a while. Mary sat in her aunt's chair watching him. He finally stood. "Maybe I'm not cut out for marriage," he said with a shrug. "I'll be off. I'll see you soon."

"Don't leave it too long, Pierce; you're all I've got, you know."

"You have Joe, and you have all those letters from Sheelagh and Colm. You never did hear from Michael, did you?"

"No, but Sheelagh tells me about him sometimes."

"He was a grand little boy. Do you remember, Mary?"

"I do, indeed, Pierce." She smiled wistfully. "We'll see him again sometime. I know we will. I keep writing to him. What about Colm? Is he still telling you about all the things he has, like he does me?"

Pierce shrugged, "We don't write much."

Mary walked Pierce out to the shop. When he left, she returned to study again the faded photographs and the small bundle of letters she kept behind the old clock.

1937

Mary

"Joe, I can't. I just can't."

He had proposed again, and again she had refused.

They went to the pictures every Saturday night and Mary, as always, invited him back for supper. She knew the neighbors gossiped, but she left the blind up in the shop door and left the door to the back room wide open. Anyone with the curiosity to look in could see herself and Joe were up to no mischief.

"Mary darlin', you know I love you. Haven't I been hanging around like a sick puppy for three years? What ails you that you won't say 'yes'? If you don't love me, then for the love of God let me know. I don't want to make a complete fool of myself."

"Of course I love you," she reached out to hold his hands, glanced at the open door, and drew back. "I can't explain, Joe."

"I've asked you many times now, Mary love. I can't keep doing it. A man has his pride you know."

Mary began to cry. She wanted to marry Joe. God knows she was lonely in the small house on her own. She wanted children, like her friends. But she couldn't get married. Her tears turned to sobs. Joe stood and closed the door then sat on the arm of Mary's chair and put his arm around her shoulders.

"What is it, Mary love? Have I wronged you in some way?"

She shook her head and continued to cry.

"Then tell me my sweet, sweet Mary. We'll deal with it, whatever it is."

She struggled to control her sobbing and took a deep breath.

"It's my Da. He would have to give me away, and *she* would have to come to the wedding." She cried even louder, "So I can't get married. I can never get married."

Joe searched his pockets and brought out a handkerchief which looked like it had been there for a very long time.

"Here, let me wipe your eyes." He did so, brushing her cheeks gently, then handed her the handkerchief. "Now, blow your nose." She did as she was told. "Sure that's not the end of the world, Mary love. We'll talk to Canon Finnegan … see what he has to say. I'm sure he'll have an answer." He kissed her gently on the top of her head. "You had me really frightened there for a while. I thought it was me!"

She looked up at him and gave a wan smile. "You know it's not you, Joe. Sure, don't I make you a cake every week? If that isn't love, I don't know what is! And me with the shop to mind and the house to look after?" Her face grew serious again. "You know what an old curmudgeon the Canon is. He'll tell me I should turn the other cheek, or one of those things he's always saying in his sermons."

"We'll go and talk to him; you don't know till you try. I'm sure he'll under-stand."

The Canon listened carefully while Joe explained.

"Can she not forgive him, son? It's the Christian thing to do. He must have had some good reason for his actions."

Joe tried to explain, though he was at a loss for an explanation himself. Mary sat demurely, eyes downcast, hands in her lap while Joe spoke for her. He explained how father and daughter had not spoken for nearly fourteen years; he shamelessly cited Brendan's drinking, and then he played his trump card. If the Canon insisted Mary have her father at her wedding, Joe said, they would prefer to go to Dublin. "We will wed there," Joe said with finality.

Joe's family was well known for their generosity to the church. Joe's father, the Glendarrig publican, had funded the stained glass window recently installed over the main altar. The Canon certainly did not want to lose the goodwill of one of his best parishioners. Canon Finnegan also knew Brendan Kelly, though he'd never seen him at confession. He did see him at Mass on Sundays, often unshaven and disheveled with the smell of whiskey so strong about him that other parishioners kept as much distance as they could from him.

"If her father were to sign a waiver, is there another family member who would stand for her?"

"I'm sure her brother, Pierce, would be willing."

"Then perhaps we can arrange a quiet ceremony. There are few enough people at a Monday Mass."

That evening, in Daly's bar, Joe's father provided Brendan with a drink "on the house" before bringing up the subject of the waiver.

"But she's my daughter, Finn, of course I want to be there and give her away," Brendan protested.

It took few more whiskies before he was persuaded by Finn's arguments.

"You don't want to upset her, Brendan. You know she doesn't want you there, and aren't weddings for women anyway?"

Brendan signed the waiver.

"It would break my Norah's heart if she was here to see how her only daughter treats her own father."

He wiped a self-pitying tear from his eye. In his maudlin state Brendan had forgotten he had another daughter.

Three weeks later Mary Kelly became Mrs. Joseph Daly at a ceremony witnessed by her brother, her friend Kathleen O'Boyle, Finn and Eileen Daly, and Joe's brother Danny. She wore a new blue dress and felt hat decorated with small blue silk flowers, and she prepared the wedding breakfast herself.

Sheelagh

At lunch Jim Porter told his daughter he wanted to have a serious talk with her. When they adjourned to the drawing room, he began.

"Your mother and I have been discussing what you should do, now that you've left school."

"Oh, Daddy, do I have to do something straight away? All my friends are taking time off. Jenny Walters is going to Switzerland for a year."

"That may be so, young lady, and it may have escaped your notice, but *we* are *not* the landed gentry."

"It can't be that expensive; they're not millionaires either. Anyway, she's going to finishing school, and she will learn all kinds of things which will be useful."

"My dear child, apart from the excellent school we sent you to, your mother has also seen fit to send you to class after class."

He held up his hand, checking the list on his fingers.

"If I remember correctly, you have learned elocution, ballet, piano, deportment, tennis, and," he paused for dramatic effect, "I believe you even tried horse riding, if my memory serves. You have more than enough skills."

"Oh, Daddy," she kissed his cheek and laughed. "That was all fun stuff, but I will learn skiing and culinary arts and all kinds of things."

"There are not a lot of snowy slopes around Bristol, so skiing is a skill I think you may forfeit. Your mother can't cook, and, quite honestly, I'm thankful for it. I can't imagine her boiling pots of tea or pushing things in and out of ovens—and her lack of ability didn't stop her making a good marriage. I am sure you will do very well, Sheelagh, with what you have. No, it's time to learn something useful."

Sheelagh cast a fleeting glance at her mother who sat in her easy chair, studiously working on her crochet. Obviously Sheelagh would get no support there. She heaved a sigh, plumped herself into another easy chair, and awaited her fate. When her father was in one of these moods, it was better to stay quiet.

"And don't give me any of those melodramatic sighs, young lady; they don't wash with me."

Sheelagh tried to look contrite.

"No, Daddy."

"Miss Dewey is getting on a bit these days, and it's time we looked for someone to replace her. Heaven knows how, but you seem to have equipped yourself fairly well at mathematics in school. You will work with Miss Dewey."

Sheelagh was stunned. "Work in the shop?"

"Correct. And don't take that tone with me. What do you think has paid for your education and kept you in comfort for the last twelve years? It's time you earned your keep, young lady. What if you don't marry? How do you think you will take care of yourself then? Do you want to end up like my sister?"

"But they are all so stuffy down there, and so boring."

"We will have no more discussion on the subject. You start on Monday. You will assist Miss Dewey, and you will learn all about being a cashier."

Sheelagh stood and flounced out of the room, though she was careful to close the door quietly behind her. She stormed down to the kitchen where Martha was preparing the evening meal.

"I've to go and work in the shop."

Martha smiled, "What's wrong with that?"

"It's a *shop,* Martha. What will my friends say?"

"It's your father's shop, Miss Sheelagh, and it could be yours one day. It's a good idea to learn how it runs."

"But I'll have to go *every day, and* sit beside Dopey Dewey."

"She's not that dopey, Miss Sheelagh. She runs the whole accounts department, and it's a big shop."

"Anyway, I will never get the business. I heard Daddy say he thinks Michael will be able to learn the trade. He said he's going to start him working there when he finishes school." Suddenly struck by a new thought, she wailed, "I would end up having my kid brother as my boss."

Martha laughed at Sheelagh's dramatics.

"I expect you'll live. Anyway, perhaps you'll meet some boys there, that won't happen if you sit around here all day."

"In a haberdashery shop?" said the young girl with scorn. "You don't understand either."

Sheelagh left the kitchen, slamming the door as she went, and stormed up to her bedroom. She would write to her sister; *she* would understand.

Colm

Edward, May, and Colm stood in the small room that would be home to Colm for the next few years.

"I have arranged with the local bank to have your allowance paid in once a month. Don't think you'll get any more. It's time you learned the value of money, Colm." Edward smiled at his son. "Come on then; let's go and have some tea while the porter takes your stuff up."

"Don't you think we should be here to make sure they put everything in the right place?" said May, looking doubtfully around the small space.

"He's the college porter, May, dear; it's not Ella. He will only deliver the trunks to Colm's room. I expect Colm will have to unpack his own things and put them away himself!"

"Perhaps we can come back after we've had tea and help him unpack."

"No, my dear. We have a long way to drive home, and he's well able to unpack his own goods and clothes."

Colm laughed at her. "Stop fussing, Mother. The other lads will think I'm a Mummy's boy if you start arranging my room. And I don't need to start off with that kind of a reputation, do I?"

May gave up, and they set off to explore the town and find a tea shop. Colm was impatient for his parents' departure but knew it would be politic not to seem too anxious.

"I've been in boarding school all my life. Why are you so concerned this time, Mother?" he asked as he finished his third cream cake and licked the last traces of jam from his fingers.

"Because you are all grown up now." She tapped his hand away from his mouth. "Don't lick your fingers like that, dear. You look as if you're starving. Use your napkin." She gave her son a wry smile. "You will probably meet some young lady at one of the College balls, and the next thing we know you will be introducing us to your new bride."

"May, he's nineteen years old with as little intention of marrying as Father John! I think we will have him pestering us for a while longer." Edward looked at his watch. "We really should be going, my dear. Let the lad unpack and settle in."

They walked back to the Hall of Residence. At the entrance to his House, Edward shook Colm's hand.

"Goodbye, son; I'm sure we will see you at half term. Don't lose sight of why you're here; study hard. I know you don't really need the degree, but you never know when it will come in useful. I look forward to handing over the reins of the business when you're finished."

Edward stepped back, and May threw her arms around Colm's neck.

"Goodbye, dear. Don't forget to write; tell us how you're getting on. Take care of yourself; eat properly, and don't do too much drinking with your friends. I've heard all about the drunken excesses you students get up to."

"I promise to get drunk only once a day, Mother; never fear."

May laughed. "You always had a wicked sense of humor."

She fumbled in her handbag, surreptitiously took out a crisp, white, five-pound note and thrust it into his hand.

"Don't tell your father, just a little emergency money." She kissed him again and joined her husband at the car. "Take care; write soon."

She and Edward waved one last time, climbed into the car, and drove out of the quad. As soon as they were out of sight, Colm turned on his heels and hurried to the porters' lodge.

"Phelps … it is Phelps, isn't it?" The porter nodded. "Has a Mr. Gough, a Mr. David Gough, arrived yet? I believe he has rooms here, too."

The porter scanned the list of residents.

"Yes sir, Room 67, in the West House, sir, just across the quad from your room."

"Jolly good, thanks." He slipped a coin into the man's hand and set off in search of his old friend.

Pierce

"I was not even invited to your sister's wedding," Freda pouted.

Pierce put a hand up to brush a strand of hair from her face. She jerked her head back, away from his hand.

He sighed. "You know why that was, Freda love. You know she only wanted a very quiet wedding so the Da wouldn't go."

"Well, Pierce Kelly, you can rest easy. I'll not be at your wedding either."

Pierce tried to hold her hand. She snatched it away. He sighed again. They had had this conversation so many times, in so many different ways.

"What are ye talking about, Freda? Don't be talking like that darlin'. Sure won't you be the center of attention at our wedding?"

They were sitting on the stone wall at the back of the graveyard. The other parishioners had long since left the church and hurried off in their different direction: some to Doonbeg, some to Glendarrig, and some to the crofter's cottages spread across the countryside and on the lower slopes of Knockglas. Freda and Pierce lingered, alone.

"No, Pierce, my mind is made up. You think more of your precious father and the business than you do of me."

"I had to build the house. You know I had to build the house."

"First it was the room, then the cart, then the house, then the lorry; you're just looking for excuses."

"Freda, the house is finished. We're buying the lorry tomorrow. We are nearly ready."

"Ready for what? What excuse will you have then? Will we be married in six months?"

He hesitated before answering, "We've to pay off the lorry first."

She jumped down from the wall and threw her hands in the air.

"You see? No more, Pierce! I've waited enough. I'm off to Dublin. I can get a job in service there, maybe even find someone who really wants to marry me. I'm sick of living with my family; there's no life for me here."

"I'll have it paid off in a year, I promise. I'll work every hour God made."

"You do that already, Pierce Kelly. The only time I see you is after Mass on Sundays. I thought if we married, I would at least see you in the evenings. I'm sorry, Pierce, but I'm off tomorrow; it's all arranged. I'm staying with a cousin in Doonbeg tonight, walking to Ballyfin tomorrow, and I've money saved for the train to Dublin. I tried to tell you before, but you're always working. Good-bye, Pierce."

She turned and ran to the road, clutching her shawl around her shoulders. Pierce stood watching her leave. He stood there long after she disappeared from view over the crest of the hill. Finally, he turned and walked slowly to his mother's grave.

1938

Mary

"Will you be godfather, Pierce?"

"I will, of course, Mary."

She pushed Joe's legs out of the way and bent to open the small oven door at the side of the range.

"Supper's nearly ready. Put some delph on the table, Joe, and see if Pierce wants another cup of tea."

"I've nearly drowned him in tea, Mary love; I've given him so many cups. It's a bottle of porter a man needs after a hard day's work, not tea." He pulled a face at Pierce.

"Don't you be trying to get round me, Joe Daly. You know I'll not have drink in this house. You can go to your father's bar if it's porter you want. Tea is what we drink here."

"Mary, my own, sweet love, no one can get around you these days; it's a wonder there's room for the three of us in here with the size of your belly."

He placed the flat of his hand gently on her stomach.

"Well, little babby, do you not think it's time you got out here and let me know whether I've a son or a daughter," he laughed.

She slapped his hand away. "It will come when it's good and ready, and you will just have to hold your patience. Now get the delph on the table, or the supper will be spoiled."

Joe set the table, Pierce fetched tumblers from the dresser, and Mary took the stew from the oven. They sat and ate.

"Who's to be the godmother?" asked Pierce as he mopped up the last of the gravy with his bread.

Joe snorted, "That's a very good question, Pierce. I understand *my* family is to have nothing to do with this child. Your sister will have it all her own way."

Mary ignored her husband's jibe. "I've asked Sheelagh."

Pierce looked up in surprise.

"Sheelagh? But she doesn't even live here. You haven't seen her for donkey's years. You don't know what she's like."

"And she's British too, don't forget that," said Joe. "My child will have a Brit for a godmother." He cast his eyes to heaven. "I never thought I'd live to see the day. A Brit!" He helped himself to another potato.

"Hold your whisht, Joe Daly. She's my sister and yours too, Pierce Kelly, and I want her to be godmother."

"And that's that. There's no point arguing with her, Pierce, I've tried."

"No, I'll not argue with her. It's a nice idea, Mary. Have you asked her yet?"

"I've written her a letter. I'm just waiting on her answer. I wanted to be full sure I could carry the baby to its time."

They continued to discuss the christening as they finished the meal. Mary cleared away the dishes.

"Will you walk in the yard with me, Pierce?" Joe gave Pierce a sly wink. "The smell of my pipe upsets the Mammy-to-be." He turned to his wife, "Will you be all right, Mary darlin'?"

"Get out, the two of ye. I'll wash the dishes and sit before the fire, I'm tired."

Joe opened the half-door, and he and Pierce walked up the garden in the dim light of a quarter moon.

"Wait up a minute, Pierce," Joe called, making a dart for the turf shed. He returned with two bottles of porter and an opener. "What she doesn't know will do her no harm," he said, opening one of the bottles and handing it to Pierce. They continued up the yard. "How's the haulage business doing?"

"It's going well enough, but Da doesn't do much any more. He's like an old man, Joe, and he's not fifty yet."

Joe waved his bottle at his brother-in-law, "Mary would tell you it was the drink," he laughed, then said in a more serious tone, "He seems to have given up, Pierce. I see him in the da's bar some nights, and he just sits there, drinking his whiskey. He doesn't even talk much any more."

"I know. I'm thinking of getting rid of the horses. He's no interest in work, and I think horses have had their day anyway."

"Are you just going to work for yourself then? What about your Ma? And himself? Will you make enough for the three of you?"

"She's not my Ma, but yes, I'll make enough for all of us."

Joe glanced sideways at his brother-in-law, "Do you want a partner, Pierce?"

"What do you mean?"

"I could well have a son in a week or two. I don't want to be working in a meat-packing factory all my life."

They stood at the top of the yard drinking their porter and listening to the silence.

"I know all about machines, Pierce. I can keep the lorry running as smooth as warm honey over a spoon. We could buy a second lorry, make a real business of it. I can learn to drive. It would be something we can hand on to our children."

Pierce smiled mournfully. "You know Freda gave up on me last year and went to Dublin. My chances of children are slim, but it's not a bad idea. What does Mary have to say?"

"Mary has the shop. What *I* do is up to me; she'll be fine."

"I'll talk to Da."

Mary

"Just once more, alanna, and we'll have it."

Annie wiped Mary's face with a damp cloth. "You're as good as your Mammy was, God rest her soul. Never made a fuss, just did what had to be done."

Mary's body tensed, her fists clenched. Choking back a scream, she pushed one more time.

"I have it! I have it. Rest easy now, child."

Annie rubbed the baby vigorously with a towel, as she had done so many times for so many mothers, and the baby cried.

"You have a beautiful little daughter. You hold her now; we're nearly done."

She placed the baby on Mary's breast. The mother bent forward and kissed her daughter's head.

"Hello, Norah love."

"Joe, Joe, she's coming."

Joe stopped digging and looked down the garden to where Mary stood in the back doorway waving a piece of paper. As he walked towards her, Mary continued to wave the paper and shout, "She's coming! She's coming!"

"Quiet, Mary, you'll wake the baby. Who's coming for the love of God? What has you so excited?"

"Sheelagh! Sheelagh's coming. She says she would love to be the godmother, and she says she wants to come over for the christening." The words tumbled from Mary's mouth. "She says we have to let her know when it is. She says she wouldn't miss it for the world." She thrust the letter at Joe, "Read it; read it. I'm so excited, Joe, I don't know where to start."

"Let's start with a drop of tea. Come on inside. I've never seen you this excited, not even when I proposed;" he added with a smile.

He put his arm around Mary's shoulder and guided her to the chair. "Here, sit down there and calm yourself." He handed her the letter, "And hold onto this. *I'll* make the tea."

"Joe, I'll have to clean out the front bedroom. I haven't even been in there for ages. Perhaps we should get rid of the piano. She would have more room in there then."

"Wait now ... wait now," he was laughing, "She's not the queen of Sheba! This is your sister, and the room will be fine as it is."

"Oh! Joe, look at this place," Mary stared in disbelief around the room, "She'll think we're tinkers. She lives in such a grand house with servants and all."

"And she lived here too, Mary. Take it easy now, and we'll have a look and see what she says." He handed her a cup of tea and read the letter. "Sure enough, she says she's coming."

"But we were going to have it next Sunday. She can't be here by then." She paused, then wailed, "*I* won't be ready by then."

"You told me yesterday you were all set. I went over and told my parents last night that it would be next Sunday. What do you mean, 'you won't be ready'?"

"The house is dirty. I want to get a new chair for in here and a rug for in front of the fire."

"One thing at a time, my love," Joe pulled his chair over in front of Mary's. He caught both her hands in his and spoke slowly and calmly.

"It's only Monday ... we have a week. I can go to the post office and send her a telegram. She will have five days to get here. We're not in America, love. She has plenty of time."

He smiled reassuringly at his wife. "If you want a new chair, then you may have a new chair. We'll get Pierce to pick one up in Ballyfin; sure he passes by here twice a day in that lorry of his."

"And a rug."

"And a rug, if that's what you want, but we'll be on bread and dripping for a month if you keep on this way."

"Oh! Joe, I'm going to see her. After all these years, I'm going to see her again."

She burst into tears.

Sheelagh

"I'm sorry, Daddy, but I *am* going."

"What about the business? What about Miss Dewey? She can't possibly cope on her own."

Sheelagh continued to search through her wardrobe and drawers and piled clothes on every available surface.

"She managed very well before I came, and she will manage very well for a week without me now."

"But she's got used to having you there."

"I'm going, Daddy; sack me if you like."

Jim Porter glared at his daughter, then turned and walked from the bedroom. Edith remained sitting quietly on the dressing table stool. When she was sure her husband was out of earshot she said, "You're right, darling, you should go. I was very sorry you didn't get invited to her wedding—though I'm sure she had good reason. Of *course* you want to go and be there for the christening."

Sheelagh looked up from her packing and gave her mother a grateful smile. "Thank you, Mummy; he's such a bully sometimes." She held up a green silk dress, "What do you think of this one? It might be nice for the Sunday."

Edith nodded, "Very nice, dear. My worry is you going on your own. Would you like me to come with you, dear? I don't mind. I've never been to Ireland, but I'm sure it's not as bad as they say."

"No, thank you, Mummy." She folded the green dress carefully. "I want to do this on my own. I'm perfectly capable, you know, and I want to spend time with Mary and Pierce and catch up on everything. You'd probably be quite bored."

"You're as stubborn as your father," said Edith.

But Sheelagh thought her mother looked relieved, nonetheless, that she would not be required to travel. Sheelagh closed her suitcase, pressing down on the lid to persuade the lock to catch.

That evening, after Jim and Edith were in bed, she sat in the kitchen talking to Martha about her trip.

"What if I don't like them?"

"Of course you will like them, Miss Sheelagh; they're your family."

"What if they don't like me?"

"Well, that could be a problem all right."

Sheelagh was startled.

"I'm joking, Miss Sheelagh, of course they will like you. Now, would you please go to bed? I've things to get ready for the breakfast, and you have to be up early yourself."

"I'm too excited to sleep, and I'm quite sure I won't be able to eat breakfast."

"That doesn't mean your father won't. Now go up to bed, will you, and let me bank the fire."

"You carry on. Do whatever you have to do, Martha. I'll go up in a minute. What if I get lost?"

"It's only Ireland, not Africa, Miss. Just ask one of the porters; they will always help you. Just remember to give them a tip."

Eventually Martha persuaded her upstairs, but Sheelagh couldn't sleep and spent most of the night imagining the meeting.

The Porters took her to the station early the following morning. Edith was tearful, and Jim was unusually quiet. Only when the guard blew his whistle, and the train began to pull out, did he shout, "Take care, my dear. Come home safe." Then he added more quietly, "We love you, you know."

Both Sheelagh and Edith looked at him in surprise. Sheelagh never remembered him saying that before. As the train gathered speed, she leaned out of the window, waved, and blew him a kiss. When the train went under the first bridge, she hastily closed the window, sank back into her seat, and heaved a sigh of relief. Her very first journey on her own, and it was to see her brother, her sister, a brother-in-law, *and* her niece and godchild. Her stomach was in knots of excitement and anticipation. Within an hour the excitement had dimmed a little, and the sleepless night and the soothing rhythm of the train had her struggling to keep awake, afraid she would miss her connection at Crewe Junction.

Two hours later, when the train finally steamed into the station, Sheelagh was confronted with the din and chaos of a major railway hub. She opened the carriage door. In the dim, dusty, light from the glass roof, she watched people hurrying in every direction. The noises deafened her: the train wheels squealing, metal on metal; guards blowing their shrill, ear-piercing whistles, and incoherent announcements echoing from multiple loudspeakers. The smells of soot and sulfur from the coal mixed with the dust made her nose itch. She stood transfixed at the open carriage door and wished her father was there to organize things. Then she remembered what Martha said and fumbled in her bag for a coin to wave at a passing porter. He changed his course immediately, helped her down from the carriage, and safely transferred her and her bags to the connecting train.

Her journey to Holyhead was uneventful, and another porter helped ease her transfer to the boat. She was violently ill on the sea crossing to Dun Laoghaire and was very glad she had arranged to stay in the port town overnight before completing the journey to Doonbeg.

The next morning, the train to Ballyfin was slow and uncomfortable. Wood-slatted seats replaced the upholstered ones of the previous day, and there was no first class section. She was relieved when it finally pulled into the station, and she wasted no time in opening the carriage door and stepping down onto the platform. She scanned the platform, unsure who would be meeting her. Mary's telegram said either Pierce or Joe would be there.

Pierce had little difficulty in recognizing his sister. She had the same tall, slim build as himself and the same curly red hair peeping from under the brim of her pale blue cloche. He came up beside her.

"Sheelagh?"

"Pierce?"

He nodded, and Sheelagh extended her gloved hand. He hastily rubbed his on his pants before self-consciously shaking hands. Both looked a little awkward.

"Oh Lord, I suppose that's a bit formal, isn't it, for a brother and sister," she said, and impulsively stood on tip-toe and kissed his cheek. "I wasn't sure how I was going to do this bit. Doesn't it feel strange after all this time?"

Pierce nodded again, unable to stop grinning. She looked so like his mother, *their* mother, except that he thought Norah's eyes were green, and Sheelagh's were a sparkling blue.

He indicated the small valise she held. "Is this your bag?"

"Oh, this is my small one; the other one is on the rack in the carriage. A porter put it up there for me, but I couldn't lift it down. It's a bit heavy."

Pierce fetched the suitcase and took the smaller bag from her.

"The lorry's outside. Mary's sorry she couldn't come. She has to look after the baby and the shop. She told me to hurry home. She can't wait to see you."

"A lorry! How novel. This will be my very first time in a lorry."

Sheelagh followed him out of the small station to where the vehicle was parked at the curbside. Pierce had spent an hour washing and buffing, polishing and cleaning the dilapidated machine. Its bodywork was dented, the paint chipped, the wheel spokes rusted, and the side window cracked, but the door handles shone, and there was not a speck of dirt to be seen on the entire vehicle.

"Here it is," he said proudly, loading her bags in the back and opening the passenger door.

Sheelagh looked at the high step into the cab and hesitated. Her suit had a slim, calf-length pencil skirt, and it quickly became obvious to both of them that she couldn't possibly climb up into the cab without hoisting it up and maybe scandalizing Pierce with a view of her stocking tops.

"Here, I'll help." He scooped her up in his arms and lifted her easily into the cab. She was a lot lighter than any of the sacks or wool bales he took to market, he thought. As she brushed down her skirt and regained her composure, he slammed the door closed and went round to the driver's side.

When he climbed into the driver's side, she pulled a face. "I feel pretty stupid."

"Don't worry about it; sure you're in now, and we're on our way. He started the engine, put the lorry into gear and they set off.

Sheelagh tried to question Pierce throughout the short journey. What did the baby look like? Who was coming to the christening? What were they going to call the child? He only laughed and said, "I've been told to say nothing until I get you to the shop. Mary is terrified she will miss something. The only thing I'll tell you is that the baby is to be called Norah." He gave her a quick sideways glance to see if she understood.

"After our mother?" she asked.

He nodded.

"All right, I'll ask no more questions. Let's see if I recognize anything."

They drove in silence, Sheelagh scanning the countryside for memories. As they rounded yet another tight bend on the narrow road, they saw the village of Doonbeg and the mountain rising behind it.

"Oh look!" she said, pointing excitedly. "I recognize that mountain. We must be nearly there. I can remember that. We could see it from Aunty Bridgie's garden, couldn't we?" She turned to Pierce for confirmation, and he nodded again.

"Knockglas—that's its name. Master Keogh said it was from the Irish. It means 'green hill.'"

"Who's Master Keogh?"

"He was the teacher at the boy's school. He's dead now."

"*The* teacher? Only one teacher for the whole school?"

He looked puzzled. "Of course, how many do you need?"

"We had nuns, but there was a different one for every subject."

"Begod! You must have had an awful lot of nuns."

Sheelagh pulled an apologetic face. "We did."

"We're nearly there."

She leaned forward and pointed, "Oh, Pierce, I remember an old woman and a girl waving from there. I can remember the sound of a horse's hooves. Is that the shop?"

"That's it, and there's Mary. Look at her! Like a hen on a hot griddle. She's been fussing ever since she knew you were coming."

A plump young woman wearing a long, loose skirt and full blouse stood outside the shop. She was wrapped in a voluminous fringed shawl. Sheelagh was surprised at how old-fashioned her sister looked. The two women smiled at each other as Pierce stopped the lorry and climbed out. Sheelagh struggled with the handle of her door. Mary also tried from the outside, but Pierce had already rounded the vehicle.

"Would you get out of the way, Mary; there's a knack to it."

He hit the door with the side of his fist, just below the handle, and the door flew open. "There, you see; it's easy when you know how."

He realized Sheelagh was going to have the same difficulty getting out of the cab as when she tried to get in.

"I don't think I dressed quite right for a ride in a lorry. Can you help me again, Pierce? Perhaps if I jump ... will you catch me?"

"Right then."

He stretched out his arms; she caught hold of his hands and jumped. She landed a little awkwardly, and her hat fell, but she quickly regained her balance. She stepped forward and threw her arms around Mary. A baby's cry came from the shawl. She stepped back in astonishment.

"Oh, my goodness, I'm so sorry, I didn't see her!" She peered at the baby tucked in the fold of the shawl. Mary rocked the infant gently in her arms, trying to calm her. Sheelagh pushed back a little of the shawl to see the tiny crumpled face more clearly.

"So this is Norah. Hello, sweet thing. Oh, Mary, she's beautiful." She blushed and put her hand to her mouth. "You are Mary, aren't you? I haven't just made a terrible fool of myself, have I?"

Mary laughed and put her arm around her sister, careful not to squash the baby.

"Yes, I'm Mary." She was both laughing and crying. She stepped away to examine her younger sister more easily.

"Would you look at you! You look just like a film star. You're beautiful. You look so like Mammy, and Pierce, doesn't she, Pierce?"

He handed Sheelagh her hat. "Yes, she does." He took the bags down from the back of the lorry; "Now, are you going to invite the poor woman into your house, or do we have to stand out here for the evening?"

Mary brushed the tears from her face. "Come in, come in. Don't mind Pierce; he's been as excited as I have. I've never seen that old lorry of his look so clean."

She ushered Sheelagh into the shop shouting, "Joe! Joe, she's here! She's arrived!" She turned to her brother, "Close the door, Pierce, and put up the sign. I'm not wasting a minute of this time. Go on through, Sheelagh; sure you know your way."

Sheelagh stepped inside. The low ceiling and the limited light from the deep-set windows made it dark. The smell of cheese was strong, competing with the smells of aniseed balls, buttermilk, and earthy vegetables. A wooden counter stood on one side of the small space, almost filling it. It held a scale, weights, and a large pewter-colored cash register. Narrow shelves lined the wall behind the counter and were stacked with an assortment of cans, packets, and jars. On the other side of the shop, where two large milk-churns stood under more narrow shelves, the walls were white-painted. The shelves there held bowls of eggs, a large block of deep yellow butter covered with a fine muslin cloth, and several rounds of cheese. At the back of the room almost hidden by sacks of vegetables was a narrow door. Four, small, glass panes at the top of the door were curtained with heavy, crocheted lace. Sheelagh touched the curtains lightly; "Oh, look at that work. Mummy would love that."

"Go on through, Sheelagh. Joe must be up the back yard," urged Mary.

Sheelagh opened the door and paused. "Oh my goodness! I think I remember this, too."

Joe was standing with his back to the range, hands thrust into his pockets.

In her room that night Sheelagh unpacked her bags as Mary watched. "I can't believe four of us shared this bed."

Mary laughed, "Two up, two down … you and I at the top, and Colm and Michael at the bottom."

"But didn't we all kick each other?"

"Sometimes, but only by accident; we didn't fight." Mary smoothed her hand over the faded and worn quilt that covered the bed. She told her sister about how she and Bridgie had made it after the other children had left and how every patch had a story.

"See that? That was part of a smock you wore. It used to be mine, but I grew out of it. You got blackberry stains all over it the day we went blackberry picking for Aunty Bridgie's jam. She wouldn't let you take it to England, but she rescued a few squares for the quilt."

Sheelagh lifted the quilt, looking intently at the square as if trying to re-conjure the memory. The two sisters finally sat on the bed, the quilt draped over their knees, as Mary pointed out individual squares.

"That piece was from the tail of one of Pierce's shirts. It was the first square I cut and sewed all by myself. The stitching is not very good."

"I think it's wonderful," said Sheelagh fascinated by the histories woven into the fragile bedcover.

"Why didn't Pierce marry Freda?" She asked suddenly. She knew all about Pierce's long courtship of Freda Quinn from Mary's letters.

"I think he's always been too busy making money and developing the business. Joe's working with him now," said Mary proudly. "They've just bought a second lorry."

She showed her sister the special children's patches surrounding the fragile, pale-yellow square in the center of the quilt—the piece taken from their mother's second-best blouse.

"Do you remember her, Sheelagh?"

"No, I don't think so. Did she always wear black?"

"No, that was Aunty Bridgie. Mammy looked very like you, except her hair was long and not so curly. She was beautiful."

"Is there a piece of our father here in the quilt?"

Brendan had not been mentioned all evening. He was rarely mentioned in Mary's letters either. Sheelagh was very curious about him and why the family had been split up. Maybe now Mary would tell her, explain it. Was it *just* because her mother died? Jim Porter always implied that Sheelagh and her brothers were abandoned. He frequently told her how fortunate she was to be living "in a civilized household."

In the few hours since her arrival, she was indeed beginning to appreciate so many things back home that she had always taken for granted, particularly servants and efficient plumbing. When she compared Mary's tiny house and shop with her own home and her father's large store, she understood how fortunate she was and how grateful she should be to Jim and Edith.

"No, I don't need to remember him," said Mary, her voice hard.

"Does he live near here, Mary?"

"Glendarrig is about three miles up the road."

Mary's answer was clipped, not encouraging further discussion, but Sheelagh wanted to know.

"Will he be coming to the christening?" she persisted.

"No."

"Why not, Mary?

"He didn't want anything to do with us, so why should I have anything to do with him?"

"He's still your father, our father." Sheelagh corrected herself, thinking how strange that sounded. "What does Joe say?"

Mary heaved a sigh and fidgeted with the edge of the quilt.

"He says it's about time I stopped all this. He says Da will die one of these days, then I'll be sorry. But I won't," she said defiantly.

"I think *I'd* like to see him."

"I'm sure Pierce will take you over there if you ask him. He still lives with Da and that woman, though I don't know why!"

"You mean his second wife?"

Mary nodded.

"Would you come with us, Mary, for a visit?" She saw the stubborn set of Mary's chin. "What about baby Norah? Shouldn't she get to know her grandfather?"

"I'll never go into that house again, not as long as *she's* there."

"Well, would you ask him to the christening, just for me?"

"I'll see," said Mary, resolutely closing the topic. She pointed to a small square in the quilt, "That one was part of our great-grandmother's favorite dress. Those tiny blue flowers are periwinkles. Aunty Bridgie told me they were the same color as her eyes. She said that's where you got your blue eyes."

Mary had changed the subject, and Sheelagh said no more about their father that night.

They talked for almost an hour more, each asking what seemed like a hundred questions and giving a hundred answers. Later, as Sheelagh lay in bed, her thoughts turned again to her father. Pierce said he would call in the next day on his way back from work in Ballyfin. She would ask him if he would take her over to Glendarrig. It would seem very strange; she knew nothing about the man, but perhaps Pierce would tell her more. She was only going to be here for three more days. It would be Friday tomorrow. She didn't have much time, and she couldn't waste the opportunity to meet her father, even if Mary *did* hate him.

Mary

Mary sat up in bed cradling Norah who suckled contentedly. Joe lay on his back, hands behind his head staring at the ceiling.

"I'm surprised at you, Joe Daly." Mary whispered, "Sulking like a schoolboy."

"Indeed, I am not sulking."

"Quiet, she'll hear you."

"I don't care if she does. I have nothing to hide. *I* don't put on airs and graces, pretending to be somebody I'm not."

"She's not!" hissed Mary. "She's been living in England for thirteen years; of course she has an English accent."

"She's turned into a Brit." Joe hissed back. "La-di-dah and looking down her nose at us." He mimicked a falsetto voice, "Oh, an outside toilet, I don't remember that! Are there spiders out there?"

"Stop it, Joe; she's my sister, and I want her to be here." Tears welled in Mary's eyes. She gently lifted the now-sleeping baby and laid her in the crib beside the bed, tucking the blanket up under the child's chin. She adjusted her nightdress, brushed away the tears, and turned to her husband. "I lost her once because of my father. I'll not lose her again for you, Joe Daly. I have dreamed of this for thirteen years. Please don't spoil it for me."

Joe sat up and put his arm around Mary's shoulder. "I'm sorry, Mary love, you're right; I didn't try." He kissed away a stray tear on her cheek. "I promise I will be on my best behavior for the next three days." He smiled mischievously, "I think I can just about manage that."

She returned his smile and gave him a quick kiss. "Thank you, my love. She's the only sister I've got, you know."

He nodded and tenderly drew her down into the bed beside him.

Pierce

It was late when Pierce drove back to Glendarrig, still thinking about his sister. He decided he liked her, though she was very different from Mary. She was pretty, and she smiled a lot. Besides, she was clearly as excited to meet them as they were to meet her. Pierce had been greatly amused by Joe's reaction to his sister-in-law. After supper the two men walked up the yard "to stretch their legs." Joe "rescued" two bottles of porter from the turf shed as they went.

"I'm sorry, Pierce, I know she's your sister, but I ask you! Who does she think she is? A film star? Where is she going with the hat and the gloves? And how long did she think she was going to be staying with the bloody bags? I nearly killed myself getting the big one up the stairs."

"I know," Pierce sympathized. "Didn't I get it off the train and put it in the lorry? Heavy as a sack of spuds, it was."

"And that accent," continued Joe, "altogether too Brit for me."

"But she's very nice, and Mary's thrilled she's here."

"Cost me a fortune, it has, getting the place ready; you'd think royalty was coming."

"It's for the christening, Joe. It means a lot to Mary."

"I know that, Pierce, but it doesn't seem right. She has her Brit sister all the way from England but won't even ask her own father who lives in the next village."

Pierce shrugged, "You know how she is."

"Well, someone is bound to tell him that Sheelagh is here, and why, and *then* he'll know he's not invited."

"I'm going to tell him tonight and get it over with."

"Good luck to you. I hope he doesn't kill you."

"He's all talk. It's a long time since he raised his hand or his fist to me," Pierce replied.

Still, as Glendarrig grew closer, Pierce recognized the tight clench in his stomach that he always felt when expecting a confrontation with his father. It was true that Brendan no longer physically lashed out at his son, but the verbal assaults caused Pierce almost as much pain.

As the years passed, the young man had grown to know his father better. He knew Brendan loved him, though his father would never say as much. He couldn't have explained why, but Pierce thought Brendan was like a wounded animal, and just like a wounded animal, he was inclined to lash out indiscriminately. Pierce was often the recipient.

His father was sitting beside the fire—a glass of stout in one hand, his pipe in the other. There was no sign of Mrs. Kelly.

"You're late."

"I was over with Mary."

"It's not a Sunday, is it?"

"No, Da." Pierce paused, reluctant to continue. "I collected Sheelagh from the station this afternoon."

"What Sheelagh?" Brendan peered at his son in the soft glow of the firelight, then his eyes opened wider. "You mean *our* Sheelagh? She's here? Why didn't you tell me? Where is she?"

"She's over in Doonbeg. She's staying with Mary."

Brendan's face grew red. He leaned forward, put down the glass, and gripped the wooden arm of his chair.

"And was anyone ever going to tell me?" His voice rose, "My own daughter … after all these years … and you sneak her into Doonbeg without a word?"

"She only arrived today, Da, and I'm telling you now, aren't I?"

"And how long have you known she was coming?" Brendan was shouting now. "Probably been planning it for months—"

"They only got a telegram from her on Tuesday. Mary never expected her to come over for the christening."

"Christening …?" Brendan bellowed, jumping to his feet. "Mary has had the child—my first grandchild—and nobody sees fit to tell me? When were you going to tell me *that* you conniving little shleeveen?"

"Da, stop shouting."

"Don't you tell me what to do in my own house," Brendan spat the words at his son: eyes glaring, the veins in his throat and temples bulging. He paused for a moment, then fell back into his chair, breathing heavily. His head turned, as if to stare into the fire. He sat motionless.

Pierce waited quietly, for a moment, but when his father remained silent and unmoving, he spoke. "Da … Da, are you all right?"

The pipe fell from Brendan's hand.

Pierce stepped forward and touched his father's shoulder. Still Brendan did not move, his breathing now heavy and labored.

"What's wrong, Da?" he tentatively shook his father. "Da, speak to me."

The heavy breathing continued. Brendan made no response and continued to stare into the fire. Pierce put a hand on his father's face and turned it gently towards him. He saw the fear in Brendan's eyes.

"It's all right, Da. I'm here." He reassured his father, then called, "Mrs. Kelly!" He heard no sound from upstairs and shouted louder, "Mrs. Kelly!"

After a moment, the woman appeared at the top of the stairs.

"What is it? What are you roaring about? I'm sure they can hear the two of you in Rathfen. Are you intent on following in your father's footsteps, now? Are you going to be drinking yourself into a shouting drunk?"

"Something's happened to Da. I don't know what's wrong, but I think I need to get him to the hospital. I need your help."

Clutching her shawl and raising the hem of her nightdress, she came down the stairs barefoot.

"I told him the drink would finish him."

Pierce put his arm around his father's shoulders and tried to pull him upright. He could not lift Brendan, who had become a dead weight, unable to support himself.

"Get down to the Quinn's; ask Annie and her husband to come up."

The woman left, Pierce remained beside his father and spoke softly.

"It's all right, Da, I'm here. I'm staying with you. Annie will be here in a minute; we'll sort this out."

When Mrs. Kelly returned with Annie and her husband, the midwife quickly assessed the situation.

"You have to take him to the hospital, Pierce." She lowered her voice, "Though I don't think there's much they will be able to do for him." She turned to her husband, "Peadar, give Pierce a hand. Will you take him in the lorry, lad?"

Pierce nodded, and the two men hauled Brendan upright and half carried, half dragged him out to the lorry. Annie held the door open.

"Will you go with them, Mrs. Kelly?" She asked.

The woman shook her head, "No."

Annie followed the men out, and the three of them pushed and hauled Brendan into the passenger seat.

"Would you like one of us to come with you, son?" she asked.

"No, I'll be fine, Mrs. Quinn. Thank you for your help."

Annie and Peadar watched the old, battered lorry drive away.

Sheelagh and Mary

Sheelagh opened the narrow door into the shop.

"I'm sorry, Mary. I've slept late. You should have woken me. Have you been up for long?"

"There's no chance of a lie-in around here. Norah wakes me for a feed before first light, then Joe has to be up and gone, and I have to open the shop. Can I get you some breakfast?"

"No, I'm fine." Sheelagh carefully sat on the lid of the milk churn. "I'll sit here and talk to you, if that's all right. Miss Dewey doesn't like me chatting with the staff in the shop."

Mary laughed. "Well I'm the only staff here, and I don't mind a bit." She stared at Sheelagh's legs. "You're wearing trousers!"

Sheelagh blushed, "Oh dear, have I got it wrong again? I felt so stupid yesterday in that skirt, getting in and out of the lorry, I thought it would be a better idea to wear these. Should I go and change?"

"Not at all. It's just, well, I've never seen a woman in trousers before, except in the films of course, like Katherine Hepburn and Marlene Dietrich, but never in Doonbeg. Does everyone wear them in England?"

"Not everyone, but younger women do. I have to say, Daddy doesn't approve, and Mummy is a bit nervous about it, but I talked them round."

"You know, Sheelagh, with all the talking we did last night, and you telling me about your new mother and father, and your house and school and everything, you never mentioned Michael."

Sheelagh shrugged, "There's nothing to say really. We're not like a real brother and sister."

"But there's only the two of you there. It's like Pierce and me; you have to stick together. You're family."

"We don't feel like that. Anyway, Daddy always thought he was a bit slow, if you know what I mean."

"Stupid, you mean?"

"Yes."

"Is he?"

"I don't think so. Daddy has even let him work in the shop. He was sixteen last birthday, you know, so he's finished with school. He went to the Christian Brothers, and Daddy says his final report was quite good."

"What's he like? He never answers any of my letters."

"He may not be getting them. I wouldn't put anything past that old dragon. There was a big blow-up about it with her and Daddy. Mike and I haven't really spoken since."

"What old dragon? Who's the old dragon? The lady who took him in? Oh don't say that, Sheelagh. Is he not happy?"

Sheelagh shrugged again, "I never asked him. He seems to be all right. He's always been very quiet; hard to know what he's thinking."

Mary was surprised and upset at her sister's indifference.

"What is his ..." she struggled for the right word, "*other* mother like? I can't believe the woman is as bad as you say."

"Mary, Aunty Wyn makes Mummy so nervous that Daddy usually goes over to visit on his own. I don't think she likes Mummy either. They are as different as chalk and cheese."

"It sounds so funny when you talk like that."

"Like what?"

Mary wrinkled her nose slightly.

"When you say Mummy and Daddy ..."

"Colm calls *his* parents Mother and Father."

"Tell me about him. Do you see him often?"

"No. When we were children, we used to go up to London to visit maybe once a year, but Mummy and Aunty May seem to have lost touch recently. It must be nearly five years since I last saw him."

"He writes to Pierce, sometimes," said Mary, adding with a wry smile, "*and* to me when he has a new car or something like that."

"Typical. He was always spoiled and showing off."

"But he's happy?"

"Oh, blissfully ..."

The small bell hanging over the shop door tinkled as a customer entered. Sheelagh quickly retreated to the back room, Miss Dewey's training difficult to deny. The baby lay in her cot. She was awake, but quiet, her tiny hand flailing as if trying to fit her thumb into her mouth. Sheelagh smiled, picked her up, and kissed her softly. When the bell tinkled again, she peeped through the lace curtains. Seeing that the customer had gone, she cradled the baby in one arm and opened the door.

"I picked her up, is that all right?"

"Of course it is. She doesn't have much time to be with her godmother."

"She is so tiny, but so beautiful," said Sheelagh lovingly. She gently brushed the baby's cheek, and the infant grasped at her finger. She looked back at Mary. "Did you think any more about her grandfather?"

"I can't, Sheelagh. I just can't. He was ready to put us all in an orphanage! Can you imagine what that would have been like?"

"That was a long time ago, Mary."

Mary turned from her sister and glanced out of the shop window.

"There's Pierce's lorry. What's he doing back from Ballyfin already? He said he would be there all day."

The lorry stopped outside the shop. Pierce climbed out of the cab, looking pale and tired. Mary went out to meet him.

"What's the matter, Pierce? You look exhausted. Are you all right? Has Da been on the drink again?"

"He's in the hospital."

"What's wrong?"

He glanced up and down the street; "Can we go inside?"

They walked into the shop, and Mary turned the sign on the door.

"Da's in the hospital," she told her sister, her voice empty of emotion. She looked at Pierce. "Let's go into the back."

She made tea, and Sheelagh gently rocked Norah in her arms as Pierce told them what had happened the night before.

"He still can't talk or move. The doctor says it's called a stroke. There's no telling if he'll ever improve."

"That's terrible," said Sheelagh.

"Where's Mrs. Kelly? Did she not go to the hospital with you?" asked Mary.

Pierce shook his head, and Sheelagh looked from her brother to her sister.

"What are we going to do?" she asked.

Pierce shrugged, "There's not a lot we can do right now. The doctor says we just have to wait and see."

"How long will it take?"

"He can't tell. No one can."

"Might he die?"

Pierce nodded.

"I want to go and see him. Can I?"

Pierce and Mary both looked surprised.

"He can't talk or move," said Pierce, not sure she had understood.

"Does he know who you are? Do you think he can hear you?"

"Yes, I think so. He looks very frightened, but I think he does."

"Then, please, will you take me over, Pierce?"

He put his hand reassuringly on her arm. "I will, of course."

Sheelagh turned to Mary, "Will you come?"

Pierce and Sheelagh waited. The clock seemed to tick louder, the baby whimpered. It was a while before Mary finally shook her head. "No, I've to look after the shop and Norah." She said dismissively, "You two go. I'll stay here."

Pierce shrugged, "So be it. I'll just finish my tea. Do you have anything I can eat, Mary? I haven't had anything yet today."

"I'll fry you both some rashers and eggs before you go."

Sheelagh gently lowered Norah back into her cot.

"I'll go up and fetch my coat so that I'm ready."

Colm

"What am I going to do, Dave? If the old man finds out, he'll kill me."

"Stop panicking, old chap. These things happen. It was an accident."

"But what am I going to do? She says she'll tell the Dean. She'll get me kicked out of university."

"She won't tell anyone; that will only make her look like a slut. All you have to do is give her enough money to go up to London."

"She says she won't do it. She's scared, says she wants us to get married."

"Silly cow! Does she really think you're going to marry a waitress?"

Colm took another large mouthful of whisky.

The green-shaded table lamp gave a soft light to the room, casting long shadows on the walls. Colm sat hunched over his desk, cradling the whisky glass in his cupped hands; staring into the remaining amber liquid. David Gough lounged back in the only easy chair, his feet propped up on the other side of the desk. A half empty bottle stood on the desk between them.

"Stop worrying, dear boy. It happens all the time. It's probably not her first. A few quid and she'll be fine, probably did it on purpose."

"If mother finds out, she'll go out of her mind."

"You've got into enough trouble in your life, old chap. You'd think she'd be used to you by now."

Colm gave a rueful grin. "She doesn't know the half of it, and what she does know, she doesn't believe. That's a mother's love for you."

"Well, you just have to send this trollop packing, and be a little more careful the next time."

"Have you got any cash, Dave? I'm a bit strapped right now."

"Good Lord, Colm, you get through it quicker than I do. Sorry old chap, getting near the end of term, pretty much out of the readies myself."

"How much should I give her?"

"Look, she wouldn't earn two pounds a week in that place. Give her ten and she'll think she's a millionaire. That's plenty. It's up to her then. If she wants to keep the brat, that's her decision."

"Where am I going to get ten quid from? I'm broke, and it's nearly Christmas. I have to buy some decent presents for the folks, you know, only fair."

"Sorry, old chap; your problem, I'm afraid."

Gough finished his whisky and stood a little shakily. "Got to go. See you tomorrow. Can't keep the ladies waiting."

He left, and Colm poured another drink. It was after midnight when he went to bed.

The porter hammered on his door. It took Colm some time before he realized he wasn't dreaming. He struggled out of bed.

"There's a phone call for you in the lodge, Mr. Colm. Your mother, I believe, sir, sounds a little upset, if you don't mind my saying so."

"I'll be down directly."

He scrambled into his clothes and checked his watch—10:30! Damn! He'd missed first lecture again. He hurried down to the lodge.

Squinting at the watery November light seeping through the mullioned windows, he listened to his mother.

"Colm, dear, I don't know how to tell you, but I just had a telephone call from the Porter's. Do you remember them, dear, from Bristol? Sheelagh's parents?"

"Yes, yes of course I do, mother."

His head was throbbing, and his mouth tasted stale.

"Well, they've just received a telephone call from Sheelagh. She's in Ireland. I won't go into details now, dear, but she said her father is in hospital. I mean *your* father. Well, your Irish father. Oh dear, this is all a bit confusing. Anyway, dear, she thought you ought to know. It seems he's quite ill."

"What am I supposed to do?" He was barely awake. He could not understand what this had to do with him.

"I know, dear. It is difficult, but Sheelagh seemed to think you should know."

He was waking up, beginning to consider the news.

"Perhaps I should go."

"Do you really think so, Colm? I'm not sure that's necessary."

"But, Mother," his thoughts were racing. "He could be dying. It could be my only chance to see him before he goes. I might never see him again."

"Well, I suppose that's true. Is that what you want to do, darling? I didn't think you would be that upset."

"He *is* my father."

"Oh, Colm!" There was reproach and hurt in her voice.

"Oh, not my *real* father, but, you know, my first one." He was floundering a little. "Anyway, it sounds like Sheelagh needs a bit of support. I think I should probably go."

"Well, if you must, dear. Would you like us to come too?"

"Not at all, Mother, too awkward for you; wouldn't dream of putting you through it. But I will need a little cash. A bit short, don't you know?"

"Of course, dear, how much will you need?"

His brain was now fully engaged. After a few calculations, he said, "Twenty-five should do it, Mother. You are a brick."

"Will that be enough, dear?"

"I'll manage. Don't want to bleed Father dry, do I?"

"I'll arrange it with your bank. You can pick it up there in an hour or so. Do let me know how things are, won't you, darling?"

"Of course, Mother. Must dash now and see about arranging boat tickets. I'll get in touch with Pierce directly. I have his address. I'll contact you when I get back."

Colm drove to the post office and sent a telegram to his brother:

SORRY TO HEAR FATHER ILL **STOP** DO LET ME KNOW IF THINGS GET WORSE **STOP** SEND MESSAGE DIRECTLY TO ME HERE IN COL-LEGE **STOP** COLM

He called into the bank, collected the money, and drove to the Tea-kettle Café. He seated himself at one of the tables by the entrance where she would easily be able to see him.

"What are you doing here?"

"Well, that's a nice greeting." He stood and tried to give her a peck on the cheek. She pulled back.

"Don't try that, Colm Kelly, after everything you said to me last night."

"I'm sorry about that, Susie. Look, I have a bit of a problem. My father is very ill, dying in fact, and I have to go to Ireland. I've no idea how long I'm going to be gone."

"Don't lie to me. Your family lives in London; you told me so."

"Ah, no! You see, they are the ones that took me in when my mother died, my real mother, that is. My real father was too grief-stricken to take care of me."

The young girl stood watching him, unsure if she should believe him or not.

"So, look, I have to go. I'm going to give you all the cash I have right now." He opened his wallet, ensuring she could not see its contents, and handed her two five pound notes. "I'm sorry, love, but that's it." He stood. "Take care of yourself. I'm sure you'll be fine." He kissed her gently on the forehead and turned to leave.

"Colm."

He turned back. "Yes?"

"Is your father really dying?"

He looked suitably solemn. "I swear on my dear mother's grave, Susie. I couldn't lie about something like this."

"In Ireland?"

He put his hand on his heart.

She nodded her head and held up the money. "Thank you."

He turned and left.

Colm caught up with his friend outside the main lecture theater.

"Come on. Let's get out of here for a few days."

David Gough looked doubtful. "I thought I might do a bit of studying. You know, catch a lecture or two."

Colm waved a pound note.

"Where did that come from? I thought you were broke."

"Had a bit of bad news. Want to help me celebrate?"

"Where?'

"I want to get out of town. I've given Susie some money. Now I want to lay low for a bit, stay out of her way. Let's go up to London."

"On a pound?"

"I have a few more where that came from."

"What about my lecture?"

Colm stared at his friend for a moment before they both burst into laughter.

"Your car or mine?" he said, tucking the money in his pocket.

Sheelagh

It took Pierce a long time to persuade the porter to allow them into the hospital.

"The nuns will kill me, sir. I'm to let no one in except the good Fathers outside of the visiting times."

Eventually the surreptitious passing of a silver coin, and Pierce's assurance that it was a matter of life and death, convinced the man he could be otherwise engaged for a few moments while Pierce and Sheelagh slipped past.

Sheelagh followed her brother through the maze of corridors that reeked of antiseptic. Despite their gloss finish, the green and cream walls were nicotine-stained and chipped, scratched and scuffed by constant passing traffic.

Pierce stopped at the double doors of Saint Margaret's ward.

"Are you ready?"

She nodded.

He pushed open the doors, and they entered. A nun sat, head down, writing at a desk, her face hidden by a large, white-winged wimple. As she looked up, she frowned. "May I help you?"

She stared with astonishment at Sheelagh's trousers. Pierce introduced himself and Sheelagh, and asked to see his father. The nun glanced at the large clock hanging below the crucifix on the far wall.

"Visiting time isn't for another two hours."

She remained sitting, her back as stiff as her white starched apron.

Pierce explained about his sister's brief visit to Ireland, how this might be her only opportunity to visit with the father she had not seen for thirteen years. Meanwhile, Sheelagh glanced nervously around the ward. She wondered which one of these quiet, unshaven men was her father.

"Well, just a quick visit then, but you really should come back later."

The nun returned to her paperwork.

Pierce thanked her, assured her they would, and led Sheelagh to a bed near the far end of the room.

"Hello, Da. I've brought Sheelagh to see you."

She looked down at the large, florid-faced man with the gray, bushy moustache. A vague memory stirred.

"Hello."

"He can't turn his head," said Pierce, "Stand beside him there; he'll see you better."

She moved to the side of the bed, and Pierce brought a chair forward for her. She sat and took Brendan's hand that rested on the bedcover.

"I'm sorry you're like this." She didn't know what else to say.

Brendan looked at her, unblinking. He tried to speak but only grunted; saliva dribbled from the side of his mouth. She squeezed his hand.

After a few minutes Pierce leaned to Sheelagh's ear and said quietly, "We can't really stay. We're not supposed to be here. We can come back later if you want."

She nodded, released Brendan's hand, and stood. Brendan eyes opened wider; he looked fearful. She touched his hand again briefly.

"We'll be back; I promise."

She took a handkerchief from her bag and wiped the side of his mouth. Pierce stood behind her and nodded at his father.

"We will, Da, at the proper visiting time. We'll just go and get a breath of air."

They stood beside the bed a moment longer, then turned and left.

Brother and sister sat in the bay window of Warren's Hotel, a pot of tea and plate of sandwiches on the coffee table in front of them.

Sheelagh frowned. "It seems so strange. He's my father, but I don't know him at all. Now I may never even be able to talk with him."

"Even if he could talk, I don't think you two would have a lot to say to each other." Pierce helped himself to a sandwich.

"Looking at him, I didn't feel as if he was my father at all. It's very sad for anyone to be like that. I feel very sorry for him, but he still doesn't feel like my father."

Pierce had stopped listening. He stared out across Market Street.

"Well, what do you know; she came after all."

Sheelagh followed his gaze. "Who?"

"Mrs. Kelly."

"You mean his wife?" She craned her neck to try to see. "Which one? Where is she?"

He pointed, "She's just turned the corner towards Emmett Street. When I brought him over last night, she wouldn't come. Maybe someone brought her over this morning. Perhaps we won't hurry back to the hospital for a while. Let her visit on her own."

"That's fine. I wouldn't know what to say to her anyway."

They remained in the hotel until the official visiting time, then walked slowly back to the hospital. The porter greeted them with a conspiratorial wink, and they made their way back to Brendan's ward. The same nun was at her desk. She glanced at the watch pinned to her apron bib and smiled.

"Is his wife still here?" asked Pierce, peering down the line of visitors at each bed.

"He's had no other visitors but you, since he came in."

Pierce and Sheelagh exchanged surprised glances, thanked her, and went to sit with their father.

Mary

"What if he dies, Mary? Won't you feel sorry then?" Sheelagh asked gently.

Mary's pressed her lips firmly together. She shook her head.

"What about baby Norah? Doesn't he deserve to see her?" Joe added his questions to Sheelagh's.

"I will *not* go and see him. I don't care what you two say. Now," she said with finality, "I have to feed the baby and take myself off to bed, if you don't mind. It's been a long day."

She lifted Norah from her crib.

"I'm going to visit him in the morning. I have a load to deliver in Ballyfin anyway," said Joe.

"Can I come with you?" Sheelagh asked.

"I suppose so."

Joe couldn't think of a polite way to refuse his sister-in-law. The thought of being a taxi-driver for a Brit galled him mightily. He'd promised Mary he would be polite, and he would, but he wanted as little to do with Sheelagh as possible. His anger against "all things British" was deep-seated, though Mary and Pierce constantly pointed out how irrational it was.

"They weren't all Black and Tans," argued Pierce.

"They took in Michael, Sheelagh, and Colm when no-one here did," added Mary.

"There's no room for Brits in this country. We're a sovereign state now," Joe insisted stubbornly.

"We are talking about family, Joe, not politics. And she's *not* a Brit."

She was from England; she had an English accent, and she was reared by English people. That was more than enough for him. She was tainted stock. The Brits had subjugated the Irish people for over seven hundred years. Irish memories were long and unforgiving. Joe *would not* like his sister-in-law.

Sheelagh, though aware of his reserve towards her, had no idea why. She thought that maybe he was a little shy.

"Thanks, Joe. I have so little time here. Mary, do you mind if I go again? I don't want to upset you."

"Not at all, you can do what you like, Sheelagh. Joe, you can pick up some things for the shop while you're there. I'm closing early tomorrow to get ready for the christening."

"All right, my love. Though I still wish you'd come with us. You're a stubborn woman, Mary Daly." He kissed her and smiled. "But I love you anyway."

Sheelagh stood. "I love you too, Mary. It's so nice to have a sister. I feel like I've been an only child for so long."

Mary blushed and smiled shyly. She lifted the baby out of her crib.

"I'm off to bed, if you don't mind, Sheelagh. Are you coming, Joe?"

"In a minute, I'll stoke the fire first."

Mary left, and Sheelagh stood to follow.

"I must get to bed, too. I'll help Mary with the christening preparations when I get back tomorrow."

Joe ignored her, busying himself with the fire.

"Goodnight, Joe."

"Goodnight."

Sheelagh

As they left Saint Margaret's ward the next morning, Joe turned on Sheelagh angrily. "That was a bloody stupid thing to do."

"I'm sorry, Joe. I didn't know what to say. It's very awkward trying to talk to someone who can't talk back. It just slipped out."

"Well, *you* can tell Mary what you did. I'm not going to."

"I thought you wanted him to see the baby too."

"Maybe I did, but only if Mary was agreeable to the idea. You know what she was like last night."

"*I* could bring Norah to the hospital; then Mary wouldn't have to come."

"Oh, yes? And how do you intend to do that, Miss High-and-Mighty-Make-Your-Own-Decisions? How are you going to bring her here? Have a car, do you?"

"I've said I'm sorry, Joe. I didn't mean to upset you. I didn't think."

"That's the truest thing you've said so far. I suppose you think I'm your personal chauffeur? I suppose that's what you're used to, over there. Well it's not the way we do things around here."

Sheelagh's eyes filled with tears. "I'm so sorry. I'll tell him I made a mistake."

The lorry lurched forward as Joe angrily pushed it into gear and stomped his foot down on the accelerator. Sheelagh gripped her seat as he swerved out onto the road in front of a startled horse pulling a loaded cart. The carter cursed volubly at Joe while trying to rein in the horse and apply the brake to his cart.

"Bloody horses, they should all be shot," Joe muttered.

They drove the rest of the way to Doonbeg in silence.

Mary sat beside the fire with Norah cradled in her arms. She smiled up at her husband and sister. "I've just finished feeding her. I'll make you a cup of tea."

"Not for me," Joe growled and continued through the parlor and out of the back door. Mary watched him go and turned to Sheelagh. "What's wrong with him?"

"I made him cross." Sheelagh explained what she'd done. "I'm sorry, Mary. I didn't mean to do it. I'll tell your father the nuns wouldn't let me bring Norah into the hospital or something."

"No, it's all right; you can take her. You can do it tomorrow before the christening. Pierce said he was going over, so he can take you. Leave Joe out of it. Don't mind him."

Sheelagh gave her sister a quick hug. "Oh, thank you, Mary. Father looks so helpless lying there. I feel so sorry for him. I just know it would make him happier to see his grandchild."

Mary ignored the comments. "If you take the baby after I feed her in the morning, I can finish getting things ready here."

"I'm so glad you're not angry with me. Thank you." Sheelagh hung her coat over the back of a chair and pushed up her sleeves. "Now, what can I do to help? And I want you to tell me more about how you grew up, all the bits you've left out of your letters."

Mary laughed. "You have to tell me more about the Porters, and your home, too. Aunty Bridgie would have loved to hear you were so happy. She worried herself so much about that."

Mary put the baby into the cot, and the two sisters set to work. Sheelagh did many of the chores she had so often watched Martha do. Under Mary's direction, she helped prepare vegetables, rolled and cut pastry, cored and sliced apples. A ham boiled in a pot on the range, and the sisters baked bread and tarts in the small oven, gossiped and chattered, and learned about their different lives and families. They shared their very different school experiences and their hopes for the future. Meanwhile, Joe worked out his temper on the vegetable plot. He also turned the turf in the shed, to help it dry, and slaked his thirst with a bottle or two of porter.

Sheelagh held the baby close, still unfamiliar with her fragile charge. The infant slept peacefully on the short drive to Ballyfin and was still sleeping as Pierce and Sheelagh entered the ward. A young nurse sat at the desk in place of the nun. When she saw the tiny bundle in Sheelagh's arms, she said sternly, "You know, children aren't allowed in here."

"Just for a minute, please," pleaded Sheelagh.

The nurse stood and lifted the soft shawl from the child's face.

"Would you look at that, what a beautiful baby, so peaceful? Is it a boy or a girl?"

"A girl," Sheelagh replied, "Norah."

"She's beautiful." She glanced from Sheelagh to Pierce. "She has both your coloring. Is she your first?"

Brother and sister looked at each other startled, and then laughed.

"No, we're her aunty and uncle. It's our sister's baby."

The nurse laughed and apologized.

"Who are you here to see?"

"Brendan Kelly, our father. Is he any better?"

The nurse lowered her voice. "No, I'm sorry. He doesn't seem to be making any improvement."

"But we can go and visit him, can't we?" Sheelagh asked.

"I suppose you can bring her in, just this once. But don't let Sister catch you. I do have a couple of forms here I would like one of you to sign. The doctor may want to do some tests."

"I'll sign them," said Pierce. "You go on down, Sheelagh."

Sheelagh walked slowly down the ward, unsure of what she was going to say to her father. She arrived at the foot of Brendan's bed.

"Hello, Father."

She moved to the side of the bed, so that he could see her more clearly. "I have a little visitor for you."

She held Norah up so that Brendan could see her.

"Here's your granddaughter. Her name is Norah."

Brendan stared unblinking at the child for some time. Tears slowly filled his eyes, spilled over onto his face, and ran softly onto his pillow.

"Oh please don't cry; you'll make me cry too." Sheelagh wiped her already wet face and sniffed. "Isn't she beautiful? She's to be christened today. I'm so sorry you won't be there. I know Mary is angry with you, but she did let me bring Norah here. I think that means she does still love you, somewhere down deep. I think, perhaps, she's just stubborn." She dabbed at his tears with her damp handkerchief. "I wish you could tell me why you wanted to put us in an orphanage. I don't believe you hated us. I know there had to be a good reason. I'm only here for one more day. I leave on Monday, so this will be the last time

I see you, for now. I hope I see you again some time, and that you'll be able to talk then. Mary has told me so many things about the family, but I would still like to talk to you."

She fell silent. Father and daughter stared at each other, their tears falling silently, while the baby slept in Sheelagh's arms.

Pierce spoke to the nurse for a long time. When Sheelagh glanced down the ward, she saw that they were laughing. She could think of nothing more to say to her father, and sat rocking the baby who was now awake and becoming restless. Pierce caught his sister's glance, excused himself, and hurried down the ward.

"Sorry, Shee. Hello, Da." He ducked his face so that his father could see him. "Well, what do you think of your granddaughter? Isn't she a grand little babby? We got a telegram from Colm too, Da. He said he was sorry you're not well."

Sheelagh nodded in affirmation. They had been surprised when the telegram was delivered the previous evening. Sheelagh realized that her parents must have contacted Colm's parents.

"Mummy loves a bit of drama in her life. I can just imagine the phone call." She smiled. "I must say I'm surprised we heard from Colm though, not like him really, from what I remember, not unless he thought there was money to be inherited."

Pierce chattered on to his father: telling him about work, what jobs he was doing, how Joe was enjoying driving the second lorry, and how Mary was fussing about the christening.

"She's even asked your brother, Pat, and his family over. I can't believe it. She's never had much time for them. I think she just wants Sheelagh to meet them all before she goes back to England. He and his wife are going to bring all their family, and Joe's family will be there, of course. His father was asking after you. I don't know where Mary is going to put them all in that small back room of theirs. We men can get out of the way up the yard. I just hope it won't be raining too hard, or we'll all be huddled in the turf shed."

Pierce, who had never had a long conversation with his father, now seemed spurred by Brendan's silence into an almost garrulous state. It was as if he was trying to make up for the years of silence between them. Eventually he did run out of things to say. Norah was whimpering.

"We'd better get going, Pierce; it must be nearly time for another feed. We have to get her back to Mary."

"Right so, I'll be in again soon, Da. Mind yourself." He edged away from the bed and walked towards the door. Sheelagh stood, rocking the baby gently to soothe her crying.

"Take care of yourself, Father. I'll try and come to Ireland for another visit before too long. I hope you get better soon." She bent to kiss his forehead lightly. "Goodbye."

She walked quickly to join Pierce who was again talking to the nurse at the desk.

"I'm ready."

"Right then, let's go before that little mite raises the roof." He smiled at the nurse. "I'll see you on Monday then, when I come in."

The nurse smiled and nodded.

Norah wailed noisily all the way back to Doonbeg.

Mary thought the christening went well. Norah, the center of attention, smiled and slept her way through the short service and the family gathering afterwards. On Mary's advice, Sheelagh decided not to wear the bright, silky, green dress she had shown her sister the night before.

"It might be a bit bright for Canon Finnegan, Sheelagh. He'll end up giving us a sermon on 'occasions of sin,' or 'Eve's wickedness,' or some such."

She wore a demure, brown, soft wool suit she had packed as an extra instead, but she couldn't relinquish her high-heeled shoes and stumbled several times on the rutted road to the church.

"That will teach me to be so vain." She laughed as she clutched at Pierce's arm yet again.

At the tea she enjoyed meeting her extended family. She wondered if her Uncle Pat was anything like her father, but when the group arrived at the house, he quickly excused himself and joined the other men gathered in the yard, close to the turf shed. Sheelagh only saw him again when everyone was leaving, and when the strong smell of alcohol on his breath made her disinclined to talk to him further. She was surprised at the smell. She knew Mary had refused to allow Joe to bring in bottles of ale and whiskey "to wet the baby's head."

"But my Da said he would bring some over from the bar." Joe had protested. "He said it would be his contribution to the hooley."

"It is not a hooley, Joe Daly. It is a christening. Do you want my sister to go back and tell everyone we are a bunch of drunkards? You can thank your father, and tell him we will be 'wetting the baby's head' with tea or water, and that will be just fine. I'll have no alcohol in my house, as well you know, Joe Daly."

He had agreed easily, but Sheelagh suspected Joe did not necessarily consider the turf shed part of the house.

On Monday morning it was time to leave. Mary and Sheelagh hugged each other tightly, reluctant to part. Finally, Pierce helped a tearful Sheelagh into the lorry. Mary stood at the shop door, dabbing her eyes with her apron.

"Don't forget to write," she called to Sheelagh as Pierce started the engine. "And come back whenever you can. We'll always have space for you," she shouted over the noise. "Norah will need to see her godmother."

Sheelagh nodded vigorously.

"Take care, Sheelagh. Thank you for coming."

Pierce edged the lorry away from the curb. Sheelagh twisted in her seat to look through the small rear window of the cab. She waved and blew kisses to Mary, until the bend in the road took the shop, and her sister, out of sight.

Pierce looked across at her. "I'm glad you came too. Don't ever be a stranger to us from now on, will you, Sheelagh?"

"No, I won't. It was so lovely to see you all. It's like another world. I can't believe I'm going back to Bristol already. I promise I'll keep in touch."

They rode in silence for the rest of the journey to Ballyfin. When they arrived at the station, Pierce put her large suitcase on the overhead rack in her carriage. He reached into his pocket and brought out a bag of sweets that Mary had given him at the shop. He handed them to Sheelagh.

"She said you might like these on the journey."

The guard blew his whistle. They hugged, and Pierce hurriedly stepped down onto the platform, slamming the carriage door behind him. Smoke from the engine stung his eyes. He stepped back and waved. The train pulled out of the station, and Sheelagh stood at the carriage window waving until Pierce was out of sight.

Pierce

The nun, Sister Patricia, sat neat and upright behind the desk. She would nod primly at him before he made his way down the ward to where his father lay. When she was not there, Nurse Egan took her place. Pierce discovered her first name was Maeve, and that she was twenty-three.

"The Mammy says there's no hope for me. I'll die an old maid." She laughed as she admitted her age.

He loved it when she laughed; her whole face lit up and her eyes sparkled. The sound was infectious. When they heard her, the quiet, pale men lying impassively in their iron hospital beds smiled too. Pierce tried to make her laugh; he practiced funny stories to tell her, or did imitations of people he met or saw. The imitations were not very good, but she laughed anyway.

"I'm sure you'd have no trouble finding a husband if you wanted one," he said.

"Good men are hard to come by at my age," she replied. "There's only mammy's boys, with no wit and less inclination, or old farmers with nothing in their pockets and too much on their minds ... if you know what I mean! No, I'll let Mammy go on storming Heaven and see what happens."

In truth, she loved nursing, and said she didn't miss "four or five small children clinging to my skirts and little enough to feed them on."

Pierce spent as much time talking to Maeve as to his father, though only if Sister Patricia was not there.

His father seemed to shrink more each time Pierce visited. Three weeks after his arrival at the hospital, Brendan had another stroke. It was Maeve who told Pierce when he arrived that evening. They both walked down the ward and stood at the foot of Brendan's bed. His eyes were closed, his breathing shallow and noisy.

"He's very congested," Maeve explained. "He hasn't got the strength to cough."

Pierce watched his father.

"Is that very bad?"

Maeve was silent, and Pierce turned his head to look at her. She nodded.

After four weeks, he was on first name terms with the hospital porters. They usually turned a blind eye to his odd visiting times, as long as there were no nuns around. This morning he made his deliveries to the market, then called in to visit his father, as had become his habit. The damp December cold numbed his hands, and he was glad of the warmth in the dark corridors. He also knew Maeve was on the early shift, which speeded his step.

Entering the ward, he saw his father's bed was empty. A screen surrounded another bed, so he waited, knowing that Maeve must be busy. As she folded the screen back, she saw him and hurried up the ward.

"I'm sorry, Pierce." She paused, and he knew. She touched his arm in silent sympathy. "Your father passed away early this morning. The doctor said it was pneumonia."

He nodded. "Where is he now?"

"He's in the mortuary. I'll get one of the porters to take you down. Are you all right?"

He nodded again, gathering his thoughts. "What do I have to do?"

"Well, you probably need to see an undertaker. Will there be a wake?"

"I don't know. Yes, I suppose so."

"You need a casket before he can be removed to the house. The people in the mortuary will be able to tell what you need to do. I'll ring for the porter."

She went to the desk, picked up the phone, and dialed. As she waited for a reply, Pierce stood staring down the aisle of beds, dimly lit in the winter-morning light. Thoughts and no thoughts raced in his head. His father's death was not a surprise. Maeve had warned him, and he knew anyway. For weeks Pierce had watched the life fade from his father's eyes, watched him struggling to stay alive with each rasping breath. Yet still, in these first few moments, though he tried to understand, he could not. So many thoughts, so much to do; yet, he was motionless.

"Pierce. Pierce!" Maeve touched his arm. "The porter is on his way. Do you want to sit down?"

He shook his head. A faint voice called from one of the beds. Maeve turned to see who it was.

"No. No ... you're busy. I'll wait outside."

"You don't have to. I'll go and see to Mr. McCauley, I won't be long. You can wait here."

She was still talking to the patient when the porter arrived. She looked up, and Pierce raised his hand slightly. She raised her hand in return and smiled gently. He left.

Mary

"Did you send a telegram to Sheelagh as well?"

"Yes, Mary; I sent them to Colm and her at the same time."

"She will tell Michael, won't she?" She looked hopefully at Pierce. "Do you think any of them will come? I don't suppose Sheelagh will. It's only a month since she left. But it would be nice if Colm came, and Michael."

"I don't suppose they will, either. It's an awful long way to come for a funeral. Don't get your hopes up."

"I know; you're right. I'd just like to see them. When are you bringing Da home from the hospital?"

"I'm going to collect him this afternoon. We'll wake him 'til tomorrow evening and then take him to the church. She says she doesn't want a wake for two nights in the house. Canon Finnegan says that's fine. Da can be in the church overnight. He says that way there's a better chance of people being sober at the funeral. It's after the early Mass on Friday."

"I'll give you some food to take over."

"Thanks. Joe says his father will be bringing over crates of porter and a couple of bottles of whiskey from the bar."

"So he should, after all the money Da spent in that place. Not that I approve, you understand, but I don't suppose you could have a wake without the drink. What is *she* doing?"

"Nothing much. She's not even cleaning the place like she usually is. She just sits staring into the fire. I don't know if she's grieving or not. Annie Quinn came over and got the place ready. She brought over the candles, and a ham. When are you coming over?"

This was the question that had been hanging between them since Pierce arrived with the news of their father's death.

"I'll come in the morning. I'll get Joe to watch the shop. I can't close it. People need their milk," Mary added defensively. "So, I won't be able to stay long."

"That's all right, Mary. I understand."

"I can't change now, Pierce. I can't stop hating him just because he's dead."

Tears came unbidden to her eyes, and she brushed them away angrily, but more came to take their place. Pierce put his arm around her shoulder. She buried her face in his jacket and sobbed.

"Why, Pierce? Why? There was no reason for them to be sent away. We lost Mammy that was enough. We didn't have to lose him, too, and then them. Why didn't he want us?"

Pierce remained silent and let his sister cry. He had no answer, probably never would now. He'd always wanted to ask his father the same question, but never quite had the courage. Now it was too late. He tried to console her.

"Aunty Bridgie wanted you; you know she did. She couldn't have managed without you. And those people in England wanted the others. Look at Sheelagh—she's doing grand—and Colm, and I'm sure Michael is too. We managed just fine, Mary. We have each other, and you have Joe and Norah, too. We're fine. Don't cry, alanna; you'll have me at it too, and that would never do."

She stepped away from him, wiping her face with her apron.

"I'm sorry, Pierce."

She took the rag of a handkerchief he offered and blew her nose.

"All right, I'm finished crying. What do we have to do? Will Joe be back soon?"

"Yes, he's over at Rafferty's farm. He said he'd be back as soon as he delivers his load."

"Are you going back to the hospital now?"

He nodded.

"They said I have to get a death certificate from the doctor. Then I will collect Da from the mortuary. It's a pine casket, Mary, and I said we didn't want brass handles. Is that all right?"

"Of course it is."

He left, and Mary sat by the fire and cried again.

Pierce

When Pierce arrived back in Glendarrig, a large group of people had already gathered in the house. Three men helped him lift his father's coffin from the back of the lorry and carry it in. They entered carefully through the low doorway, mindful of the shallow step. The casket was gently set down on the table in the center of the room, and Peadar Quinn, helped by another neighbor, carefully pried open the lid. Annie put the candlesticks at the four corners and Peadar lit them from a taper. The neighbors gathered around the coffin.

"Begod, he looks awful sick. He must have had a terrible time in that hospital," said Jack Connors, an old friend of Brendan's from Daly's bar. Jack's wife gave him a swift elbow in the side, and he raised his glass to his friend. "Rest in peace, Brendan."

Mrs. Connors took Pierce's arm. "God rest him, Pierce; your father had his troubles, but he's at peace now."

Uncle Pat arrived, shook Pierce's hand, sympathized with the widow, then poured himself a glass of stout and went to stand at the foot of Brendan's coffin.

People filled the small cottage. Some prayed, some drank, and some exchanged stories. Annie Quinn offered tea and sandwiches, welcomed new visitors, and bid goodbye to those who were leaving. Mrs. Kelly continued to sit by the fire. She drank tea at Annie's urging but ate nothing. She accepted people's commiserations, thanked them for coming, but she didn't cry.

Pipe smoke filled the room, and the babble of talk increased as the evening grew late. Eilish O'Doherty, an old woman from Knockglas, took her place beside the fire and began to keen. Covering her face with her apron, she rocked back and forth, wailing her lament in wordless, high-pitched sounds.

Annie led a decade of the rosary after which Mrs. Kelly was finally persuaded to go to bed and rest.

The wake continued through the night and, in the early morning, the women took over from the men as the chief mourners.

Mary

Mary's heart pounded as she lifted the latch and entered the cottage. She walked slowly through the crowd of people to where her father lay. She stood, gazing down at him. Annie joined her.

"How are you, Mary love? I'm glad you're here."

Mary smiled wanly and looked around.

"It hasn't changed much in here. It looks very grand from the outside, with the new roof and all the windows."

She looked back at her father's body.

"Is *she* here?"

"She's resting upstairs; she'll be down soon."

"The last time I was here Mammy was in a coffin on this table."

Annie put her arm around the young woman's shoulders.

"We put flowers around her, in blue and white jugs." Mary continued, glancing towards the dresser. "There aren't any flowers now."

"No, sure it's wintertime child; few flowers show their faces now. Can I get you a cup of tea, alanna?"

"Yes, please."

Annie left to fetch the tea. Mary continued to stand looking down at her father.

"Here, child, come and sit by the fire and warm yourself with this."

She put the mug of hot tea in Mary's hand and guided her towards the settle. Two other women, strangers to Mary, sat with her.

When her tea was finished, Mary returned to her father's coffin and blessed herself.

"Rest in peace, Da. May God have mercy on your soul."

As she turned to leave, Mrs. Kelly stepped out of her bedroom at the top of the stairs. Their eyes met. Though they had seen each other often at Mass in the village, even at the Ballyfin market, they had never spoken. The widow came down the stairs. The mourners quieted and slowly parted to allow her to cross the small room to Mary. The two young women stood, facing each other. Mrs. Kelly spoke first.

"Thank you for coming."

Mary's tongue seemed stuck to the roof of her mouth, and her hands were shaking. She held the edge of the coffin.

"Thank you. I'm sorry about …" She didn't know how to finish, she indicated her father. Mrs. Kelly nodded. Mary stepped away from the table. "I have to go. The shop … Joe, my husband, is minding the baby."

Mrs. Kelly nodded again.

Mary, flustered, turned quickly and left the house. Mrs. Kelly stood looking at her late husband for a while then took up her place beside the fire once more.

By early afternoon the men were back, unshaven and tired, to continue their farewell.

Pierce

Pierce slept in his clothes. Annie Quinn had persuaded him to go to bed just before dawn, and he quickly fell into an exhausted sleep. It was early afternoon when the growing murmur of men's voices woke him. When he woke, he remembered. He struggled out of bed … his head throbbing … put on his boots, and ran his fingers through his matted hair.

Peadar was talking with a group of men at the bottom of the stairs. He looked up as Pierce opened the bedroom door.

"Hello, lad; we thought we were going to have to drag you out of bed for the removal. You slept well?"

"Yes thanks, Peadar. I think I might have had a drink or two too many last night. Is there any danger of something to eat? My mouth is in a terrible state."

Jack Connors laughed, "Not used to the drink, that's your problem. Should have had more practice, like your Da. Good man for the practice was your Da, almost had it perfect. God rest him." He raised his glass to Pierce.

Peadar glared angrily at his friend. "Don't mind Jack, lad. Annie's gone home for a sleep, but I'm sure one of the ladies will make you something."

He scanned the small room, tight packed with people, and caught the eye of a dark-haired woman in black dress and shawl. He beckoned her over. The woman made her way through the crowd towards them.

"You just missed your sister. She was here not an hour since. She said she would be back with Joe and the baby for the removal." The woman waited. "Pierce, this is Martha Ryan. Her husband is one of the crofters up on Knockglas; she'll mind you, lad."

Peadar returned to the conversation with his friends. The woman led a sleepy and slightly bewildered Pierce through the gathering of people towards the back door.

"Oh God, no one is looking after the pig."

"Don't you worry about it, lad. Annie has it all sorted."

She indicated a small stool beside the half-door, and Pierce sat.

"I'll have some food to you in two minutes. You stay where you are."

She edged her way back through the crowd towards the fire, and Pierce lost sight of her.

As he sat trying to clear his head, he became aware that the din in the room was quieting. Everyone had turned towards the front door. He stood and craned to see over their heads. A young man was standing at the door. He was well built with brown hair, neatly parted at the side, and a thin moustache across his top lip. He wore a dark, double-breasted suit, a white shirt, and dark blue silk tie with a matching silk handkerchief tucked casually into his top pocket. He carried a brown leather valise.

"Is this the Kelly house?"

Peadar stepped forward, "It is. Can I help you, sir?"

The young man gave a nervous smile as he peered into the smoky dimness of the room. "I'm looking for Pierce Kelly, is he here?" He scanned the group of villagers.

"He certainly is, sir. May I ask who is looking for him?"

"I'm his brother, Colm."

An audible gasp came from the assembled friends and neighbors as they looked from one brother to the other. The crowd parted slowly, making a narrow path to where Pierce stood looking incredulously at his younger brother.

"Colm?"

Colm squinted his eyes against the smoke and stared at Pierce.

"Pierce, is that you?"

Pierce nodded, and Colm walked towards him. It was only then that he saw the open coffin. He stopped abruptly.

"Oh, good God, is that him?"

Several people nodded, and Peadar, still at his elbow, said quietly, "Yes Colm, that's your Da."

Colm walked around the coffin and took his brother's hand.

"Hello, Pierce, old chap, bit of a strange way to meet, eh?"

Pierce nodded. He was tired, disheveled, and hung over, and he now wished he'd shaved.

"I didn't think you would come." He looked over Colm's shoulder. "Is Michael with you?"

"Michael? Good heavens, you mean *brother* Michael? I haven't seen him since we were kids. No, he's not with me. Is he coming?"

"I don't know. I don't think so."

"Would you like a jar, son?" Peadar offered Colm a small tumbler filled with tawny liquid. He took it, drank it in one gulp, and gasped. When he regained his breath, he handed the glass back to Peadar.

"Thanks. This is all a bit bizarre." He glanced back at the curious mourners. "I had the devil of a job getting here. Not too many taxis in this part of the world, are there? The station master in Ballyfin finally found someone to drive me here. He said he owns the local drapers."

"That's Niall Mahon," said Pierce.

"Right. Well he said to tell you he'd be over later. Nice enough chap."

Pierce struggled for something to say. The dark-haired woman pushed her way through the people and thrust a steaming mug of tea into his hand. She put a plate of ham, cold potatoes, and a hunk of bread on the stool beside him and turned to the crowd.

"Will you all stop goggling at the two of them, and get on with your own business. These lads have a lot of catching up to do, and they don't need all of you gawping at them."

She turned back to Pierce.

"Why don't you go out in the back yard, Pierce? You can have a bit of privacy out there. Would you like me to put the pig away, so he's not annoying you?"

Colm looked in some alarm at the woman. Pierce nodded. Martha let herself out of the half-door, closing it behind her, and returned a few minutes later.

"There you are, lads, out you go. He's shut up out of your way now."

She stepped aside, and Colm followed Pierce into the small yard.

The acrid sweet smell of the pigsty assaulted Colm's nostrils, and he hastily pulled the handkerchief out of his top pocket and held it over his nose and mouth.

"Oh, my God, that's awful. What is it?"

"I can't smell anything. Maybe it's the pig."

Pierce sipped the tea and looked at his brother. "Sorry, would you like a cup?"

"No, thanks, but I wouldn't mind another drink."

Pierce shouted over the half-door, and a bottle and a glass were held out. Putting down his cup, he took them and poured Colm a drink.

"You're looking very smart, Colm, just like a bank manger."

Colm looked down at his crumpled suit. "I'm a bit of a mess after the journey. Thought I'd better wear the navy one, with a funeral and all. Good thing about having a father in the tailoring business, always guaranteed good suits, and a good fit." He laughed awkwardly. "Well you know what I mean, the *other* father. I've some fresh shirts in the bag."

He took a large mouthful of the whiskey and coughed. "Wow, this stuff has a bit of a bite to it. So, what do we do now? What are all those people doing in there? And why is the lid missing from the coffin?"

Pierce gave his brother a puzzled frown. "It's a wake, Colm. Have you not been to a wake?"

Colm shook his head. "Seems a bit barbaric to me. What the hell's a wake?"

Pierce tried to explain, and Colm tried to understand. As they spoke, Peadar leaned over the half-door.

"Sorry to interrupt, Pierce, but we should be leaving in a while. Your Uncle Pat and I will help carry the coffin, along with the two of you. Mary said Joe would be here as well, so who do you want for the sixth? You know every man here is willing."

"Is Jack Connors sober enough?"

"I'll make sure he is, lad. We'll be closing the coffin soon. Do you want to say goodbye to your Da?"

"We'll be in directly."

"*I* have to carry the coffin?" asked Colm, eyes wide. "Don't you have an undertaker? Don't *they* arrange all that?"

Pierce shook his head. "We carry him to the Church ourselves, Colm; that's how it's done. It's only about a mile and a half. Come on in to say goodbye to him. We can talk after the removal. Mary will be here soon. I'm sure you can stay with her tonight. She will be so pleased to see you."

"We have to go and look at him … now?"

Pierce nodded, slightly amused at his brother's obvious discomfort.

"Yes, Colm, come on; it'll be fine. It's lucky you get to see him before he goes to the church."

"I'm not sure that was such good timing," said Colm, reluctantly following Pierce back into the house. He stopped suddenly. "Wait a minute. I don't know how to carry a coffin. What if I drop it?"

"There will be five more of us, Colm, and he doesn't weigh that much now. You'll be fine. We'll show you how to do it. Aunty Bridgie was my first, and I think she was heavier than Da. He lost a lot of weight in that hospital."

Mary

Joe helped Mary down from the lorry. She wrapped the baby close in her shawl, protecting her from the cold wind. He opened the door of the house and let his wife step into the crowded room ahead of him. Kitty Farrell saw her immediately and hurried to her side, determined to be the one to give Mary the news.

"Mary, Colm's here, your brother Colm. He looks like a young prince, Mary. Wait 'til you see him. He's with Pierce. Peadar just went to bring them in. They were talking out in the back yard. He's come all the way from England, Mary, and you should see the bag he has with him. It's leather, and polished so you can see your face in it."

The woman stopped for breath, but Mary was no longer listening; she was looking across the room, searching for Pierce and her younger brother. Her heart was beating fast, her face was flushed, and she held Norah tight to her breast for security. He *did* come. After all these years she would see him again, talk to him. Kitty stepped aside, and Mary saw the two men standing at the foot of the coffin, their faces strangely lit by the flickering candles. One was Pierce, tall and lean with a mop of unruly red hair, his face unshaven and his clothes ill-fitting and worn thin with age. The young man standing beside him was shorter, plump, and dressed smarter than any politician she'd ever seen. She thrust the baby into Joe's arms and hurried to greet her younger brother.

Colm stepped back, startled, as a young woman called his name and threw her arms around his neck, crying. He glanced over her head at his brother, his eyebrows raised questioningly. Pierce put his hands on Mary's shoulders and gently pulled her back.

"Easy, Mary, you've frightened the life out of him; he doesn't know who you are. Colm, it's Mary."

Colm looked at the pale-faced woman in the drab dress and shawl. Her straight, brown hair, which had been knotted in a bun, was now disheveled, and loose strands hung about her face. Despite her tear-smudged cheeks, she was smiling warmly up at him.

"You look so grand," she said, standing back to admire him. She wiped the tears from her face and looked for her husband. "Look, Joe! It's Colm! He's grown into a man." She laughed and pointed to his face. "See, he has a moustache, just like Ronald Coleman in Lost Horizon." She hugged her brother again.

"Mary love, I think they want to say the rosary and close the coffin," said her husband. Then he lowered his voice. "Stand back there a bit, love. I think Mrs. Kelly will want to be here."

Pierce and Mary had forgotten their father's wife. She was standing now, watching the two young men and their sister standing beside their father's casket. She walked forward slowly.

"I'm glad you're all here. It's right that you are." She glanced at Brendan. "He and I had our differences, but I'm sorry for what happened to ye." She looked directly at Pierce. "After the funeral, I want to talk to you, Pierce. I've been doing a great deal of thinking these past couple of days. We need to talk."

Pierce nodded. Mary's face showed her surprise. Having only spoken to the woman for the first time earlier that day, she expected hostility, but there was none. She studied the woman who had taken her mother's place, who married her father and moved into her home. She was surprised to see the widow was still a young woman. Her lean frame, pale face, and thin, bird-like hands had only made her look older from a distance. She looks tired, Mary thought; she looks very, very tired.

"I *am* sorry for your loss, Mrs. Kelly," she said, with more sincerity than she would have believed. "It must be hard to lose your husband. I couldn't imagine being without my Joe."

The woman glanced again at her deceased husband lying in his coffin, rosary beads twined in his hands.

"I've arranged for him to be buried beside your Mammy. I thought you would like that. I think he would too."

The three stared at the woman in astonishment.

"But I spoke to Canon Finnegan; I arranged a plot ..."

"I know, Pierce, but I spoke to him too. Kevin Moody has dug a grave beside your mother's. I'll be going elsewhere."

Peadar gently touched the woman's elbow. "Mrs. Kelly, will we close the coffin now?"

She nodded, and Peadar blew out the four candles. Three men stepped forward, and Brendan Kelly's widow, Pierce, Mary, and Colm stepped away from the table.

Eilish O'Doherty blessed herself aloud and began to recite "The Creed." The mourners put down their glasses and cups and joined her in the prayer of belief.

"I believe in God, the Father Almighty, Creator of Heaven and Earth...." Peadar and Jack Rogers took the lid from under the table and put it in place.

Eilish began the "Our Father" and the people chorused their response. The men were hammering the nails in place as she announced "The First Sorrowful Mystery, the Agony in the Garden."

The thirty or more people who were crammed into the dark room chanted the response to the "Hail Mary" over and over. It was a religious mantra that united family, friends, and neighbors in their prayers for the deceased.

> "... Holy Mary,
> Mother of God,
> Pray for us sinners, now, and at the hour of our death, Amen."

She brought the prayers to a close with the final prayer:

> "Glory be to the Father,
> And to the Son,
> And to the Holy Ghost,
> As it was in the beginning,
> Is now, and ever shall be,
> World without end, Amen."

The mourners blessed themselves in silence.

Mrs. Kelly walked behind the coffin. The six men stumbled occasionally on the rough road, but helping hands ensured no mishap. Brendan was received into the church by the Canon, and more prayers were said as his casket was placed in front of the altar.

After the brief service, Joe returned to Glendarrig with Pierce to collect the lorry. Annie Quinn, along with other friends and neighbors, accompanied Mrs. Kelly home, while Mary waited for Joe in the church porch. It was decided Colm would stay with them for the night, so he waited with her. Mary, rocking Norah gently in her arms, took the opportunity to ply Colm with questions. He laughed at her obvious fluster and excitement and answered her last question first.

"I will have to leave the day after the funeral. It's coming up to Christmas, you know. I have a few things I have to do."

She was disappointed, but two days were better than nothing. The shop would be closed tomorrow anyway, in mourning and for the funeral. She could spend time with him then, and there was always this evening.

Mrs. Kelly

Mrs. Kelly had no opportunity to speak to anyone alone. The house had been full of people since the morning after Brendan's death. Though she sent a message to her family in Rathfen, they did not respond. They had disowned her many years before. None of them came to the funeral, not even her uncle.

She sent a message to Ballyfin, writing briefly of her husband's death and the funeral. She closed the note with ...

Please come to Glendarrig on the evening of the funeral. Bring all that you own with you. We can be together now.

After the burial, the mourners slowly drifted from the graveyard. Mrs. Kelly took the opportunity to tug Pierce to one side.

"Can I have some time in the house alone? Just a few hours ... I want you to come back later, and bring your brother and sister. I have things I need to say. And I need your help, though I'm not sure you'll give it."

She glanced around her to see if others were close by, then turned back to Pierce. She looked beyond him to the mountain.

"It's time to tell the truth. He can't stop me now. I wanted to speak a long time ago, but he said he could never face the shame, and I didn't have the courage to defy him."

Pierce looked puzzled, his stomach tightened in anticipation. Was he finally going to have an answer? Now, just when he thought it was too late? She returned his hard stare, unblinking, her chin raised. His thoughts tumbled over each other, and he took a deep breath to steady himself. Would she really be able to explain why—why his father had abandoned his brothers and sisters? Why he kept Pierce? And why this woman, this small, tired-looking woman, not much older than himself, hated him so much? He broke his gaze and nodded.

"I'll be there before it's dark, Ma'am, and I'll bring Mary and Colm with me."

They drove over from Doonbeg, the three of them squashed into the small cab of the lorry. Mrs. Kelly was waiting for them, sitting in Brendan's chair beside the fire. They entered the house in silence, and she gestured for them to sit. All three took their places on the wooden settle.

"I would ask you to listen to me carefully, and not to get angry before you hear me out."

They stared at the frail young woman.

"Pierce, you must know that this house is now mine."

He took a breath to speak, but she held up her hand. "Please hear me out."

He nodded and remained silent.

"I have no wish to live here. This house has no happy memories for me: I came in sorrow; I lived here in sorrow, and I do not wish die here; though I *will* stay here until I die, if I must."

Mary exchanged glances with her brother. What the woman was saying made little sense, but they remained silent.

"I want you to buy the house from me, Pierce."

Again he opened his mouth to speak, but the woman silenced him with a look.

"I am not unreasonable. I know that this is your home, and if I must continue to live here, then you may live here, too. However, if you want this house for yourself, and I'm sure nothing would please you more, then I need money to help me go. I know you are careful with your money, Pierce, and I know you have money saved. I need your help. I want to leave, but without money, I cannot."

"I think you are careful with money yourself, Ma'am," said Pierce sharply. "A good deal of money left this house that neither my father nor I benefited from."

"He spent every penny he could lay his hands on the drink. You know that well enough, Pierce Kelly. There was no point in leaving it for him to drink away. I handed up money for the roof, though I had better use for that money. I needed it."

"So you could take it for your own use? What needs did *you* have? You were always housed and clothed and fed."

"I did not take it for myself."

Their two voices were rising in an argument that mirrored a hundred previous arguments in the house. Mary put her hand on Pierce's arm.

"Wait, Pierce. Do you want to fight with this woman for the rest of your life? There was never peace between you, and I think there will be no peace now that Da has gone. Listen to her for a while longer." She turned to Mrs. Kelly. "What exactly do you want?"

"I want the price of passage to America for *two*, and money enough to allow me to start afresh."

All three jumped to their feet. Colm was the first to respond, and Pierce heard echoes of his father's voice as fury spewed from his younger brother.

"For *two* ...? We just buried your husband today, and you have the bare-faced nerve to tell us you want to run off with another man, *and* make my brother pay for it? You slut!" He spat the words at her. "Don't give her a penny, Pierce. Show her the door. No woman can be trusted. They are all the same, nothing but lying, scheming bitches."

"So, this is why you and my father were always fighting—another man!" shouted Pierce. Now he thought he understood. "It was you. It was your fault all along. That's why he didn't want us in the house. It was you! I don't know why he didn't throw you out years ago. I *knew* it wasn't his fault."

She stood to face her accusers, almost crouching like a cornered animal, her back to the fire. "I am not a slut," she screamed at Colm. Then she turned on Pierce. "And I'm not running off with another man, not in the way you mean. All that I asked was that you hear me out, but I might have known you're not civil enough even to do that."

There was a silence. The young woman and her husband's eldest son stood in angry confrontation breathing heavily, years of anger and hatred etched on their faces.

She lowered her eyes and sat back in the chair.

"He wanted you in the house, and so did I. I never wanted any of you to leave; I swear to God." She began to cry.

No one heard the latch or saw the young man enter. He crossed the room and put his arm around her shoulders. She looked up, startled for a moment, then looked across at the three young adults. They stared dumbfounded at the stranger.

"This is my son, Cathal."

Mary was the first to sit back on the settle, followed by her brothers.

"Mrs. Kelly," Mary said, very quietly, "I have no idea what is happening here, and I would dearly love you to explain. Pierce, will you please hold your tongue, and let the woman speak? And, you too, Colm."

"Thank you." The embattled woman looked at the young man beside her. "I'm sorry, Cathal. I thought I would be finished before you arrived." Her son still had his arm around his mother's shoulders. "Will you wait outside while I finish? I'll not be long."

He nodded and returned to the door. "I'll be close by, if you need me."

He stepped outside, closing the door quietly behind him. She watched him go, then looked back at her stepchildren.

"When I was young, before I married your father, I had the misfortune to discover I was having a child. My mother was very angry and told my father. He wanted to know who the father was, so that we could be wed. I could not tell him." Her voice dropped almost to a whisper. "I knew a marriage was not possible." She looked straight at Mary, "It was not my fault. I didn't want it to happen. I didn't know. I was only a child myself."

"They sent me to the Magdalene's, the Sisters of Mercy in Dublin, though it's little mercy they show. I was told I must work in the laundry. When my time came, they told me they would take the child and, if no parents were found, it would be reared in an orphanage. I didn't want to do that to the child. *No* child deserves that." She looked at Mary, "They told me I wasn't fit to rear a child, that I would never see it again. How could I leave my child like that, in an orphanage?"

The room was heavy with silence. The young woman sat, staring into the fire, before turning again to her antagonists.

"I ran away. I worked for as long as I could. I cleaned houses, washed bottles in a bar. When I couldn't work any more, I wrote to the father. He sent me enough money to keep me for a month and to pay for the birthing. I told him I wouldn't part with the baby, so he said he would try to arrange a marriage for me, one where I would be able to keep the child. Until he did, he said, I should put the child with the nuns in the Sacred Heart in Ballyfin and come home. It would only be for a short time, so I did. At least if the baby was close by, I could visit him sometimes."

"My parents believed the child was given up. I did everything to try and make amends to my family, but I visited my child whenever I could. I would not let him be adopted. We were going to be together; I made him that promise."

"But, why did Da marry you?" asked Mary. "If anyone found out about your bastard"—Mrs. Kelly flinched at the harsh word—"he would have been shamed before the whole village. How could he live and work here after that?" She shook her head in disbelief. "Didn't your family tell him?"

"They wanted to get rid of me. I was tainted stock." Again the woman lowered her voice. "The father said he would arrange it."

Pierce frowned. "So, did Da find out?"

"I told him myself, the morning after we were wed. I tried to explain to him. I said I would be happy to look after you all, as long as Cathal could be part of the family, too. That's what the father told me to say."

"But, Da didn't agree," said Mary.

Mrs. Kelly shook her head. "He said he'd take no bastard into his home." She began to cry. "I told him I would tell everyone about my child if he made me care for you. I'm sorry. I didn't mean it to happen like it did. I thought he would give in and let me have Cathal here, but he said he'd give his own children away first. He said he would put you all in the orphanage, that it would be better if you were reared by women who truly honored God."

She paused, her head bowed, crying quietly. "I had nowhere to go. My family would not take me back when they learned what I'd done. I wanted to tell your Aunty Bridgie when she came here, but I was afraid of him. He had a terrible temper, as you know, especially when he had drink taken. He told me we had made our vows before God, 'until death us do part.' I was never to shame him, or make him look a fool, by telling anyone about Cathal." She looked at Pierce. "You know how angry he got." She took a deep breath. "But, in the end he couldn't get rid of *you*, Pierce. He said you were just like your mother. I hated that. He said you would be helpful with the horse, and around the house, but the truth was he loved you too much. He couldn't let you go. You were his eldest, his first-born."

Pierce dropped his head and gripped his two hands together.

"I hated you." She continued, "He could keep you, but I couldn't keep mine. I was so angry."

In the silence, a spark from the fire flared and burnt itself out on the hearth. No one noticed.

"I have visited Cathal almost every week. I bought him little treats and decent clothes; that's where a lot of the money went. That's where I went on Sundays, though your Da never knew why I went to Ballyfin. Now, I'm free to keep my promise. If you'll help me to go to America, we can start again. I'm a widow with a young son. No one need know. We could get work there, have a new life."

Still there was silence. A small child could be heard crying in the lane outside, and a woman laughing.

"But, if I can't go, then he'll live here with me. I'd choose to be shamed in front of the whole village before I'll give him up again. He'll live here, and I don't care what they say."

She stared defiantly at the three somber faces watching her.

"My things are packed. I will leave nothing of me behind. Only tell me that you will help me, and I'll leave tonight. I can stay with a friend in Ballyfin for a few days until the arrangements can be made. I want to go, Pierce; I just need help."

The silence extended for some time. Outside, it was dark, and in the small room only the firelight's glow illuminated the tense group.

Pierce looked up at his stepmother and nodded slowly.

She rose, walked to the stairs, and pulled out two small bags from under the steps. Turning back to Pierce, she took a piece of paper from her pocket.

"This is where I'll be. Please arrange it soon. We can only stay there a short time."

He nodded again.

After Mrs. Kelly left the cottage, Mary, Colm, and Pierce stared at the closed door for some time. It was Mary who broke the silence.

"Do you have enough money, Pierce?"

He nodded, still staring at the door.

She touched his arm lightly. "I can lend you some if you need it."

"I wouldn't give her a penny." Colm snorted. "She wouldn't dare bring her bastard back here."

Pierce looked at his brother, then his sister.

"Can I drive you both back to Doonbeg, now? I'm very tired. I'll come over to the shop tomorrow." He gave Colm a wan smile. "We'll have time to talk then, before you go."

"Will you be all right here on your own tonight, Pierce?"

"Yes, thank you, Mary. I'll be fine. It's been a long day. We can talk tomorrow."

They left the cottage.

The woman and boy stepped to the side of the road as the battered lorry and its three occupants passed them on its way to Doonbeg.

End of Book 1.

Michael

The man rapped impatiently on the door, stepped back and almost stumbled over the small child tucked close behind him.

"For heaven's sake, boy, keep out of the way."

Taking a watch from his fob pocket, the man glanced at it, gave a snort of exasperation, and hammered on the door again. A few moments later they heard the slide of a bolt and the door opened slightly. The boy peeked cautiously from behind the man's legs. He saw an old woman peering out, she seemed very cross-looking. She opened the door a little wider. He saw she wore a long black dress, neatly fastened at the neck and wrists with small black buttons. Her mouth was gathered in a tight purse of disapproval, and the boy could see a small dark moustache across her top lip. Deep frown lines creased her forehead.

Jim Porter turned, caught the boy roughly by the arm, and pushed him towards the entrance.

"Get in boy. Get in, and stop getting in the damn way."

The surprised woman stood slightly to one side as the man pushed the child into the dark hallway....

"Michael" is the second book about Norah's children ... to be published soon.

Glossary

Alanna:	From the Gaelic, a leanbh (a lanav) meaning child.
Amadan:	Fool.
Banns:	Notice of an intended marriage, posted for three consecutive weeks in the porch of the parish church, and read from the altar.
Childer:	Children.
Delph:	Earthenware, usually blue and white, originally from Delft in the Netherlands.
Gosters:	Colloquial, children.
Gob-daw:	Idiot.
Girleen:	Little girl.
Hooley:	Party, celebration.
Jar:	An alcoholic drink.
Keen:	A wailing lament for the dead.
Lorry:	Truck.
Porter:	Black beer.
Shleeveen:	Derogatory term, meaning sneaking or mean.
Whiskey:	The Irish spelling from the Gaelic, uisce beatha, meaning water of life.
Whisky:	The Scottish spelling.
Whisht:	As in 'hold your whisht' meaning 'say nothing.'

978-0-595-40654-8
0-595-40654-8

Printed in the United States
R3175100001B/R31751PG76670LVX6B/6}